DOMINO

I0547723

UNFILTERED
creative

DOMINO

KIA HEAVEY

ALSO BY KIA HEAVEY

Night Machines

Underlake

DOMINO

ONE

Domino set off at a brisk trot with every intention of completing his morning rounds on schedule. He had passed the ancient hickory and made it all the way across the clover-laden lawn before a sunny patch of dirt lane undid him.

He stepped onto the soft dust and the warmth came right up through the pads of his feet. The change from shade to bright light made him blink, and that made him sleepy. After all, he had spent most of the night on patrol.

Domino surrendered and flopped onto his side, rubbing his cheek along the ground. He rolled onto his back, stretching his legs as far as they would go and rubbing himself into the soft, warm dust. With his belly exposed to the sun, Domino closed his eyes.

Just as he dozed off, there was a commotion over in the chicken coop. Instantly alert and on his feet, Domino pricked his ears forward, lowered his carriage close to the ground, and crept ahead. His eyes never wavered from his destination. He took cover twenty yards up the lane alongside the grassy bank and raised only his head, periscope style, to gather information.

Three fat hens scurried down the gangplank from the coop. In their haste, they trailed a scattering of airborne down and indignant exclamations.

"Help! Murder!"

"Can you believe this?"

"Absolutely not! And in broad daylight, too."

"What is this world coming to?"

Domino tuned out their squawking and focused on the entrance to the coop. In a flash, he had noiselessly placed himself beneath it. He could hear the shrieks of a guinea hen from within, as well as the unmistakable foul language and rough tones of a rat.

With no kits of his own, Domino had never felt the primal rage of a parent protecting his young, and he certainly didn't think much of the personality of an egg. What *did* get his blood boiling was that the eggs and the hens belonged to the Browns, for whom he worked, and it was his job to keep precisely this sort of thing from happening.

Up the gangplank in a blur, Domino burst into the coop in a rage of bristling fur and furious howl. The frantic hen flapped on the edge of her roost, in the center of which an exceptionally large and ugly rat simultaneously fended her off, cursed at her, and attempted to purloin her precious egg.

Domino was nothing if not professional. He held his rage at the rodent's presumption in check as he snapped into full enforcement mode. Jaws open, he leaped at the filthy beast's throat.

The rat was unusually quick for its size. Domino was left with only a mouthful of gray fur as his quarry bolted. Trailing a stream of urine in its terror, the rat seemed to fly as it leaped from the roost and tore down the gangplank.

Domino followed at full tilt. In an adrenaline-fueled rush,

he shot out the exit too fast and tumbled down the gangplank. He quickly regained his feet, only to be blinded by the harsh sun in his sensitive eyes.

"That way! That way!" clucked the hens.

Domino spun in time to make out the form of the fleeing rat as it gained the shadow alongside an ancient stone wall a dozen yards away. There it paused to look back at its pursuer.

Domino locked eyes with his quarry and stalked to within a few feet of the nasty beast. He soon halted, knowing the rat had only to take two steps to disappear into one of the wall's many crannies. Domino had spent the better part of the summer staking out the low wall before he had been able to capture the chipmunk that had taken up residence there. He knew from experience that a frontal assault at this point would net him nothing.

The rat's back end was invisible in the sharp shadow alongside the wall, but its front end was starkly lit in the harsh midday sunlight. It was still panting from its recent dash for its life, but with its would-be killer safely in sight, it soon regained its typical arrogance. "Well, well, not so fast today, are we, cat?"

Domino's sensitive ears flicked at the squeaky tones of the rat's voice. "I'm not the one who was so scared I pissed myself," he replied. While he spoke, his eyes scanned the scene, seeking a way to approach the creature.

The rat laughed. "Maybe so, but I'm not the one who ran through it. Even now, I can smell it on you. When you bathe later, enjoy the taste," it taunted. "That's what you like anyway, isn't it?"

"And you little sociopaths wonder why we kill your species whenever we get the chance." As Domino bantered, his mind raced. If only he could gain the shadow, he could slither along the base of the tumbledown wall. He took a tentative step closer.

The rat stiffened. "Uh, uh, no you don't." It shook its head in feigned disgust. "My tail, you really are as stupid as you look. I can see you, remember?"

"And yet, your ego prevents you from scurrying to safety. You could easily get away from me now, yet you choose not to. Who's really stupid?"

Seething rage seemed to flame up in the rat. "I'm not the stupid one," it squeaked. "Go ahead and bully me while you can, cat. Your days of running this territory are coming to an end."

A wrathful fervor glowed in the rodent's eyes, and Domino momentarily paused in his attempt to approach. He didn't care for the rat's rebellious tone or its cryptic threat.

Domino meowed a chortle. "I see. And who, pray tell, will end my reign of terror?" He was running out of repartee. Again his eyes swept the area around the rat. The sun was so bright that his vision was unable to penetrate the sharp contrast of shadow and light. Everything looked as black and white as his own fur. If only he had the advantage of hiding in the shadow... The shadow! Something odd was happening in the shadow beside the rat. Intent on taunting him, the rat didn't see it, but Domino did.

The shadow became somehow blacker, and then it was fluid. In a flash of motion, it engulfed the defiant rat, lifting it from its crouch and into the air.

Domino's eyes widened in disbelief. Right in front of him, a black cat emerged into the sunlight, head high, the apoplectic rat wriggling in her mouth.

"Gaaaah!" squealed the rodent. "Put me down, weasel! I'll tear your eyes out. Cat turd!" It swept at her face with impotent claws but could gain no purchase on the stranger's sleek fur.

Domino held his aggressive stance and quickly brought his shocked features under control. "You've got a hell of a nerve," he growled, "hunting another feline's territory." He hoped his admiration for her invisible stalk was not evident in his voice.

Her mouth full, the female only winked at him in the strong sunlight.

"You there! Could you be less of a tom?" The rat thought it saw an opening. "This weasel came onto your turf and took me right in front of you. What are you, neutered? Haven't you got anything under your tail besides a bunghole?"

Technically, the rat was right. The appropriate response would be for Domino to thrash the stranger and run her off his hunting grounds, with plenty of wounds to lick later while she rethought her behavior. But something about her brazen look as she stood right in front of him—with his rat in her mouth and she barely half his size—stayed him.

"That squealing is hurting my ears," he told her.

She obliged him by lowering the rodent to the ground and grasping it with her front claws. She thrust her jaws deeper around its throat and firmly squeezed off the stream of curses and threats.

Rooted to the spot, Domino watched her. As black as the shadow from which she had emerged, she wore smooth, radiant fur that glowed in highlights emphasizing her compact shape. Even her tight, quick movements were finely controlled. She was small but powerful for her size, her grace a cover for her strength.

"You do have a lot of nerve, hunting my rats right in front of me," he felt compelled to repeat.

The stranger replied by doing something even more insulting: she looked away from him, the universal animal sign that means *I do not consider you a threat*. She idly licked a bit of rat from her foreleg

"Oh!" sputtered Domino in outrage. This diminutive female utterly undid him. Her actions somehow had the opposite effect on him than they should have. Instead of hurling himself at her and teaching her a lesson, he only wanted to watch her and admire her.

The black cat lowered her head and delicately tore the still-twitching rat's throat open. Then she drew a great yawn and stood, taking a long look at Domino. He held himself straight and lifted his head, trying to look bigger under her scrutiny. With an almost-smirk, she bent her head to take the dead rat in her mouth. She turned and leaped lithely to the top of the wall before streaming over the far side and disappearing.

Domino could only watch her go. "How do you like that?" he muttered to himself.

"Did he get it?"

"Did he kill it?

"I thought I saw another cat, too."

"Domino would never allow that."

As the clucking behind him grew louder, Domino became self-conscious. Still facing the stone wall over which the strange cat had vanished, he yelled, "And don't come back!" Then he turned and, head and tail high, paced away from the agitated yard birds to continue his morning rounds.

Soon he reached the dilapidated toolshed that stood between the coop and the stone wall. The aging wooden building had a moss-covered cedar-shingle roof and leaned at an angle that suggested it was less than structurally sound. The Brown children used it as a clubhouse, and Domino often joined them at their play. Just now it was empty; the children had boarded the large, flashing bus as they did most mornings. They wouldn't be back until afternoon.

The shed door frame was more of a parallelogram than a rectangle, so the door never closed all the way and Domino could enter whenever he pleased. Inside was a dusty square room. An ancient worktable was pushed up against the single window. At the moment, the surface was spread with sketch pads, tools, wires, and other things the children kept there. A wooden bookshelf against the opposite wall held more tools, books, toys, experiments, and a lone, despondent frog in a fish tank.

Domino jumped lightly to the tabletop and surveyed the land outside the grimy window. Satisfied that all was well, he leaped back to the ground and sniffed around the edges of the floor. A mouse had been here recently and probably more than once. Domino made a mental note to come back in the evening and sort it out.

As he left the shed, the emptiness in his stomach left by the purloined rat began to make itself known. Perhaps this was one of those days when Mrs. Brown would leave some leftover chicken (maybe even some tuna!) outside the kitchen door for him.

But first, Domino made a wide loop around the yard to pass close to Thor's doghouse. The German shepherd lay in the doorway, lazy as always. His head snapped up, and he gave Domino a baleful look as the spotted cat swaggered along a precise route just beyond the dog's reach.

The days of Thor racing toward him, barking ferociously, only to be brought up short by the painful yank of his collar were over. Back when Thor was new to the Brown territory, Domino would sit in a relaxed pose, watching with amusement as the tethered dog hurled himself at him again and again. As a bonus, sometimes one of the Browns would come out and yell at Thor to quiet down. The poor beast would become frantic, trying to get them to see that there was a cat sitting *right there*. Domino would look away in disgust, infuriating Thor even more, before sauntering off.

As usual, Domino made sure to walk by with casual indifference. He watched Thor out of the corner of his eye as he went. Thor knew that Domino knew that Thor couldn't touch him. Humiliated, the dog could only stare at him in futile rage. Domino languorously finished his parade and approached the back porch of the big, old farmhouse.

As luck would have it, Mrs. Brown came out of the kitchen door just then and called him. He picked up his pace to meet her. Up on the porch, he rubbed against her legs and accepted her pats and ear scratches. Then, as hoped for, she placed a small piece of chicken on the floorboards in front of him. Quite hungry now, Domino gobbled the morsel and looked up, meowing, "More?"

"Sorry about this, big boy," said Mrs. Brown. She scooped him up and placed him in an open pet carrier, which Domino only now noticed had been sitting on the bench in anticipation of his arrival.

"What are you doing?" he raged. But Mrs. Brown only held him firmly until she had closed and latched the door. "Let me out of here," Domino demanded. She didn't answer; instead she picked up the carrier and put it on the seat of the waiting vehicle. The slam of the door erupted into Domino's sensitive ears and he yelled out. Then Mrs. Brown got into the other side of the vehicle and slammed that door, too. "Ow!" Domino yelled again.

"I know, I know. Poor Domino," soothed Mrs. Brown. She began driving.

Domino could see her through the wire door of the carrier. She had shiny long fur (on her head only, as with most humans). It was the color of late-afternoon sunlight on stone, and looking at it soothed Domino. Then the vehicle lurched around a turn, reminding him of her maltreatment. "Where are we going?" he howled, though he knew the answer.

Since coming to the Brown territory, he had been taken in the car precisely twice, and both times he went to the veterinarian. The first time had been when he was about a year old for something the Browns called a "checkup." The second time had been the following fall, when he developed an abscess after a fight with a tabby cat that had thought to cross his territory. The veterinarian had made Domino sleep, and when he woke, the wound felt immensely better.

Mrs. Brown carried him into the reception area. He heard her tell the woman behind the desk that he was here for a checkup. That meant he would be stabbed with needles. He wailed in anticipation, "I hate it when you do this to me."

Mrs. Brown spoke to him though the carrier. "There, there, it's okay, Domino. You're a good boy. This will only take a minute, and then you'll be good to go for a whole year."

Domino turned his head as a door opened. Through the mesh door of the carrier, he saw a dog come into the room. "Oooohhh!" he yowled. He arched his back until it bumped against the carrier ceiling. His fur stood up straight and he bared his teeth, making himself look enormous and fierce.

"Settle down, Domino." Mrs. Brown lifted the carrier and turned it so he looked into her face. She gave the carrier a light shake to distract him.

"You can come in now," said a male human voice.

"Good morning, Dr. Mundy." They went into the examination room and the door closed behind them, barring any escape.

The exam was every bit as horrible as Domino remembered. He was lifted, poked, prodded, and weighed. "Fifteen pounds," exclaimed Dr. Mundy. "What a big boy."

"I'd appreciate it if you wouldn't patronize me," spat Domino through gritted teeth.

"Okay, take it easy," the veterinarian said. He lifted Domino's tail. "Still not neutered?" he asked Mrs. Brown.

She laughed. "Oh, no, Bill wouldn't hear of it."

Dr. Mundy laughed, too. "Well, he is a working cat. I guess he needs his moxie."

Domino growled low and deep.

"Okay, big guy, almost done," the vet assured him. Then came the stabbing of the needles and in a trice, Domino was back in his carrier.

He complained and berated Mrs. Brown the entire drive home. She put on some music and drowned him out. When they finally arrived at the house, she left the carrier on the back porch while she went in the kitchen door. Without an audience, Domino sat silently and waited. As the familiar smells of his beloved territory filled the small space, he began to feel calm again. When Mrs. Brown returned, she didn't let him out right away but instead placed a large piece of leftover chicken on the decking nearby. The intoxicating smell wafted to Domino, and his neglected stomach began to rage. Soon the chicken was the only thing he could think about. Mrs. Brown finally opened the carrier and he sprang out, his jaws open to the meat even as his paws hit the ground.

Mrs. Brown squatted beside him while he ate. She stroked the top of his head and told him what a good boy he had been. Domino permitted her affections, even though she had betrayed him that morning. The pats felt nice, and the chicken was very good. When he had finished the meal, he rubbed against her legs once before glancing out over the backyard with an air of authority. He noticed a sparrow taking a dust bath in the lane and immediately headed out to see to it. His ears swiveled back once when the kitchen door closed.

No longer hungry, Domino didn't bother to stalk. Instead, he charged the small bird and ran it out of his yard. Satisfied that everything was in order, he made his way back to the barn, where he had started his busy day.

Domino went in the open barn door and stalked past three antique jeeps. Mr. Brown and the two older children had gotten one of them running, and they sometimes drove it around their territory or away down the road. The one that worked was painted green with a white star on the door. Soon, the jeeps would be joined by the Browns' powerboat, which would spend the winter in the barn.

Domino climbed a narrow stairway to the hayloft. The Browns didn't keep livestock other than hens, so only boxes and seldom-used tools were stored up here. Last spring, the children had brought up some old fleece blankets and made Domino a fine bed. It was in the perfect location, in front of the open hay door, high above the ground. Not only was the view of the yard expansive, sunlight fell directly on the bed for much of the day. Domino retired to this fleece haven now. With a full belly, a sore backside, and the sun on his fur, he suddenly remembered how tired he was from patrolling all night and that he had been robbed of his morning nap. He wanted to be rested up for that night's Prowl, where he expected to meet up with many other cats. And so, with a last blinking survey of his territory, he gave himself over to a long, deep nap.

. . .

THE MOON HAD BEEN UP for several hours when Domino left the Brown property to cross the now-empty road. (It was a full moon, and Thor had howled at it like an idiot when it rose. Domino really felt sorry for him sometimes.) A brief westerly trot brought him to the wooded area alongside the Neighborhood, which was a collection of houses where many families of people lived. And with them lived their domestic animals, including many cats. Nights like tonight, with crisp, scented air and enough moonlight to cast shadows, were ideal for a Prowl. Domino expected to meet up with many others and gather much intelligence. But there was one cat he always sought out first.

The woodland trees gave way to a cultivated euonymus hedge. Domino passed into its shelter to sit unseen and look into the backyard of a house. There he spied an enormous cat sitting atop an outdoor dining table. The table was pushed up against the house, so the large cat could see into an open window. Inside the house, separated from her suitor by the mesh of a screen, a sleek Siamese female perched on the windowsill. She and the large male were touching noses through the screen. Domino grinned. He could hear them purring all the way back in his hiding place.

Bats wheeled above the yard. Their high-pitched chirps made Domino flick his ears in annoyance. He broke cover and stalked through the grass to the table. It was not his finest work, but the cat couple was too involved with their sniffing and nose touching to notice him anyway. He launched himself onto the tabletop without warning, frightening the large cat so that he fell back into a defensive posture, hissing, his fur on end and his mouth open to show enormous teeth.

Domino sat nonchalantly and began to clean his paw. He

looked up as his friend began to deflate. "Good evening, Flufferdoodle," he deadpanned.

The large male regained his composure quickly. "I wasn't scared, you know." At his friend's smirk, he grumbled, "You are such a rat, Domino."

Domino turned to the graceful female behind the screen. "Good evening, Meg."

Meg had a gentle disposition and had noted his abrupt arrival with friendly curiosity. "Hello, Domino. I suppose you've come to take Fluff to the Prowl."

"I have indeed."

"I wish I could go with you." Meg looked melancholy. "I wish I were an outdoor cat, like you guys."

"I am just as pleased that you are safe indoors," said Flufferdoodle with a note of chivalry in his voice. "At the last Prowl, a dog was off-leash and he chased some cats. And Tiger says he saw a coyote in the Gully the other day."

Meg lowered her head. "I know. It's just that I get so envious of your adventures. What must it be like to roam where you please, to climb as high as you want, to smell all the world, to have only moonlight and your whiskers to guide you?"

"Eh, it ain't all it's cracked up to be," said Domino.

Meg smiled at him before looking at Flufferdoodle. Her deep blue eyes were luminous in the moonlight. "What must it be like to run wild with you, my love?" she said quietly.

Domino looked away, muttering, "Oh, brother."

"Someday I'll get you out of here, I swear," Flufferdoodle promised her. "But for now, I must tend to the business at hand."

"Yes, of course. Go." She stretched her slender neck to touch her nose to the screen once more. Flufferdoodle met it with his own. Then he turned and took a powerful leap to the ground.

"Stealthy," commented Domino, as the concussion of Flufferdoodle's landing vibrated through his paw pads. He turned to say a quick good-bye to Meg before leaping to join his friend.

They jogged from Meg's yard to the adjoining one, which was Flufferdoodle's territory. As they wove through the jungle of playhouses and swing sets, Domino spoke. "Some moon tonight, eh?" He passed by three poles crowned with bird feeders. "I can actually see how orange your fur is."

"It's nights like this I wish I had your markings," said the larger cat. "You look like a collection of moon shadows."

Domino snorted. "I wish I had your size."

Flufferdoodle dodged around an abandoned bicycle with training wheels as they passed through the front yard. "I only have a few pounds on you."

"That may be, but your *fur*—my paws, it makes you look as big as a bobcat."

"Yeah, you'd think. But on the other paw, you haven't lived until you've yakked up a Flufferdoodle-size fur ball."

Domino shuddered. "Yeah, I could probably do without that." They crossed the street in front of Flufferdoodle's house, passed quickly through the light from a streetlamp, and slipped into a bank of hostas alongside the paved sidewalk. Once they were safely in the cover, Domino spoke again. "Have you seen any new cats around here lately?"

"Have I," grunted Flufferdoodle.

"A black female?"

"No, that's not the cat I'm talking about."

"Then who?"

The pair paused at the edge of the hostas to survey an

expanse of lawn. Once they deemed it safe, they proceeded out into the open. "New guy," said Flufferdoodle. "His people just moved here from some big city."

"What's he look like?"

"A little bit like Meg, actually. He's definitely got the Siamese in him. Tipped ears and tail, crossed eyes, and he sure likes to talk." He paused for a second. "Bit of a strange cat, actually."

"What's that mean?"

"I'll let you see for yourself. I'm sure he'll be at the Prowl tonight."

"What's his name?" asked Domino.

"Socrates."

They had reached a wooded space between two houses. Here, the ground dipped down from the edge of the road into the Gully, a strip of wild land between the lawns and hedges of the Neighborhood with a ditch along the bottom. When the rain was heavy, the ditch became a torrent that carried runoff away. Through this patch of woods and at the far end of the Gully was another road lit by a streetlamp. In the bright circle it cast, on the open pavement between lawn, hedge, and woodland, cats convened on certain nights to exchange greetings and news.

The two friends proceeded stealthily through the woods along the edge of the Gully. At length, when Domino looked ahead through the trees, he saw that a good number of cats had already arrived at the Prowl. He and Flufferdoodle left the cover and sifted into the overgrown grass by the pavement. Domino squinted at the gathering as he approached. There were perhaps ten or twelve cats, all of whom were sitting and looking at one cat in particular. "What the...?" exclaimed Domino.

The cat at the center of attention had positioned himself just under the streetlight so that his face was in shadow, though he could easily see all the cats assembled before him. But odder still was his position: he was sitting up on his haunches, like a squirrel when eating a nut. But this cat wasn't eating anything. He was holding forth, and the other cats were listening.

"That's Socrates," said Flufferdoodle in a low voice. "See what I mean?" he added.

"Yeah, I do."

Domino and Flufferdoodle broke from the brush and entered the circle of light on the pavement. Domino called out loudly, "Sorry we're late, guys."

The gathered cats all turned to greet them and there was much meowing and touching of noses. Only Socrates did not move.

"Come here, you've got to meet the new guy," said a tabby cat with the predictable name of Tiger.

"Looking forward to it," said Domino. Since Socrates had not moved, he allowed himself to be led to the odd cat. "Welcome," he meowed when he reached him.

Socrates didn't look at Domino so much as he evaluated the way the other cats treated the barn cat: with deference and respect. His eyes narrowed before he finally returned Domino's look. "Nice of you to join us," he said finally. He did not come down from his strange sitting-up position.

"I know you're new to the neighborhood," began Domino, "but around here, we greet by touching noses."

"How quaint."

Domino's tail began to twitch with annoyance. He tried again. "I am unable to greet you properly while you sit up so high. Why do you sit in that strange position?" His eyes remained locked on Socrates's, which were slightly crossed and so pale a color as to appear almost white. Domino felt an unpleasant quaver in the pit of his stomach.

"Where I come from, all the cats sit like this," declared Socrates.

Domino could hear Flufferdoodle chortle behind him. "Exactly where do you come from?" he asked.

"The City," said Socrates with obvious pride. "A place to which I am certain you have never traveled."

"You'd be right," answered Domino. "Why would I go to a place where cats don't even know how to behave like proper cats?"

Their meows had risen in volume with each word, and a calico female quickly stepped between them. She rubbed sweetly against Domino's cheek. "Domino," she said, "Socrates has some really interesting things to say. Yes, he's from a different place, and, yes, his ways are different from ours. But he knows so much. You should listen to what he's saying. He's really smart."

Domino dropped his attention from Socrates to greet the calico cat. "You're right, Cricket. Where are my manners?" But he didn't look at Socrates again, preferring to blink lazily while Cricket groomed the impossible-to-reach spot on the back of his head. She made a soft chirping sound when she purred, and since she was always purring, the other cats had given her the name Cricket. She had no people and lived alone in the woods at the head of the Gully. But she was so sweet and gentle that she had no trouble finding plenty of human benefactors in the neighborhood.

The other cats had all grown silent, looking from Domino to Socrates. Still sitting up high, Socrates kept a composed demeanor, but his twitching tail tip gave away his annoyance at the interruption. At last, another male tabby (this one was called Mister) walked back to Socrates, sat respectfully before him, and said, "Will you please explain what you were saying before, about cats being tran... tran-*scen-dent* beyond the *pre-sup-po-si-tion* of others?"

Domino and Flufferdoodle exchanged amused glances at the unaccustomed words from a cat they had known their whole lives. But Cricket's head popped up as she exclaimed, "Oh! He's going to talk again." She abandoned Domino to join Mister and sit at Socrates's feet. Most of the other cats did the same. Domino gave Flufferdoodle a questioning look, and the big tom shrugged in reply. They stepped back to make room for the audience, preferring to stand at the back of the odd gathering.

"Yes, please do share your pearls of wisdom with us," muttered Domino under his breath. Flufferdoodle snickered.

"Not just cats, *all* creatures are transcendent." Socrates spoke in a voice of authority, in the guttural tones of a Siamese. Domino felt a pang of envy. His own voice was deep and strong, but he could never make the exotic, attention-commanding sounds of that breed.

There were murmurs of enlightenment from the cats gathered closest to the speaker.

"Cats are transcendent," boomed Socrates.

"Of course!"

"Naturally!" came the replies.

"Dogs are transcendent."

Less enthusiastic responses of "What?" and "Hmm."

"Even birds, mice, rabbits, and rats are transcendent."

This time Socrates's words were greeted with gasps of disbelief.

"I don't understand. What do you mean?" called a female tuxedo cat over the murmurs.

"I'm glad you ask, Lily." Socrates's entire expression transformed from the glare he had recently shown Domino. Now his eyes seemed alight with inspiration as he stared into the space over the cats' heads. He appeared to be seeking and finding higher orders of knowledge in the very ether. "I mean that cats are not, simply, hunting and killing machines, all claws and teeth and no mercy for smaller creatures."

"Speak for yourself," grumbled Flufferdoodle. Domino huffed in agreement.

"I mean that dogs are more than unintelligent eating-sleeping-pooping machines."

The crowd's murmurings took on a note of understanding.

"And I mean that even rats and mice have a purpose, and it isn't simply to steal and spread filth."

More sounds of enlightenment from the onlookers. Domino began to feel uneasy. He called out, "Then what is it?"

Socrates's distant gaze locked suddenly onto him. "Why don't we let *them* tell *us* for once?" he thundered. "Why do *we* get to decide what *they* are? Why do we *presuppose*? Who put cats in charge of defining other living creatures?"

For once in his life, Domino didn't know what to say or do. The growing sounds of approval from the gathered cats didn't help him think, either.

Beside him, Flufferdoodle was shaking his head. "This guy's out of his mind."

Socrates continued, "And why are we so sure that it's perfectly all right for cats to kill and eat other creatures, based only on our own *presuppositions*?"

Again, sounds of wonder and amazement came from the listeners. Some moved closer still to Socrates and he looked down upon them with benevolence.

"I suppose we don't really *need* to kill them," a ginger tabby near Domino said. "I mean, all of us have humans who feed us."

Domino turned to her. "Well I, for one, have a job to do. Mr. Brown would not only not feed me, he would throw me off my territory and get a new cat if I were to let rats take over Mrs. Brown's henhouse."

The tabby only looked at him in confusion.

A battle-scarred older tom sidled up between Flufferdoodle and Domino. "He's lying, you know," he said softly.

"How do you know, Rudy?" asked Domino.

"I used to live in the City," replied the stray. "I hung out in the meat-packing district, back when I was young and strong enough to hold the respect of the others. There were a lot of us there, and I never once saw a cat sit up like *he* does." He inclined his head with a scowl at Socrates. "Any cat who put himself above the others like that would have been knocked down in a hurry."

"Huh," said Domino.

"In fact," continued Rudy, "cats like him never even saw other cats at all in the city. Pet cats live in apartments, which are rooms inside a building. They are never outside at all. A cat like our friend here wouldn't have had any contact with other cats whatsoever."

"DOG!" yelled a cat on the other side of the crowd. Instantly, every shade of fur stood on end as all the cats arched their backs.

Every cat except Socrates. "Be still, you fools," he hissed.

Frozen in fear, the cats obeyed him. Domino watched, fascinated, as a medium-size, yellow dog raced into the group from just outside the ring of light. He came to a halt and looked from cat to cat, barking and snarling and showing his teeth. Everyone gasped in fear.

Suddenly, Socrates was in the dog's face. "Be quiet, Max," he meowed sternly.

The onlookers all drew in their breath in horror, awaiting Socrates's inevitable murder. But instead of clamping his jaws around the cat's neck, the dog stopped barking and stood still. Then, in an inexplicable display of what could only be called *transcendent* animal behavior, he touched noses with Socrates. To everyone's amazement, the dog began to wag his curly tail.

The reaction from the crowd was powerful. Cats exclaimed out loud at the miracle they had just seen. And though Domino still felt wary of Socrates, he was speechless for the second time that evening. Even he had never seen a cat perform such a sensational act as commanding an angry dog to be quiet. And while he was pretty sure Socrates's theory of "transcendence" was so much cow dung, he was unable to explain what he had just seen in any other way at that moment. But from the sounds around him, the other cats were firmly convinced that Socrates was wise and powerful, more so than any cat any of them had ever met before.

AS HE JOGGED BACK toward the edge of the Neighborhood at Flufferdoodle's side, Domino stewed. "I don't like that guy," he said at last. "He's trouble, mark my words."

Flufferdoodle laughed. "Oh, come on, Dom. You can't let him bother you." He shook his head. "He's a ridiculous clown. Anyone can see that."

Domino slowed to a stalk and waited until Flufferdoodle noticed and turned to look back at him. "Unfortunately, Fluff, not everyone does see that."

Flufferdoodle growled in exasperation, turned away, and continued padding across the grass. Domino ran a few paces to come alongside him again. "I'm not kidding, Fluff. You saw how everyone reacted when he somehow tamed that stupid dog."

Flufferdoodle kept walking. Domino ran ahead of him and stopped in front of him so that Flufferdoodle had to hold up and look at him. "Seriously, Fluff," Domino meowed. "You saw it, too. They looked at him like he was one of the Great Cats or something."

Seeing his friend's agitation, Flufferdoodle relented a little. "Yes, I saw how starstruck some of the cats were. So what do you want me to do about it, Dom?"

"I—I guess I don't really know." Domino felt an unsettling mixture of confusion and apprehension. "It seems as though he's already won everyone over. Even if I knew what to do, it feels like it's already too late." He stared despondently into the distance.

Flufferdoodle smiled indulgently at his friend. "Then it's already too late. All the silly cats in the neighborhood are convinced that a pretentious, smooth-talking, new cat is just *too cool*." He chuckled. "But, my paws, even you have to admit that was a pretty neat trick with the dog."

"Of course, it was," admitted Domino. "But it was just that —a trick. He called that dog by name—he knows him somehow. And anyway, it doesn't mean he's right about that other nonsense."

"Of course not." Flufferdoodle gave an enormous yawn. Domino stared at his cavernous mouth and formidable teeth with envy. "Well, old friend," said the larger cat, "I've had enough Prowl for one night. I'm heading into the house to see if there's any food left in my bowl. Then I'm going to see which person is sleeping the soundest and snuggle up for a good, long nap." He began walking again.

Domino fell in beside him. "You housecats," he teased, trying to dispel his own unease. "You all keep the same hours as your people. The night isn't even half-over, and you want to go to bed. You're going to miss all the action." He shook his head in mock disappointment.

"Goodnight, Domino." They had reached the back door of Flufferdoodle's house. The giant tom turned and went through the cat door, a clever human invention that somehow knew to let only Flufferdoodle pass through.

"Goodnight, Fluff," called Domino. He watched his friend vanish before heading for the bushes at the back of the yard. And though he stalked and sniffed and scratched at several tree trunks and even gobbled up a hapless mole, for the entire way home, Domino could not shake the apprehension he had been feeling since he first spotted the strange new cat sitting up affectedly like some sort of demented prairie dog, spouting his bizarre notions.

TWO

Domino caught a squirrel!

Amazed by his own prowess, he danced and hissed around the dazed creature. "Where's your sense of superiority now, tree rat?" he taunted.

In his whole life, Domino had never been able to catch a squirrel. The bushy-tailed rodents were just too cautious, too quick, and could climb a tree faster than any cat ever could—facts they never let cats forget. Every cat Domino knew who had tried to catch one had instead gained only an hour of abuse hurled down by the obnoxious beast from the safety of a lofty bough.

Every humiliating near miss in his life came back to Domino now, and he gave the expiring creature a hearty swat for good measure.

"Impressive."

Domino looked up sharply to see who had spoken. Atop a nearby boulder, with the sun reflecting off her ebony fur in a thousand dazzling shades of blue-white, sat the female who had stolen his rat two days earlier.

"I caught a squirrel!" Domino meowed. What luck, for her to have happened by at this very moment.

"So I see."

Domino sat up straight, basking in his triumph. In a last burst of frantic energy, the squirrel leaped to its feet and ran for the woods, shrieking, "No! No! No! No!"

Domino produced his deepest, most lionlike roar. "Oh no you don't!" In a flash he was atop the fleeing rodent. He clamped his jaws on its neck, grasped it with his front claws, and pushed off with his hind legs to roll the two of them over onto his back. The disoriented squirrel squeaked and struggled with every bit of its fading strength. Holding tightly, Domino brought his rear feet up and kicked over and over until he heard the dull snap of the squirrel's neck.

His sides heaving, Domino posed awhile longer with his quarry, making sure the strange female got a good view. Then he cautiously stood, lifting the carcass and laying it on its side. He sat tall beside it and tried to look as regal as possible for his visitor's benefit.

"You going to eat that?" she meowed.

Her voice delighted him. Though she was clearly a mature female—he guessed she had two years, like he did—her voice had a high-pitched, kittenish quality to it. This was probably because she was a small cat, but Domino had seen for himself the power and prowess she packed. Yet her lilting meows somehow made her seem more approachably feline, an intriguing contrast to her sudden, mysterious appearances.

Domino had already eaten well that morning. One of the children had brought a plate out to him with an uneaten portion of eggs, milk, and butter. The squirrel was nice and plump in anticipation of the coming winter and surely held more meat than he could eat. "Is that the only reason you come around here?" he asked his visitor. "The food?"

"What do you think?"

"I think you like me."

She didn't answer. But as she sat on the sun-warmed boulder, Domino could have sworn that she winked at him.

Domino let himself admire her compact cat shape, her slender legs (a little on the long side for her size), and her slim tail wrapped elegantly about her paws. Her fur looked as lustrous as a star-filled night sky. "I suppose you could have a bite or two," he meowed.

A thrill ran through Domino. He had never before allowed a strange cat to so much as wander onto his territory without a fight. He had certainly never invited anyone to share his kill. The invitation had been a thoroughly un-Domino-like impulse, as though another part of him altogether had made the decision without running it past his brain first. This dazzling little female had such a strange effect on him.

"Thank you," she said in her dainty voice. She leaped lightly from her perch and came to him with cautious steps. He was, after all, much larger than she. To reassure her, Domino sat back from the kill and looked away to the side. He glanced back only when he heard the sound of rending flesh.

He watched her work. Her teeth were white and healthy looking, and she kept her claws exquisitely sharp. The squirrel was soon opened up so that both cats could easily access the meat. Domino leaned in for a bite, making sure to take a perfunctory swat at the stranger's head. After all, he didn't want her to think he had no regard for custom whatsoever. Without letting go of the strip of meat she was chewing, she gave the swat right back to him. Feisty. He liked it. He issued a warning growl. Still holding tight to her morsel, she moved aside almost imperceptibly so that he might lower his head and enjoy the kill as well.

Here was another first for Domino: sharing a kill at whiskertouch with another cat. Once or twice, Flufferdoodle had visited him and they had nibbled together at the scraps the Browns sometimes left on the back porch. But Flufferdoodle was so well fed by his own people that it had been more of a social pastime than a meal.

Eating the squirrel with this glossy little female was a new experience altogether. First, there was the pride Domino felt in having taken the squirrel with her there to witness it. But then there was a new feeling, similar to the sense of accomplishment he got from keeping the Brown territory free of vermin. He had performed a service for his new friend. He had hunted so that she might eat. He felt a quiet joy in having provided this meal for her. After all, as far as he could tell, she was on her own in the woods, where she had no people to help her through dry hunting spells, and she had real enemies to avoid, like raccoons, coyotes, and bobcats. He was glad she had come to his territory, where he could feed her and protect her.

He bent his head to the meal alongside her. She flicked her ear as his whiskers tickled it, and likewise he felt her whiskers caress his cheek. He half closed his eyes and chewed the sumptuous meat, even as she did the same a mere breath away from him. It was the most sensuous, enjoyable meal he had ever eaten.

After they had taken their fill, the two cats found a sunny patch of grass where they could rest. Domino slid onto his side and made sure to stretch out as far as he could so she could see how long his body was. Though she didn't comment on it, he caught her looking. After a moment, she came to him and began grooming his face and neck. Domino closed his eyes and

27

purred. Soon the visitor was purring, too. She settled down near him, lying on her stomach with her legs tucked beneath her, her golden eyes even now keeping watch on him. Domino was almost asleep when she asked, "What's your name?"

"Domino," he said. "Mr. Brown named me when I was a kitten." He struggled to stay awake. "What's yours?"

"Celine."

"Celine... that's nice. It suits you." His eyes closed. Domino could hear her purring drowsily. The autumn sun was generous with its warmth today, and he absorbed it happily. Soon he was asleep. And when he finally awoke, Celine had vanished again.

DOMINO SPENT the afternoon and evening making repeated rounds of his territory. Every time he approached the area beyond the ancient toolshed, where the tumbledown stone wall delineated lawn from woodland, he slowed and looked around carefully. This was the spot where he had first seen Celine and where she had slid over the wall with his rat to disappear among the undergrowth. It was also near where he had caught the squirrel only a few hours earlier, and she had been there to share it with him. Approaching the picked-over carcass now, he saw that it had been discovered by late-season flies. He passed it by and doubled back to the wall. He climbed up to the highest point he could find and sat, gazing long into the woods, searching for a glimpse of midnight fur. His head turned at every falling leaf or rustle of sparrow foraging among the litter. At one point, he caught himself on the verge of calling her name.

"Good grief, tom up, Domino," he said to himself. Turning, he leaped gracelessly from his vantage point and padded back toward the yard, his head low and his ears flat. He didn't acknowledge the hens as he passed them. They took the occasion to resume their incessant clucking.

"What's eating Domino?"

"I don't know, but something certainly is."

"He looks like he could bite your head off."

"Like he did to that squirrel. I was behind the shed. I saw it."

"Poor beast."

"Nonsense. They never have anything nice to say to us."

Tuning them out, he headed for a favorite bathing spot near Thor's run. But in his foul mood, Domino forgot all about blithely pretending he was unaware of the dog's proximity. Rather, he sat glaring in Thor's direction. Thor stared back at him, tired from an outing with Mr. Brown and not interested in being the fall guy to cheer Domino from his mood.

The waning moon was high when Domino finally retreated to his bed in the loft. He cleaned his belly and back, then licked a paw to run over his head and ears. He remembered Celine's ministrations that afternoon and bitterly stopped washing; it wasn't nearly as nice as when she did it for him. Frustrated, he flopped onto his side. The nights were becoming cooler and he pushed himself up against the wall of the fleece nest.

Just before dawn, Domino stirred then woke abruptly. Celine was curled alongside the crescent of his body, purring in her sleep. His heart had begun pounding in alarm at the nearness of another creature, and it continued to pound when he realized it was she. "How did you sneak up on me like that?" he asked softly. Pleasure at seeing her tempered the indignity in his tone.

She opened her eyes just enough to see him. "I am ninja kitty." She winked.

"Come on, no cat is *that* good."

She closed her eyes again. "Let's just say, you're a very sound sleeper." Her breathing became rhythmic and soon, basking in the unaccustomed warmth of another cat's body next to his, Domino slept again, too.

After that, the Brown territory became Celine's home, too. Though the two cats separated in the mornings to make their respective rounds—Domino of the Brown property and Celine of the woods—they always joined up after moonrise to share a brief patrol before retiring to the loft.

ON CELINE'S first day at the Browns', Domino showed her around his route. They exited the barn through the cat door, which Mr. Brown had installed when Domino first arrived to work the territory. He took her past the henhouse and showed her inside the children's mossy-roofed clubhouse. Then they crossed the edge of the lawn and worked their way alongside the ancient stone wall to approach the main house. Domino brought Celine up onto the back porch to check for breakfast. (That day there was a bowlful of dry cat food.) Finally, he showed her the invisible line along which to strut to torment Thor most effectively.

Celine's first outing went brilliantly. Thor had been asleep when the scent of a strange cat wafted past his nose. Before waking completely, he was already barreling toward her in full assault mode. He might not have been there at all, for all the notice she paid him, coolly cleaning a paw as though she had not a care in the world.

Thor's dripping jaws were mere centimeters from closing around her neck when he was brought up hard by the tether, his raucous bark choked off to a yelp. Only then, in his painful humiliation, did Celine seem to see him. Her smug expression sent Domino into a swoon of admiration as he watched from the shadow of the barn.

Outraged, Thor set to barking viciously at the new cat. As his mouth was only a few inches from her sensitive ears, Celine lifted tail and swaggered decadently away with a look of annoyance. She joined Domino by the barn, where they could look at Thor and gloat together. The dog would not calm down, however, and he strained at the end of his tether to bark as loudly as he could at them.

"Crude but effective," commented Domino, as the annoying racket continued unabated. The cats sauntered away past the hens and the children's clubhouse to the peaceful grassy spot beside the stone wall. The enormous oak that shaded the area all summer had shed its leaves, allowing the weakening sun to cast what little warmth it might unimpeded. Domino rubbed his head along Celine's side. He loved the way her dark fur gathered heat from the feeble sunlight and gave it back to him. He thought her black coat looked exceptionally fine, contrasting against the brightly colored leaves all around.

"That was one of the best dog baiting runs I've ever seen," he complimented her. "You walked the razor's edge."

She blinked demurely. "Actually, it was a total thrill."

"I admit," said Domino, "I was almost frightened for you at the last second. It seemed like he might reach you."

"I wasn't afraid," she said. "I knew you wouldn't have steered me wrong."

Thunderous purrs erupted from Domino. He head-butted her happily, almost knocking her over in his delight. What had he done to earn the trust of this extraordinary cat?

. . .

AS WINTER CAME ON, the children brought an old cooler with a cat-size doorway cut into the side up to the loft. They had lined the makeshift den with fleece blankets. Inside it, in a jumble with Celine, Domino basked in the heat coming off her body. He was as cozy as any hearth-side lap cat, and he happily fell into the habit of sleeping better than he ever had.

One morning, with head high and ears forward, Domino sniffed the northwesterly breeze. The first snow was coming.

He had already completed his morning rounds and taken a tasty sparrow for breakfast. Celine had vanished over the stone wall for the day, and he was antsy. For the past few weeks, he had been happily distracted by his new companion. But now that their lives had settled into a routine, his mind returned to its previous concerns. Domino suddenly wondered what Flufferdoodle was up to as he realized he missed the big tom's company. And then he remembered the new cat in the Neighborhood, Socrates. "I certainly hope he doesn't think he has cowed me from roaming there if I please," meowed Domino to no one in particular.

And he was off, trotting down the Browns' driveway, pausing to check for cars, and crossing the road. He wove through the thin woods and arrived in the bushes behind Meg's house. As there was no sign of his friend there, Domino continued into the neighboring yard.

He still didn't see Flufferdoodle there, so he went around to the front of the house. He finally caught sight of the huge orange cat lolling on the front doorstep. Domino came up to him briskly. "Hey, Fluff," he said.

Flufferdoodle rolled onto his impressive stomach and grunted a greeting.

"Enjoying your nap?" asked Domino.

"Not really," the big cat grumbled. "This flagstone was

warm from the little bit of sun this morning, but it seems to have cooled off now." He lifted himself to his feet with a sigh. "I may as well get up." He yawned and sat. "How have you been, old friend? Long time no see."

"Yeah, I know. Sorry about that."

"That's cool. I mean, Meg's family closes the window now that it's cold, and I can't visit her, then you disappear... whatever. I'm fine, don't worry about me."

Domino head-butted his friend. "I apologize. It's just that, well, there was this little black cat that came out of the woods over at the Browns'—"

"Let me guess: a female."

Domino hung his head, grinning. "Yes, a female."

"Say no more, Dom. Say no more." Flufferdoodle stood and took a step toward the street. "But since you're here now, what do you say we patrol?"

"Lead the way." Domino fell into step alongside Flufferdoodle as they crossed the pavement and began moving alongside the border of dead hostas. "How have things been in the Neighborhood? Any news?"

"Nothing, really, except that clown, Socrates, has been spreading his addle-headed mush around." Flufferdoodle stopped walking and looked Domino in the eye. "Really, I'm shocked that so many cats are listening to him."

Domino kept walking. "Told you he was trouble."

As they reached the edge of the cover and contemplated crossing an open lawn, a foul stench reached their nostrils. "Ugh, what is that?" snarled Domino.

"Ah, that... that is a gift from our friend, Max the dog," explained Flufferdoodle. "He is a poster puppy for one of our favorite canine qualities—leaving one's poo lying around."

They skirted the pile with disgust and continued toward

the woods around the Gully. "Oh, and you were right about Socrates and Max," continued Flufferdoodle. "They do know each other. They share people. They live together."

"So what? I share my people with a dog. But we aren't friends, and he certainly doesn't obey my commands."

Flufferdoodle shook his head. "I know. I don't get it, either. I gather they were adopted when they were a kit and a pup, and they just don't know any better."

"Well, be that as it may, how is it that Max is free to litter the neighborhood with his feces?"

"Oh, this will thrill you," Flufferdoodle said drily. "Socrates claims that he has figured out how to open the door at his house."

Domino stopped in amazement. "What? Socrates figured that out?" His eyes were as wide as a bat's and his mouth hung open in an undignified, not-very-catlike manner. To cats, opening a door is the pinnacle of feline intellectual achievement, a goal attained only by the most brilliant animals. "Wow." Ears slightly flattened, Domino moved forward again.

"Listen, just because he's highly intelligent doesn't mean he's very smart," Flufferdoodle consoled him.

"Good point." Domino regarded his friend. "Flufferdoodle, have I told you lately how glad I am to know you?"

"No, but now is as good a time as any."

As they worked their way through the trees, they heard a meow of greeting. Cricket came to them, her calico coat almost invisible against the litter of brown leaves. "Hi, Domino. Hi, Flufferdoodle," she purred in her chirpy voice.

"Hey, Cricket," the toms greeted her. There was much touching of noses, head-butting, and purring before the friends settled in for small talk.

"Snow's coming," Domino said. "You ready for it, Cricket?"

"Oh, yes," purred the calico. "I got a cozy little den all set up and ready to go. Come on, I'll show you." She led the way down into the ravine and over a few boulders. Then she squeezed through a narrow space between the roots of a fallen tree and disappeared. Domino looked at Flufferdoodle, who shook his head. "No way I'm fitting in there. You go check it out. I'll wait out here."

"Okay."

Domino was long, but he was slim and wiry. He snaked his way under the fallen tree and emerged in a sizable den that had been formed by the unearthing of the roots. The space was large enough for both cats, but small and snug enough that it would hold Cricket's body heat during the cold months ahead. The industrious female had pulled in moss and leaves to line the space and create a cozy sleep nest. "You like it?" she asked as her guest looked around.

"I think it's very nice," Domino purred. "You'll get through the winter in comfort and style."

After taking their leave of Cricket, Domino and Flufferdoodle continued through the brief woodland and came out on the pavement near the Prowl meet-up site. Even now, a few cats were getting in a last bit of socializing while the ground was still dry. Domino looked more closely as they approached. "What the...?"

Lily was sitting like a normal cat, but facing her were Tiger and Mister, and they were sitting up as Socrates had done when Domino first saw him. He trotted up to the threesome in an agitated posture. Tiger and Mister saw him coming and meowed a greeting.

"Meow to you, too," Domino answered. He came to a halt and sat beside Lily, facing the two tabbies. "So, um, what are you guys doing?"

Tiger and Mister looked at each other in confusion, then back at Domino. "What, you mean sitting up like this?" asked Tiger.

"Yes, that."

"I don't know. Why not?"

"You should try it," added Mister. "It puts you up high and you can see better. It makes you feel bigger and more important."

"Which is why I don't care for it," said Domino. "It makes some cats feel bigger and more important."

"Yeah, but any cat can do it, so it's not like it actually *does* make anyone bigger and more important," Tiger pointed out.

"That is true," admitted Domino. "But then those who choose not to do it are made to feel lower."

Mister shrugged. "That's their choice."

"Yeah," agreed Tiger. "So why would any cat *not* choose to sit up high?"

"Because it isn't catlike behavior," Domino hissed.

"Great Cats! Settle down, Domino," Lily meowed. "It's really not that big a deal. Look." And she sat back on her haunches, lifted her forepaws, and sat up high, too. "See? It's easy. Try it."

"No thanks," demurred Domino. "I'm not some kind of *squirrel* or something." He pronounced the word *squirrel* with contempt, which earned him another disapproving look from Lily. "Now what?" he meowed.

"It's just that it's not very nice to use the names of other kinds of animals as an insult. How do you think it makes the other animals feel?"

"What? Who cares how they *feel?*" Domino didn't know what to make of this new line of thought. He felt the fur on the back of his neck prickle as though it might rise, even though there was no physical threat to him.

By now Flufferdoodle had sauntered up to the group to sit beside Domino. He was so large that his eyes were level with those of the cats that were sitting up high, negating the effect. Domino smirked when he saw this.

"How's it going, cats?" Flufferdoodle meowed in his deep voice.

"Hey, Flufferdoodle," the others meowed.

"Smells like snow is coming," observed Mister.

"Oh yes; I'd say by tonight, for sure," added Tiger.

Lily looked sour. "Guess it's time to start spending more time indoors with the people."

Domino was only listening with one ear while the other one rotated constantly to take in information from all directions. Soon he detected a rustling sound from the grass that bordered the woods behind him. Turning his head, he saw a chipmunk picking seeds from pinecones along the edge of the ground cover.

The chatter of Domino's companions faded into the background as his eyes and ears locked onto the rodent. His tail twitched and he went into a crouch. Every muscle rigid, Domino waited for the chipmunk to look away. When it went to work on a new pinecone, Domino took two stalking steps toward it.

Distantly, he could hear the other cats murmuring. He heard Lily snicker. Eyes locked to prey, he did not turn his head to see what was funny. He took another nearly invisible step toward the chipmunk.

Suddenly, to Domino's bewilderment, Lily loped past him, approaching the rodent with no stealth at all. "Shoo," she called to it.

The chipmunk saw her. It froze momentarily in terror before turning and shooting like a bolt of lightning to a nearby stone wall, where it disappeared.

Domino sat up in wrathful amazement, his ears pinned back and his baleful glare fixed on Lily. "What wretched behavior was that?" he spat.

Lily sat to face him, looking more annoyed than anything else. "I just didn't feel like watching you tear apart a poor, defenseless creature, that's all," she said. She lifted a forepaw and began cleaning it dismissively.

"Poor, defenseless creature?" Domino sputtered. "Great Cats, where do you get this stuff?" Even as he asked the question, he knew the answer. "Listen, *vermin* are not poor, defenseless creatures," he began. "They are mean-tempered and destructive. They carry disease and fleas."

"Which is why our people give us shots and flea drops," answered Lily.

Again, Domino's mouth hung open before he remembered to snap it shut. "Not all cats," he reminded her. "Not Cricket. Not Rudy."

"Well, that's their problem," said Lily. "Cricket could go live with people anytime she wanted. They love her."

"But she doesn't *want* to," said Domino. "She wants to be a wild cat."

"Whatever. That's her choice," Lily concluded. It was plain she thought it the wrong choice.

Utterly frustrated, Domino was bereft of answers to counter this new way of thinking. "You guys must all have rabies or something," he grumbled. He glared around at the other cats, announced he was going back to his territory where cats were free to act like cats, and stormed off.

He soon sensed the heavy tread of Flufferdoodle as the large cat trotted to catch up with him.

"Wait up, I'll walk you back to my place," he said.

"Thanks, Fluff."

Though Domino was glad to have the companionship of his friend, the two cats said nothing the entire way back to Flufferdoodle's yard. As they approached the gray-shingled house, Flufferdoodle shoved his face into Domino's shoulder. "Seriously, don't let them get to you, Dom. They're just over-thinking things. It's stupid. It won't last."

Before Domino could answer, the door to the house opened and a small girl came out. "Flufferdoodle, there you are," she called.

"Later," said Flufferdoodle. He went to his mistress, looked up, and meowed a greeting. She scooped him up in her arms, an impressive feat of strength for the small girl who had given the enormous cat his name a few years earlier, when she had just four years. Flufferdoodle touched noses and rubbed his cheek against hers. Holding him, the girl closed her eyes and smiled. "I love you, Flufferdoodle," she said.

Domino watched his friend in the girl's warm embrace. It was a touching sight, and when he turned to head back to his territory, he felt comforted. The rage that had flared at Lily's obnoxiousness faded. *What a silly cat she is,* he thought as he passed through the hedgerow behind Flufferdoodle's property. *She wouldn't last a day in Celine's woods.*

THREE

The snow came and settled the Brown territory under a white layer. The smells, the scurry of animals, even the percussive clucks of the hens were muted. Domino and Celine made their way more slowly than usual on their morning rounds, pausing to sniff and test the snow as they patrolled. When they reached the stone wall, Celine touched Domino's nose before turning to leap over the wall and vanish into the woods.

"Happy hunting," he called after her.

He continued on, taking morning inventory of the grounds. He cast a watchful eye over the hens as he sniffed and investigated every new set of tracks. Mostly they had been made by small birds poking through the snow for errant grains of chicken feed. All seemed to be in order. Domino crossed the driveway, passed Thor's run, ducked through the winter-bare bank of hydrangea, and headed for the northern perimeter. He traversed a small field until, once again, the Brown territory dissolved into woodland. Domino had worked his way through these woods the previous summer and knew they were not extensive. The road bordered them to the west and the large meadow to the east. If he went straight north, the woods would end at another territory, similar to the Browns', though those people kept neither a cat nor any other creature.

Domino followed the near edge of the woodland and monitored spoor—mostly rabbits' and birds', punctuated by a possum's and a raccoon's. Then his lips pulled back as he came across a new set of tracks. They were nearly the size of a rabbit's though lacking the large back footprints, and the stink of rat hung over them like a malodorous haze. Domino's ears went back as he raised his head and made a visual scan of the area, breathing through his open mouth to catch any additional information in the air. He saw nothing out of the ordinary, so he bent his head to the tracks and followed them. They traced the edge of the trees, often disappearing into ground cover (although the reek was still easy enough to follow) and came out at last on the edge of the road. Domino wasn't sure, but he thought there were several sets of rat tracks here, although it could have been the same animal going back and forth along the roadside.

After a thorough search of the area, he concluded that the creature or creatures had returned across the road in the direction of the Neighborhood. He turned and headed back to the house. It was chilly out and he had run a wide patrol over snow-covered ground. A bowl of cat food would hit the spot.

Later, with a full belly, Domino leaped onto the wide rail of the Browns' back porch for a midmorning nap in the winter sun. But he dozed fitfully, the fresh rat tracks prominent in his thoughts. Uneasy, he found himself wishing Celine were with him. She was as skilled a hunter as he was fearless; she would doubtless have some insights about the new development.

Domino stood and stretched deeply then leaped to the

ground. Soon he was perched atop the stone wall. Thanks to the fresh snow, he could easily see the route Celine had taken. He paused to look around and scent the air. All was clear, and he stepped down from his vantage point to the wild side of the wall.

Domino had explored these woods briefly when he was new to the area. Unlike the woodland at the north side of the property, this went on seemingly forever. With no human settlements or dogs to give it order, the forest was both fascinating and formidable. One time, Domino had narrowly avoided a prowling raccoon and another time, he had come across coyote fur lodged in the bark of a tree against which the beast had rubbed itself. *It's probably riddled with fleas,* Domino had thought at the time. With a large territory to work and fields beyond the barn for sporting, he had plenty to do without placing himself in danger. A judicious animal, Domino had not sought to add the woods to his territory.

But today, knowing that Celine had passed this way, he felt safe following her path. He looked around and sniffed the air one more time before proceeding farther. With the leaves down, the place wasn't as dark and there wasn't as much concealing cover as the last time he'd explored. Domino knew his black-and-white fur worked well against the snow-mottled ground. He tracked Celine's trail. She had followed what appeared to be a deer path for some distance. Then she had crossed an area of turkey scratches. By the patterns in the snow, Domino saw that she had given a dropped feather a hard time before carrying on.

The ground dipped and Domino came to a depression. The dry autumn had passed and the bowl-shaped area had begun filling with water. It was frozen over now but would become a sizable vernal pool. Celine's tracks skirted the pool and went away to the east, and Domino followed.

The forest floor became dense with fallen trees, dormant undergrowth, and leaf litter. Here were more boulders and gullies as well. A feeling of rightness and strength came over the barn cat as he climbed and leaped, slunk along the edges of logs, sniffed and sprayed. The air was crisp and bright with a light breeze bringing fresh smells. Domino coiled and sprang, alighting soundlessly on a snowy stone top and taking pleasure in the strength of his muscles and the skill of his body. Up high again, he lifted his head regally and looked all around. There were countless holes to explore and objects to climb. Everywhere, birds foraged and vermin skittered. Domino breathed deeply. "I can see why Celine likes it here," he said to himself.

He finished admiring the view and returned to his tracking. The dainty paw prints clearly marked Celine's path, and he followed them fondly. Then all at once, his back was up and his fur stood out straight. Another set of prints had joined Celine's. They were feline as well but much larger than a regular cat's.

"*Bobcat*," Domino hissed. He looked about wildly but saw nothing. Every instinct in his body screamed for him to return to the safety of his territory, but Domino thought of Celine and forced himself to investigate further.

Since it was certain Celine would not keep company with a deadly predator, Domino could only conclude that the big cat was stalking her. "Oh, Celine," he moaned. Ears flat and fur still on end, he took several brave steps along the path. He looked ahead constantly but could see no movement of anything larger than a squirrel. Whatever had transpired here had taken place hours earlier, while he had been investigating rat spoor on the farthest edge of his territory.

A silent shadow passed over him. With an involuntary sideways leap, Domino landed in a crouch and looked up. Just above the bare treetops, a red-tailed hawk cruised past. Domino met its eye as it coldly assessed him, sizing him up for a possible meal. Domino glared back. "Come down here and try it," he yelled. The bird didn't bother to answer as it glided on, its icy gaze searching among the trees for smaller prey.

Grateful yet again for his size, Domino nonetheless backed into a hollow in the dead tree behind him. The bobcat's tracks followed by the raptor's shadow had unnerved him. Though his winter coat kept him warm, he shivered.

Domino knew himself to be a courageous and dedicated hunter. He also had a keen understanding of the rules of the hunt. In nature, size and strength win. Domino was big and strong—for a cat. He could take plenty of animals with ease. But he also understood that there were other animals that could take him just as easily. He grasped the difference between courage and foolishness.

And though his heart quailed with apprehension for his friend, Domino knew that tromping through the woods until something ate him would not help Celine. "She grew up here and she lived here until she came to me," he reminded himself. "Celine knows what she's doing."

It was a blow to his pride, but Domino recognized that he did not have the awareness that the diminutive black cat possessed of the rules of the woodland. And the rules were the rules; a cat could learn them, live by them, even use them in his favor, but they would not change for a cat or for any creature. Domino would not challenge them today.

On high alert, he made his cautious way back along the trail of paw prints. When he at last crested the stone wall, he paused to look back. Silent and shadow crossed, the woods gave no clue as to Celine's fate. With one last meditation for her safety, Domino returned to his side of the wall. He felt better the instant his paws landed on the frosted sod of his own territory.

He spent the remainder of the afternoon dozing on the fleece blanket in the hayloft. As he watched the sun lower to the horizon, he at last spotted Celine crossing the yard to approach the barn.

"WHY DON'T you go see your friends anymore?" Celine's meow was gentle but insistent.

"I don't know. It's been kind of cold, I guess. I hate the feeling of ice between my paw pads."

"Well, it's warm today."

It was true. A rare spell of autumn-like weather in the dead of winter had set in. Snow melted off all the hard surfaces, and branches were bare and black against the sky. It even smelled as though there would be rain before long.

"Yeah, I guess." But Domino's tone was not enthusiastic.

Celine mentioned the ultimate incentive. "I bet there'll be a Prowl tonight."

The waxing moon was low and heavy in the evening sky, highlighting the earth with a metallic-looking glow. A balmy, damp wind carried recently awakened scents as creatures of all sorts took advantage of the warm weather to stretch their legs, wings, and tails. Domino could not deny the conditions were perfect. "Yeah, probably," he allowed.

Celine stretched playfully onto her back, showing Domino her belly. "Well, I, for one, am bored. Enough staying close to the den because of the winter! It's nice out. Let's take advantage of it." She rolled onto her stomach and fixed him with her golden gaze. "I'd really like to meet Flufferdoodle and Meg."

Domino looked down at her. He always wanted to please her, but he was reluctant to head back to the Neighborhood. "You probably won't be able to meet Meg," he predicted. "Her people will have the window closed against the cold."

"Maybe not. It's as warm as an early fall day. And I can still meet Flufferdoodle. And Cricket," she added.

"Well, that's about all of them that I'd care to see these days."

"Oh, come on. Tiger and Mister are your old friends. You told me so."

Domino stared out through the open hayloft door. "Yeah, but they're not as fun as they used to be," he said.

Celine was on her feet, going to him and pushing her head into his chest. "You don't know that. I bet they've figured out what a weirdo this Socrates cat is by now." She began to purr. "Maybe his people even packed him and that dog up and moved back to the city."

"I wouldn't count on it." But Domino was purring, too.

Celine won and the pair set out to the Neighborhood. As they left the Brown territory and approached the road, Domino was certain he sniffed rat again. The odor was near the same area he had found the tracks after the first snow of the winter. "Do you smell that?" he asked his companion.

Celine paused to lift her pointed little nose and scent the air. "Hmm, I think I smell something."

"Rat?"

She sniffed a bit more. "Could be. Not sure, with all the other smells in the air." She noticed his intense look and added, "but it could be."

They passed through the thin woodland. "Here's the hedgerow behind Meg's house," Domino said. They moved through the cover and stopped at the edge of the lawn to survey the open expanse. "Well, I'll be ..." Domino uttered.

The night was so balmy that Meg's people had indeed left the kitchen window open. "Is that Flufferdoodle?" Celine whispered. She had spied the enormous longhaired cat perched on the patio table, where he could nose against the screen.

"Yes. Come on." Domino led the way, stalking noiselessly across the yard. Celine moved at his side, a silent moon shadow slicing through the rough winter grass. At the same moment, they leaped onto the tabletop.

Flufferdoodle flung himself sideways to slam against the wall with a percussive bang. He landed facing them, his tail puffed out as big as a raccoon's. He was confused at first to see the small female who confronted him. Then he saw Domino and his bared teeth were replaced with a scowl. "Will you ever grow up, Domino?" he growled.

Mirth was evident in Domino's voice as he said, "Fluff, meet Celine. Celine, this is my best buddy, Flufferdoodle."

Annoyed at being flustered when finally meeting his friend's new acquaintance, the ginger male pulled himself together quickly. "Good evening, my dear," he meowed suavely.

"Hello." Celine stepped forward delicately on her long legs and lifted her chin to touch noses with him. "It's wonderful to finally meet Domino's friends."

"The feeling is mutual." Flufferdoodle stepped back so Celine could approach the window screen. "And this is Meg," he said.

"Hi, there," meowed the winsome Siamese.

"Hello," said Celine. She and Meg sniffed one another as best they could through the screen.

Domino and Flufferdoodle sat together and watched the females. "Good, they seem to like one another," said Flufferdoodle in a low voice.

"Yes, it seems to be going well," agreed Domino. "Although you never know, especially with females."

"I love your points," Celine was complimenting Meg. "Black tips and paws are just so *elegant*."

"Thanks," purred Meg. "But I've really always wanted to be all one shade, like you. All that midnight fur just makes you look so *sleek*."

"Oh, brother," said Domino.

Celine turned to hiss him into silence before resuming her talk with Meg. Chastened, the toms sat patiently until the females had finished their conversation about grooming and nail-sharpening techniques. At last, the outdoor group bade Meg farewell and left her alone on her windowsill to look out into the night and imagine.

New smells struck the cats almost as soon as they left Flufferdoodle's territory. "I say, you Neighborhood cats have gotten really lazy," Domino critiqued. "It stinks of rat around here."

"Yeah, about that," Flufferdoodle began. "There have been some rather unfortunate changes since your last visit."

"Let me guess," said Domino. "No one hunts vermin anymore."

"Oh, it's even worse than that," said Flufferdoodle.

"That doesn't even make sense," Celine protested. "What kind of cat can see a rat or a chipmunk or a sparrow within range and not make a go of it?"

"You got me," was all Flufferdoodle could answer.

They eventually made the small woodland by the Gully and passed through it to collect Cricket. She and Celine touched noses like old friends, and the toms sat patiently while Cricket showed off her cozy den to the new cat. As the females returned, the calico was just finishing up with, "...and I haven't been even a little bit cold all winter!"

As Cricket passed him, Domino noticed moonlight reflecting off her side and delineating clearly visible ribs. He began to pace alongside her. "Cricket, are you getting enough to eat?" he asked.

"Oh, I'm doing okay," she replied. "I got a new patron, a sweet old lady, but she's all the way across the Neighborhood. Sometimes, when the snow is too bad, I don't get over there every day."

"But these woods are full of tracks and scat," Domino noted. "You must have plenty of prey."

Cricket smiled indulgently at him as though he were missing something obvious. "Oh, no one really hunts anymore," she explained.

Domino's throat tightened so that any words he may have uttered were choked off.

"I never thought about it," Cricket continued, "but smaller animals aren't really any different from us. They've got to eat, they've got to stay warm, they've got babies to feed." She looked into Domino's staring eyes. "They've got feelings, too, you know?"

"Cricket," he managed to sputter. "You're a cat. *You* have feelings. *You* have to eat. You have to *hunt*. You have to—"

"There's really no point." Flufferdoodle sidled between Domino and Cricket, detouring his old friend away to speak privately. "You can't talk to any of them. I've tried."

"But it's crazy," Domino exclaimed in a controlled howl.

"Yes, it is. And there's naught you can do about it."

Domino quick-stepped ahead of Flufferdoodle to look at Cricket again. Celine was chatting with her now as they walked. Cricket wore the same open, friendly expression on her face that she always had, but now she looked different to Domino. Her eyes seemed vacant, missing the crucial feline light of critical thought. Her sweet, accepting personality, which all the cats—people, too—had always loved about her, now revealed itself for the first time as an unfortunate trait.

Domino slowed his pace and dropped back to walk alongside Flufferdoodle again. "Like I said," repeated the big cat, "there's naught you can do about it. I recommend you just ignore it and enjoy hanging out otherwise." He bumped against Domino, nearly knocking his old friend over. "Come on, it's a perfect night," Flufferdoodle went on. "I bet the whole Neighborhood contingent will be out."

Flufferdoodle turned out to be right. Cats were prowling along the side of the road and across lawns, sharpening their claws on tree trunks and pouncing at random objects. Tiger and Mister, inseparable as always, were executing a standoff with Izzy, a large calico female with white chin and paws. "Oh, I love this," exclaimed Flufferdoodle. He trotted over to join the trio and added his basso profundo yowls to the strains.

Domino stood nearby with Celine and Cricket and watched. Before long, a meow of greeting reached him. He turned his head to see Lily strolling over to them. "Hey, Lily," he meowed back. He had decided to try Flufferdoodle's recommendation to ignore the strange new customs and just have fun, so he had already resolved to forget about her silly behavior with the chipmunk the last time he had been in the Neighborhood. The tuxedo cat touched noses with him before noticing Celine.

"Why, hello," said Lily.

"Lily, this is Celine," Cricket explained. "She came with Domino."

"So I see," answered Lily. "Welcome to the Prowl."

"Thank you." Celine stepped forward shyly to touch noses. She was the smallest cat at the Prowl, and a shaggy winter coat had replaced her summer sheen. A housecat, Lily had black fur, too, but with clean white patches at her chest and paws. Sleek and well fed, she was an impressive animal.

"So, where'd Domino find you?" she meowed.

"Actually, she found me." Domino came to sit beside Celine. "She appeared alongside the stone wall at the edge of the woods on my territory."

"The woods?" Lily looked from Domino back to Celine. "So, are you a wild cat?"

"Well, not exactly," began Celine. "I had people once, when I was a kit, but they had a male child who wasn't very nice. So as I got bigger, I spent more time out on my own. I became a pretty good hunter and the better I got, the more I really enjoyed—"

"So how did you meet our Domino?" Lily cut her off.

Confused, Celine hesitated at the interruption. "Well, it's kind of a funny story, actually," she began again. "I had been working the woods near this house for a while. I could smell that they kept chickens there, and where there are chickens—"

"—there's chicken feed," Domino finished for her. "And where there's chicken feed—"

"—there are rats." Celine smiled at him before turning her attention back to Lily. "So anyway, I was stalking along the shadow of this stone wall when all of a sudden, I hear this crazy squeaking. I look up, and here comes a huge rat, barreling right toward me—"

"Uh oh, I'm not sure I like the way this story is going," laughed Lily.

Celine stopped speaking, baffled.

"Why? What's wrong?" asked Domino. "It's a funny story, really."

"If it involves a rat and a wild cat," Lily explained, inclining her head at Celine, "it's probably going to end up with somebody getting hurt."

"If by *somebody* you mean the rat, you're absolutely right," meowed Celine. The note of feline pride in her lilting meow caught at Domino's heart, sparking his protective instinct.

Lily transferred her attention to Cricket, who had been looking about at the numerous cats prowling the area. "Nice turnout tonight, hey, Cricket?"

"Oh, I'll say," answered the calico. "But where's Socrates? Isn't he coming?"

Domino felt the follicles tighten all along his back at the Siamese's name, but he pretended not to care one way or the other. He began to inspect a lifted forepaw as he listened to Lily's answer: "I'm sure he'll be here any time now."

"Oh." Cricket looked around at the gathered cats some more. "Hey, what about Rudy? Has anyone seen him lately?"

"Not me," answered Lily. "But I think Mister saw him a few days ago." She glanced away as a gray female came into view across the pavement. "She's got a nerve, coming here," Lily muttered under her breath. To the small group, she said, "I'll see you guys later. I have to go take care of something." With flattened ears, she stalked across the pavement to confront the newcomer.

Domino chuckled as the tuxedo and gray cats postured at one another and began yowling. "That Lily, she is such a drama queen," he said.

"Rudy doesn't really come to Prowls anymore," Cricket went on. "He hangs around the Gully plenty, though, but all stealth-like." Her voice lowered to a whisper. "He goes there to *hunt*, you know. Even though we all know that's wrong now, he doesn't care."

Celine looked at Cricket in confusion. "Wrong? How can it be wrong? It's the most basic job there is for a cat... besides sleeping," she added fondly.

"It's like this," Cricket explained. "Hunting may be fun for us, but for the prey, it's a horror show." Her eyes widened with empathy. "How would you like to be torn apart by a larger, stronger animal?"

"I wouldn't like it at all," Celine answered matter-of-factly. "In fact, I take great care to avoid such an outcome when I patrol the woods."

"Yeah, but that's wrong, too," Cricket said. "No one should hunt. No one should do anything that hurts anyone else."

"I see," Domino meowed coldly. "Is that what you tell an angry dog as it prepares to bite your head off?"

"Max is perfectly nice," Cricket replied. "He hangs out with us cats now."

Domino turned away and shuddered. "Disgusting," he muttered to himself.

A breeze crept low along the ground but with an implied urgency, heavy and wet and laden with smells. Domino scented many things on it, some of them unpleasant, some downright disturbing. The stink of dog washed over them, and a moment later Socrates strolled into the center of the pavement, where the streetlight drew a sickly glow from his pale fur. Just behind him paced Max, who stopped and sat obediently, opened his mouth, and dropped his tongue like an anchor.

The Siamese sat up in his customary squirrel-like posture and called out in a loud meow, "Good evening, everyone. What a glorious night for a Prowl."

All around, feline activity ceased as cats headed toward the illuminated circle. Cricket stopped talking to Celine midsentence and went quickly to sit near Socrates. Other cats jostled and butted one another to claim a good spot. Socrates waited patiently, a benevolent expression on his face, until the cats had settled down and all were sitting up high like him, waiting expectantly.

At the back of the gathering, Domino and Celine had turned to look at him as well, though they held their position and sat normally. Flufferdoodle sauntered over to Domino's side, his former howl-mates having abandoned him to join the audience. "I wonder what entertainments Suck-rat-ees has in store for us tonight?" he growled to his old friend. Domino tried to smile back, but it was more a grim tightening of his lips.

With Max seated just behind him and to one side, Socrates gazed at each cat in turn. "A glorious night for a Prowl, indeed," he repeated. "It is wonderful to see you all gathered here, enjoying yourselves and one another, exchanging greetings, making your music. You are truly a shining example of what felines—indeed, all creatures—can be when they allow themselves to transcend their lower instincts and instead be their highest, best selves. Simply a beautiful sight," he meowed, again looking at each cat in turn.

Lily turned her head slightly down and to the side, and Domino caught a look of self-satisfaction on her face. He imagined more than one cat wore the same expression, though he couldn't be sure because they were all facing away from him to see Socrates.

The Siamese began to address some of the cats by name.

"Mister, hope you are having an enjoyable Prowl. Lily, my pet, it is always a joy to see you." The tuxedo bowed her head at his praise. At Domino's side, Flufferdoodle made a sound like he was working on a hairball. Domino snickered.

"Domino, what a rare pleasure to see you," Socrates boomed. All humor left Domino as he looked up to meet the strange cat's pale eyes, fixed upon him with a disturbing intensity. "We are all so glad you've seen fit to join my humble address."

"*Your* humble address?" Domino sputtered. He felt the scrutiny of all the gathered cats as they turned to look at him. "It's the *Prowl*."

But Socrates had moved on to the next cat, drawing all attention back to himself. After several more greetings, he paused and gathered himself. His expression of benevolence intensified. "Tonight, I want to show you all something very special. I have invited guests to this evening's gathering, and I'd appreciate it very much if you would show them your most courteous—your most *transcendent*—good behavior." He turned to look at the meaty dog hunkered behind him. "Are they here yet, Max?"

"Yeah, yup, here they are," the dog woofed. He bent his head to nudge two small creatures as they came timidly from behind him and stepped into the ring of light. Edging forward, they moved alongside Socrates and sat up like squirrels, blinking in the light and looking at the cats gathered all around.

Domino felt his eyes might eject from his skull, they had sprung open so wide. Yet again, his mouth hung open in un-cat-like amazement. Socrates had summoned forth two large, gray rats, and they now sat beside him as though they had every right to be part of a cats' Prowl.

"Everyone," meowed Socrates over the sudden murmurs,

"these are some friends of mine. They have a few words they'd like to say." Socrates waited for the cats to quiet down before turning an encouraging look upon the larger of the two rats. "Go ahead, Sunflower Seed."

"*Sunflower Seed?*" sputtered Domino so that only Flufferdoodle and Celine heard him. "Since when does food have a name?"

The larger rat, a male, stepped forward and coughed politely to clear his throat. "Uh, hello, fellow creatures," he began in his squeaky rat voice. "Uh, my name is Sunflower Seed, and this is my mate, Meadow." He half turned and indicated the female beside him. She nodded shyly as he went on. "I—I just want to start by saying what an honor and a privilege it is for us to be invited to an actual Prowl. I mean, gracious, here we are at an honest-to-goodness cat Prowl. Us. Two rats!" He shook his head in amazement. "I never thought I'd see such a thing ..." He faltered, apparently overcome with emotion.

Domino couldn't look away from the odd sight. The two rodents were definitely rats, but they were somehow different from the occasional rat he came across on his territory. They were larger. Also, their fur was cleaner than any rat he'd ever seen, as though they had taken great pains to tidy themselves up for the occasion in a way that would be pleasing to cats. But Domino had never known a rat to tidy itself thus. A sickening thought sprang into his mind: *It's almost as though a cat groomed them.* The contents of his stomach roiled and he shook his head to clear it of the absurd idea.

Sunflower Seed had recovered himself. "Wow, I mean, this must be a first, right? I think we're all really lucky to be present at such a momentous occasion. This is something we can all tell our babies about someday." He froze as though realizing he had committed a faux pas. "I mean those of us who aren't fixed."

He appeared horrified at his misspeak. "Uh, sorry," he stammered. "I hope I didn't hurt anyone's feelings." The cats were silent as he tried to correct the situation. "Please excuse my error. I'm used to being among my own kind. I have a lot to learn about what's normal for cats. You see, humans don't care for us rats the way they care for you cats. Humans would never take us into their homes and feed us and take us for medical care."

Several cats nodded in understanding.

Encouraged, Sunflower Seed spoke with renewed confidence. "You see, humans aren't very kind to us rats at all. They don't just shut us out; they actively try to destroy us. They poison us. They trap us. They poison our babies. And sometimes ..." and here, he hung his head, clenching his eyes as though his next words were almost too painful to bring forth. "Sometimes," he continued in a small voice, "they even send cats to kill us."

Sunflower Seed's shoulders heaved once. Meadow scampered closer to him. She sat up again to place a comforting paw around him and Sunflower Seed clung to her as emotions overtook him. All around them (to Domino's astonishment), cats were murmuring soft meows of pity.

Meadow looked up at the gathered cats. "Please excuse my mate," she squeaked. Her voice was even higher pitched than Sunflower Seed's, and Domino's ears twitched with displeasure. But the other cats had moved slightly closer to sit in sympathetic postures. "We been through some tough times," she explained. "We used to live in the City, but our building got exterminated. We just barely got out, but we lost all our family—parents, litter mates, cousins, and like that." Her beady eyes welled.

"You don't have to do this, Meadow," Sunflower Seed told her tenderly.

She smiled at her mate. "No, it's okay. I want to talk about it." He nodded and she returned her attention to the cats. "Anyway, we got out, me and Sunflower Seed. But it was winter by then, and we had nowhere warm to live." More empathetic murmurs came from the crowd.

"And I was pregnant, of course," she added with a sad chuckle.

The murmurs from the cats were even louder.

"I know, right?" Meadow said in a plucky voice. "So, anyway, we kept moving. Every time we thought we had a safe place to stay, humans would spot us and we knew it was time to move on. We had to be so careful about what we ate, since they would try to poison us all the time. And me so hungry with the babies growing in me." She gave that sad, brave laugh again. "Anyway, not far from this Neighborhood, we were laid up in a shed with the cold wind whistling through the holes in the wall and not a crumb to eat, when the babies came. I nursed them the best I could, of course, and Sunflower Seed did his best to take care of me. But the very next day ..." and she stopped talking as a spasm of tragedy overcame her. Now it was Sunflower Seed who put his paws around her and held her. She sobbed once then went on in a rushed voice, spitting the painful words out as quickly as possible. "The next day a cat got in, and we couldn't save the babies." She broke down in quick, squeaky, rodent sobs.

Cats everywhere meowed their sorrow and hung their heads in shame. Domino sighed in exasperation at their sympathetic reaction. Beside him, Flufferdoodle sat stock-still, fascinated at the spectacle of two rats weeping in front of a ring of cats. Domino looked at Celine, who was sitting on his other side. She grinned at him. "Well, what did it expect?" she purred. "Everyone knows babies are the most tender."

Domino barely refrained from laughing out loud, but Celine's dear face and amused expression were the best thing he could have wanted at that moment.

Up at the front of the group, the two rats were holding one another and emitting raspy, maudlin sobs while Socrates looked down upon them with solicitude.

Then Lily stepped forward and went to the pair. Noticing her approach, the rats lifted their faces to her. Domino watched, transfixed, as she lowered her head and *touched noses* first with Meadow, then with Sunflower Seed. Domino's mouth became awash with saliva as the contents of his stomach swirled precipitously and hurtled up his throat. Head low, he vomited onto the pavement. The world spun as his body strained to wretch up an unidentified sickening agent.

He heard Flufferdoodle's low voice near his ear. "Whoa, Dom, take it easy, tom." On his other side, Celine broke into an urgent purr and butted at his head. Crouched low with mouth agape, Domino panted in the cool, damp air. Gradually his head cleared enough for him to sit up again. "I'm okay," he growled to his companions without meeting their eyes.

All the cats were now taking turns greeting the two rats. Still nauseated, Domino was fastened to the spot in horror as he watched. Sunflower Seed and Meadow were walking from cat to cat, followed by Socrates, and just behind him, Max. The rats would sit up when they came to a cat, and the cat would lower his head and touch noses with them. There was an aura of breakthrough and unity and good will—indeed, of transcendence itself!—around each meeting. Escorting the rats, Socrates observed the proceedings with benevolence.

Unsure what to do, Flufferdoodle and Celine waited for

Domino's lead. But Domino was still dizzy and it was too late when he realized it was his turn to greet the newcomers.

The rats crept right up to him and looked him directly in the eye as though they were his equals. A rat had never approached him in this posture before, and in the blink of an eye Domino's back was up, his fur on end and his tail a bottle-brush. A venomous hiss burst from his mouth.

The rats instinctively flung themselves back, slamming against Socrates and knocking him off balance. Annoyance crossed the Siamese's face as he scrambled to his feet and sought to regain his composure. "Domino, if you please, do show our guests some manners," he meowed.

He had forced his voice into a normal, almost cordial meow, but Domino would have none of it. "I'd rather die than touch noses with a *rat*," he spat.

The two rodents stood petrified between the glaring cats. Flufferdoodle and Celine shifted nervously on either side of Domino, darting nervous glances from him to Max and back again. All the other cats stood captivated by the unfolding drama.

"Domino?" Socrates said in a warning meow.

Domino's only reply was a higher back and a louder hiss.

Socrates kept his cross-eyed gaze locked with Domino's as he spoke down to the rats. "You'll have to excuse Domino; he's a bit of a country bumpkin, but he'll come around."

"Not bloody likely," snarled Domino.

Neither cat blinked. "Max," meowed Socrates tensely, "would you be kind enough to escort Sunflower Seed and Meadow as they greet Domino?"

The yellow dog licked his chops. "With pleasure, Socrates." The fur on his shoulders rippled as he stepped forward with teeth bared.

With an earsplitting yowl, Domino launched himself off the cowering rats' backs and exploded into Socrates's face, where he became a blur of claws and teeth. Socrates utterly forgot to be transcendent and instantly transformed into a spitting ball of fur in response. But Domino was already up and over him and all about Max's head. The dog snapped his jaws at the black-and-white tempest. Domino felt a burning tug in his left rear flank. He locked tooth and claw onto the dog's neck and raked his hind feet over the animal's snout repeatedly, finally tearing his leg loose from Max's teeth in the process.

Max shook his head viciously. Domino allowed himself to be flung free and hit the ground running. He was off the pavement before Max had stopped shaking his head. The enraged dog pursued the black-and-white cat to the base of the nearest tree, but Domino had already put twenty-two feet of vertical space between them. He looked down at the furious beast barking his head off and hurling himself against the tree trunk.

Domino panted with his mouth hanging open. His heart hammered and his torn leg throbbed. He was still caught up in the euphoria of terror, and the furious dog appeared to him as a ferocious mythical beast, a ravenous wolf or a rabid hyena.

Then he remembered Celine and Flufferdoodle, and Domino scanned the area where the Prowl had just been. The two rats had vanished. Domino watched the other cats leave the area, some trotting nervously, some outright running, seeking the safety of their homes. Cricket had already streaked into the shelter of the trees, her eyes glazed as she ran on sheer instinct. Flufferdoodle and Celine fled past his tree to disappear into the wooded Gully.

Socrates was the only other creature who remained visible in the ring of light on the pavement. He sat deathly still and glared up at Domino with such intense malice that the big barn cat shook with dread and loathing.

Eventually, Max's racket became too irritating for the Siamese to endure. He stalked up to the baying canine, inserted himself between Max and the tree, and swatted the dog smartly across the snout. Max yelped in pain.

"Shut up, stupid," growled Socrates. "Do you want Animal Control to come get us?"

Max's eyes were watering from the painful scratches on his nose. He shook his head.

"Come on, let's go," Socrates said. He shot a last baleful look up the tree at Domino before turning and slouching away with head low and ears back.

Max looked at Socrates, looked back up at Domino, gave one more angry bark, and trotted off to follow the furious cat.

Domino's death grip on the branch beneath him did not loosen. "I'm shaking like a leaf, guess I belong in a tree," he mumbled in an attempt to humor himself. His teeth chattered and his leg throbbed. He could feel warm blood matting down the fur around the wound. Then the damp wind unleashed a torrent of long-promised rain. With no leaf canopy above him, Domino was quickly drenched. But with the memory of Max's wrathful yowls, hot breath, and snapping jaws still fresh in his mind, he held his position to be sure the dog was truly gone.

The wind began to whip around to the north, transforming the cold rain to sharp ice pellets, which it drove into the cat's eyes and nose. Domino figured he was no longer shivering from fear but from cold, and it was time to descend. His injured leg worked about half as well as his other hind leg on the way down the tree. When he leaped from the trunk, it gave out beneath him and his hindquarters flopped gracelessly onto the ground. He hoisted himself up quickly and loped unevenly into the cover of the trees. The leg was painful and the going slow until he was halfway through the woods and he heard the most beautiful sound: the sweet notes of Celine's meow.

He halted and turned his head toward her as she came up to him. She bumped her face against his. "Domino, thank the Great Cats you're okay," she fussed.

"Well, my back leg is a little off, but nothing too bad," he meowed. He forgot the pain and the cold and his wet fur and the pelting sleet as he happily head-butted Celine.

"Come on," she said. She turned and trotted briskly toward the far side of the Gully. "We need to get to Flufferdoodle's yard. There's shelter in the hedge behind his house."

In the short time he had been standing in the cold, Domino's leg had stiffened considerably. He lurched along behind Celine as she led him in the direction of his old friend's territory, and their home beyond that. The cold gale blasted harshly as the cats made their way. Wet and shivering, Domino became shakier with each excruciating step. He kept Celine in sight and plodded on. In spite of the pain, he noticed she had somehow kept herself dry while he had been exposed in the tree. She had probably sheltered beneath an overhanging rock or a dead tree while she waited for him. He shook his head fondly, in awe as always of her wild-cat skills.

They reached the edge of the trees and paused so Domino could catch his breath. "You stink of blood," Celine told him. "Let me take a look while you rest."

Domino leaned onto his good hind leg and extended the injured one away from his body for Celine's inspection. He felt her whiskers tickling the flesh around the wound as she sniffed and licked. "Oh, yeah, he got you good," she said. She returned to his side. "Listen, Domino, you've just got to make it a bit further. Once we get through Flufferdoodle's yard, there's that hedge where we can rest and recuperate."

Domino felt defeated. It had cost him almost all his strength just to pass through the Gully, and it was that far again to Flufferdoodle's territory. He swallowed hard. "You promise I can rest?"

"Oh, yes. And it'll be nice and dry, I'm sure of it."

"Okay, let's do it."

They passed from the relative shelter of the bare trees and began to cross the first lawn. Domino's leg was on fire now. His teeth chattered. Ice pellets packed themselves into the spaces between his paw pads. "I hate this, I hate this, I hate this," he chanted as he plodded through the sleet.

"Come on, you're halfway there," cheered Celine. She stopped to push her nose against his shoulder, then trotted on ahead again.

An interminable period of time passed before they were finally making their way through Flufferdoodle's yard. As they headed for the hedge at the back of the territory, the big orange tom emerged from his cat door and trotted over to join them.

"Dom, thank goodness you made it. I was getting worried," he meowed. "If it weren't so crappy out, I'd have come back to look for you."

"Wow, Fluff, I'm touched, I really am," Domino said through gritted teeth. "But lucky for me, I was with her." He nodded at Celine.

"His leg's pretty rough, but he'll survive," Celine apprised Flufferdoodle. "But let's get out of this weather. We need to rest and clean up the wound."

The trio kept moving until they reached the euonymus hedge and crawled underneath. An evergreen still in full leaf, the dense plant maintained a miraculously dry cavern beneath its branches, just as Celine had promised. Domino's injured leg had stopped working altogether by this point. He dragged himself into the center of the space and flopped on his side, his ribs heaving and his muscles trembling with cold and exhaustion. Within seconds, he slept.

"I'll see to that wound. Why don't you see if you can warm him up?" Celine meowed softly.

"Yes, ma'am." Flufflerdoodle circled the sleeping tom and curled his enormous tufted body along his friend's back. He laid a massive paw across Domino's shoulders before resting his own head on the dry bed of leaves. "May as well catch up on some shut-eye myself," he mumbled. "You crazy wild cats keep me up too late. I'm usually asleep by now." His voice slurred out as he joined Domino in the land of nod.

Celine sat to catch her breath. In the dim light she could just make out the sleeping toms curled together like sibling kittens. She spent another moment listening and sniffing to make sure they were in a safe place. Satisfied, she went to Domino.

Celine carefully cleared away the debris that clung to the wound from Domino's awkward journey, as his haunches had given way more than once and the injury had hit the ground. Then she removed the clotted blood. She took care not to irritate the wound but made sure to be thorough, and after a long time, the work was done. The bleeding had stopped, and the bite was clean and exposed to the freshening air. Celine assessed the damage—a tear in the big muscle that ran along the front of Domino's back thigh. She nudged the position of his leg with her nose until the wound closed itself.

Finally satisfied, Celine found that she was exhausted, too. She lay down and positioned herself carefully along Domino's belly. She felt his breathing, now slow and steady. Flufferdoodle's mass seemed to have warmed Domino so that his shivering had stopped. She felt her own heat exchanging with his along the meeting of their bodies. She was warm and relatively safe and so tired. At length, she slept as well.

FOUR

Domino gobbled up the dry cat food with gusto. Three days after the disastrous Prowl, his leg had healed considerably, and he was once again filled with restless energy. He figured he would stoke the furnace in his belly with a hearty breakfast before heading out to patrol the meadow, away behind the barn.

The kitchen door closed quietly behind Mrs. Brown as she came onto the back porch. "Hey, Domino, how's it going?" She squatted next to him.

"Oh, brother," muttered Domino to himself. He laid his ears back and scooped up one last huge mouthful.

Mrs. Brown placed a soothing hand on his back. "How's the leg coming, big guy?"

"Here, let me show you," Domino meowed. He skittered off the porch and down the steps to the yard.

As he trotted away, he heard Mrs. Brown say, "Pretty good, huh? Okay, then, I guess you don't need me."

That morning, Celine had deemed him well enough that she felt comfortable leaving to go work her woods. Domino was on his own for the day. He skirted the barn and headed for the meadow. Almost immediately, images of the miserable Prowl began flashing into his mind, as they had done frequently over the past few days, and Domino didn't want to think about it. He didn't want to think about how the Neighborhood cats seemed to have been infected with madness, like rabies or some sort of mental distemper. He didn't want to deal with the natural order of the world being deconstructed and reassembled into something bizarre and unrecognizable by a cat who had never actually lived as a cat. He didn't want to relive the nauseating sight of cats—once noble and proudly feline cats!—greeting rats—filthy, corrupt, destructive, nasty rats!—as though they were equals. *Actually touching noses with them.* The memory of Sunflower Seed's carefully groomed fur came back to him and he gagged abruptly. He didn't even want to try to get his head around the disturbing mass delusion.

He wanted to hunt, to run, to stalk and pounce. He wanted to be a cat, and he didn't want to have to delve into *why* he was a cat and whether he *should be* a cat and if it was *all right* for him to be a cat. He just wanted to *be*.

The lawn gave way to long, whispery brown grasses. Domino's trot altered to a methodical high-step over the clumps and tufts, punctuated by the occasional leap. A crispy coating of sleet and ice capped the hay and crunched under his paw pads. The air was sharp and clear, stinging his nose and burning his eyes. The low winter sun blared light, even if it gave no warmth.

A rabbit—that would be just the thing. Something large enough to give him a good fight and the glorious moment of hard-won victory. Something to make him feel like a cat again. And so, Domino worked his way deeper into the long grass, sniffing and looking for tracks and scat.

Before long, he found rabbit pellets. This was no surprise; the meadow was full of rabbits. He began moving low to the ground, concealing himself behind hummocks, and silencing his movements. His spots disappeared among the harsh shadows of the bright winter day. Soundless and invisible, he moved across the westerly breeze, scenting. The smell of rabbit was strong. It wouldn't be long now.

Up ahead, he spotted a patch of brown fur, almost invisible among the dead grasses. Domino froze, ducked, took an invisible step forward, and cautiously lifted his head again. The fur remained in the same position. He hadn't been seen.

He stalked forward several lengths of his own body before chancing another look. He could see most of the rabbit this time. It was lying on its side, which was unusual out in the open in the cold of winter. Something seemed off. Domino sniffed the breeze, now that he was close enough to get more specific information. The scent of rabbit was strong, but there were other smells as well. Blood. Fear. Vermin. Death.

Rage came over him. He gracelessly hopped the last few yards and came to the rabbit's corpse. The creature lay where it had fallen, its back to Domino. He walked around it and saw it had suffered myriad injuries. A great many small rips, tears, and shreds. Fur rent, eyes raked, and innards strewn. Flesh torn and fouled but not eaten. Damage done by creatures not built for hunting animals this size. Rodents, with tiny razors on their claws and in their mouths.

It had to have been more than one; no single rat could have killed a full-grown wild rabbit. And it had to have taken a long time. Domino noted the trampled grass, the spattered blood, and the multiple pellets—rat and rabbit—expelled in terror and excitement. Finally, he looked at the rabbit's face. Destroyed and plundered, yes, but still frozen in an expression of pure terror. The stink of rat hung over the whole scene.

Fur riffled along Domino's back. He flattened his ears and bared his teeth, spinning and scanning the blowing grasses all around. He glanced at the dead rabbit again and saw how stiff and icy it was. It had been there a day at least, maybe two. There was no immediate threat. As Domino's adrenaline rush faded, he felt the now familiar roiling of his stomach contents. His mouth watered but he forced himself to lift his head and take gulps of bracing air. Turning from the carcass, he skulked all the way back to the barn.

He spent the day in the loft, lolling on the blankets in front of the open hay door. His healing leg exacted a painful toll for the morning's excursion, and though adrenalin from agitated instincts coursed through his system, he was obliged to rest and recover. But he kept watch over the yard from his vantage point. He spent the midday hours observing the hens as they worked their way into the kitchen yard, scratching and complaining. Mrs. Brown came out of the house at one point and threw them some stale bread crusts. Domino snickered as the plump birds jostled and upended one another in a frenzy of clucking and floating bits of down.

Over by his doghouse, Thor paced restlessly. He glanced up at Domino once before studiously ignoring him. Domino smiled, amused. Thor went back to his pacing, his eyes raised to the distant meadow to the east and the strip of woods to the north. Domino figured he had caught wind of the rats that had invaded the territory, maybe even the fouled rabbit carcass. Truth be told, it unnerved Domino as well. He thought of the unfortunate creature that had been savaged in the meadow. He couldn't stop seeing the rabbit's face, contorted and frozen in uncomprehending terror. For a fraction of a moment he felt empathy for the prey, even as he himself could not comprehend the disturbing new sentiment that had infected the Neighborhood. He quickly shook his head to dispel the notion, laughing at himself. "Imagine a hunter like me, empathizing with a rabbit. How ridiculous. How *transcendent*," he mocked.

He slipped into a troubled doze and dreams beset him. As usual, they involved hunting. Back in the meadow, Domino crept through blowing grasses. A high moon dappled the ground with harsh shadow, and a strong breeze concealed his scent from prey ahead. Rat stench hit him in the face and he crouched, listening and looking. Scuttling noises gave away the rodent's location. Domino approached in a transport of stealth. The rat was a big one, and Domino watched as it plundered the hatchlings from a bobwhite nest. The tiny, naked birds chirped and cried piteously, but the evil rat stuffed one after another into its foul mouth. It ground the tiny hatchlings in its jagged yellow teeth and let the bits fall to the ground in long strands of saliva. It laughed as it terrorized the dwindling number of helpless baby birds.

With a pounce, Domino was upon it.

The fight was vigorous at first, but soon the rat ceased trying to injure its opponent and instead began wriggling and squirming in an attempt to free itself. "Please," it pleaded in its ugly, screechy voice. "Please don't hurt me. I have babies at home." Domino only laughed and pinned the beast on its back on the ground. He fastened his jaws on the rat's throat and raked his hind legs across the gray belly. The rat screamed horribly, the sound universal to all field animals in mortal danger, a high-pitched shriek of terror. Domino clamped his jaws tighter to silence the disturbing yowl. It was a rat shrieking, then a weasel, then a hawk, then a rabbit, and finally a cat. Then the sound died altogether. But Domino's fur was raised at the feline end to the death cry. Lifting his head in alarm, he looked down to see the dear face of his Celine, the once-bright eyes already beginning to glaze over.

"Ugh!" Domino meowed as he snapped awake. He was on his feet, his back arched and his fur on end, his ears pricked forward in confusion. It took a moment before he came to himself. "What an awful dream," he exclaimed. He quickly looked over the interior of the empty hayloft then spun to scan the view out the open door. All seemed to be in order in the yard below. There was no physical threat to be found. "Dung," growled Domino. "That stupid rat-cat is getting to me. He's even messing up *my* thoughts."

He began cleaning his legs angrily. Before long, he heard Celine's light footstep ascending the narrow stairs at the back of the loft and her lilting meow of greeting.

"Hey," he answered. He was still haunted by the disturbing dream, and it did his heart good to see his sleek mate trotting toward him across the ancient wooden floorboards. She looked strong and healthy and beautiful as always. "How were the woods today?" he asked.

She lifted her fine nose to touch his in greeting. "Oh, very productive. I took care of an obnoxious chipmunk. Lots of raccoon tracks, though, so I thought I'd get back here before it got too late and they started coming out."

"Good thinking." Domino hesitated. He didn't want to tell her about the virulent rats that were apparently visiting the northern reaches of the territory over near the road on the way to the Neighborhood. But on the other hand, there was a new threat in the area, and Celine should be aware of it. "Did you see anything unusual in the woods today, by any chance?" he began.

She considered for a moment. "Unusual? No, I can't say that I did. Why?"

"Well, I felt a lot better this morning, so I thought I'd go try to get a rabbit in the meadow."

"With your leg still healing? Ambitious. Did you get one?"

"Well, no, but someone did."

Celine blinked her golden eyes in confusion. "What do you mean?"

Domino told her about the rabbit.

"Great Cats, why would another creature do that?" she meowed. "I mean, it's one thing to sport with your prey a bit, once it's safely in hand. But to join up with others to viciously shred a creature you have no intention of eating ..." She shook her head. "Do you think it's the same rats from the Neighborhood?"

"Who, Sunflower Seed and Meadow?" Domino thought for a moment. "Well, them or others like them. We certainly never had a rat problem like this over here before they showed up over there. So, yeah, I'm pretty sure they had something to do with it."

Celine was turning the situation over in her mind. "I can see why they would come over here to do it. If they did it where the Neighborhood cats could see, it would destroy Socrates's whole stupid transcendence theme."

"You're right," agreed Domino. "But why do it at all?"

"Right, that's what I can't understand," said Celine.

But suddenly Domino did understand. "It's a warning," he said.

THE DAYS of convalescence were interminable. Every waking moment, Domino's heart beat fast and hard with apprehension.

He knew the rats were up to no good—the rats which that idiot Socrates had invited in, and which he had somehow convinced the other cats to accept. Even now, Domino was sure they had become entrenched in hollows and under garden sheds and in sewers throughout the Neighborhood. They were probably bringing in friends from the city, taking over bird feeders, displacing chipmunks and field mice, and, of course, breeding, breeding, breeding. Soon there would be so many of them that a whole army of cats wouldn't be able to bring the population back under control. There would be disease and spoilage and fleas. The once bright and balanced Neighborhood would be as sordid and unhealthy as the worst skid row in the most decayed urban armpit. Domino growled in frustration whenever he thought of it.

A regular threat he could fight. He loved a good fight, in fact. Woe to the uninvited tom who thought he could simply sashay onto Domino's territory and help himself to a sparrow or a mouse. Domino would confront him immediately and assertively. There would be posturing, raised fur, and dire yowls of warning. Then, at an invisible signal, the combatants would hurl themselves at one another. Domino was large and heavy, and his active life made him strong and quick. He had never lost a battle, though he had a scar or two to show off.

But Socrates had never physically challenged Domino, as any self-respecting feline should. Socrates had never hissed or blown up to twice his regular size. He had never indicated that he presented any sort of threat whatsoever. He had come instead as an apparent friend and had used only his novel-sounding ideas and mellifluous Siamese voice to weave his unnatural spell.

The Neighborhood cats had been taken unawares. Accustomed to their easy, comfortable lives, they had lost their natural suspicion of strangers. They accepted Socrates uncritically, taking him at his word and welcoming him into their society. Then his dog. Then his rats.

Domino had plenty of time to think about it as he waited for his hind leg to become strong again. In retrospect, he saw it all so clearly. Socrates had presented himself as an interesting cat with new ideas from another place. He had prepared the way by capturing the cats' imaginations with his talk of transcendence and friendship among all creatures. *And why not?* the foolish cats must have said to themselves. They had zero experience of anything threatening in their lives. They had been eager to prove themselves just as sophisticated as their exotic new acquaintance. By the time Socrates brought the dog, it was already too late; any cat who wanted to cause trouble would lose the fight. (Domino swore he felt his leg throb every time he thought about Max.) And when it came time to introduce the rodents, the Neighborhood cats had already convinced themselves that a friendly greeting was the only appropriate response—and Max was there to remind them of this if any of them balked.

Like Domino had.

Three days had passed since his excursion to the meadow where he had found the slaughtered rabbit, and now his leg was much stronger. But black thoughts continued to fill his head, making his teeth chatter. Full of nervous energy, he decided to head for the north woods. He told himself it would be good exercise for strengthening his hind leg, but his real motive was to patrol. He wanted to make sure the Neighborhood rats weren't getting a foothold in his domain. He slipped through the leafless hydrangea, emerged into meadow grass, and proceeded straight until he came to the edge of the wood. There, he turned and followed along the tree line, toward the road.

Snow squalls had deluged the area throughout the day. As each one passed, the sun battled its way through fast-moving clouds to glow pale and impotent in the winter sky. Domino blinked as he stalked into the lowering sun. Immediately, a fresh bank of clouds overtook it and the air was again filled with sifting flakes. The squall was sudden and intense, and Domino could barely see a few inches ahead. He pushed on, guiding himself by following the line where the meadow grass gave way to woodland. He concentrated so hard on keeping his bearings in the low visibility that he paid scant attention to anything else. Abruptly, he realized he could hear an animal tracking alongside him not two feet away in the brush that hid the roots of the trees.

Domino gave a small leap and spun to face the woods. His tail was out straight and every strand of fur stood at attention. He flattened his ears and bared his fangs as he tried to scan the space in front of him. After a brief pause, a pale cat emerged from the densely whirling white spots. The visitor fixed Domino with ghostly, colorless eyes, and Domino recognized his nemesis, Socrates.

"Don't even think of setting paw on my territory, freak," Domino spat. This was his turf, and he wasn't about to use Socrates's weapons of repurposed words and unarguable assertions. He would fight like a cat, with his honest strength and claws and teeth.

But Socrates only sat, smirking and fading in and out of sight amid the flurrying flakes. Yet again, Domino felt sickening bewilderment at how to proceed against a foe who would not fight honestly and properly. In his confusion, he could feel his fur begin to lie back down, and his flattened ears pricked forward in spite of his fury. Immediately, he raised his back again and hissed menacingly.

"My dear tom, I have not come to fight," meowed the Siamese. He continued to sit and stare at the black-and-white cat. His eyes reminded Domino of the winter sun—nearly white, aglow with some sort of inscrutable energy, and cold.

"Then you better turn tail and head back across the road, because there's nothing else here for you," Domino warned. Socrates's ghost eyes were giving him a creeping feeling in the pit of his stomach, and his fur once again rose on end. Fight-or-flight adrenalin was surging through his body, though his opponent gave no indication of physical threat. Confounded, Domino remained frozen in place with no apparent course of action.

Socrates ignored his warning and said, "I have come to see for myself this majestic territory of yours. You see, I have big plans and I'm not sure the Neighborhood will be large enough. I will need room to expand at some point."

"You can't be serious," hissed Domino.

Socrates feigned being taken aback. "Why would I joke about something like that?" he meowed. His slightly crossed eyes were disturbing; Domino never knew which to focus on.

"And naturally, with such big plans, I will require assistance," Socrates continued. "So the other reason I have come is to satisfy my curiosity about *you*. About how you run your territory and what kind of cat you really are and whether you might be a good partner to oversee the future phase of my expansion."

Domino's skin prickled all over his body. "You've got to be kidding," he growled.

"No, seriously. You know, you really impressed me at the Prowl the other night." Socrates shook his head ruefully. "You got me all worked up in spite of myself. Not very transcendent, huh? And in front of all the other cats, too." He gave a small chuckle. "Took Max and me a few days to settle everyone down again. But we got it done. We convinced them." Domino made no answer besides a low growl, so Socrates sat up on his hind legs and craned his neck as though looking past him into the distance. "Hey, where's your cute little mate?"

"Don't you even mention her," Domino exploded in a guttural yowl.

Socrates lowered himself into a normal sitting position again and met Domino's eyes. "My, my, no need to be so defensive," he said. "Anyway, she's a bit... *uncivilized*... for my taste. But I can see how that might be appealing to you."

Domino felt like he would explode at any second. The light was beginning to fail, the snow was still falling thickly, and he feared he would lose track of his enemy in the diminishing visibility. He needed to make Socrates go away. "For the last time, get off my territory," he demanded in an aggressive screech. His body was taut, ready to do battle.

And still, Socrates only smirked. It was maddening. At last he said, "Well, I have already been here for most of the afternoon. I've seen what I wanted to see." Domino felt a thrill of fear at this revelation, but Socrates kept talking. "I was just planning to return home for some kibble and a bit of catnip. But I'm so glad I ran into you. Do promise me you'll think about my offer. No telling what we could accomplish if we were to join forces."

Domino was ready to jump out of his skin by this point. "You crazy cat, I will never join you," he shrieked.

Socrates dropped his jovial expression and became simply cold and evil. "That's fine with me, because I don't need you," he said in a low hiss. "I already have everyone else."

"Not everyone," Domino protested in a wail. "Not Flufferdoodle."

"We shall see about Flufferdoodle," Socrates meowed. Domino didn't care for the way he said that, and he took a step toward his unwelcome visitor. Socrates stepped back into the underbrush.

"Not Celine," Domino yowled, taking another step forward.

Socrates laughed. It was an ugly sound, low and throaty. He stepped back again as a gust whipped the snowflakes up and around, wrapping him in a particulate mantle. His pale fur mingled with the flurry until he became impossible to see, though Domino could still hear his unnerving chuckle. Then he disappeared altogether.

FIVE

Celine laughed incredulously. "So now you say I *should* spend my time in the woods? Since when is the Brown territory more dangerous than the woods?"

"I'm telling you, this tom is off-the-wall, bat-crap crazy. And evil," Domino said. "And don't even get me started on those rats of his. And the dog," he added.

Celine smiled and blinked her golden eyes at him. "A dog I can outrun and outclimb. And a rat I can kill," she reasoned.

"Yeah, but can you kill many, many rats, all of whom are attacking you at once?"

"Well, that is an unusual situation."

"Yes, it is. And it's our situation now."

She went to him and butted against his shoulder gently. "Fine, you're right. This is a strange time. I promise I'll take it seriously and be more careful."

"Thank you. That's all I ask."

They sat side by side in the open hayloft door, looking out over the morning yard. Mr. Brown brought Thor out of the house and over to the doghouse, where he clicked the tether onto the dog's collar. The German shepherd shook himself before looking up expectantly. Mr. Brown patted him on the head then walked over to his truck. As he drove away, Celine remarked, "Thor sure must be soft if he has to sleep in the people house in the winter."

"Yeah," sniffed Domino. "Though in all fairness, he doesn't have a companion. I've been much warmer at night now that you're here."

They left the barn and passed where the dog could see them on their way to the back porch. They reached it just as Mrs. Brown was filling the food bowl. "Hang on, guys, I'll get you some fresh water with no ice on it," she said to them. By the time she returned, they were both hard at work on the kibbles.

Back in the yard, they touched noses and went their separate ways for the day. Domino watched as Celine slunk through the shadows alongside the driveway. Soon, she trotted up the bank to check the henhouse and shed before continuing to the stone wall and the woods beyond.

A short while later, Domino was halfway across the road when he paused to investigate a road kill. His lips curled back as he recognized the stink of rat. "Ha, ha, that's what you get for trying to sneak over to my territory," he mocked at the flattened corpse. But as he continued on his way, he wondered how many others had made it. He figured they were staging in the north woods. He would have to add the area to his regular patrol. His leg was a lot better, but not perfect. Maybe he could ask Celine to do it—she was a woodlands expert—but the thought of his petite mate going up against more than one of those huge, nasty rats was unacceptable. He would have to do it himself, but maybe she could handle the southern portion of the territory from the stone wall to the chickens. He sighed as he trotted along. There simply weren't enough hours in the day.

With management concerns occupying his mind, Domino soon reached his first destination and sat crouched beneath the euonymus hedge at the back of Flufferdoodle's yard. He took a moment to observe the territory. There were no small creatures to be seen, he noted with admiration. Fluff kept the place in good order. At last, he spotted his enormous, shaggy friend rounding the corner of the house. Domino burst forth from the cover and trotted to meet him.

"Hey, Dom," meowed Flufferdoodle. A wide cat grin spread across his face. "Guess the leg is finally better, huh?"

"Better enough," Domino agreed. "And thank you again for your help getting home after the incident."

"Least I could do," said the massive tom. "Didn't want you limping and bleeding all the way back without an escort. And, yes, Celine is a great cat, but let's face it, she's also not very big," he finished in a stage whisper. He sat on his padded rear. "So, what are you up to?"

"Recon." Domino briefed him on Socrates's visit to his territory the previous day.

Flufferdoodle huffed in annoyance. "What is that weirdo up to?" he wondered. "Why can't he just leave everyone alone?"

"That's the question, all right." Domino was utterly perplexed when he thought about it. "Hopefully we'll figure it out someday. But in the meantime, I'm more concerned about what he's up to. So I figured the best place to start is with you. Care to fill an old friend in on the latest happenings in the Neighborhood?'

Flufferdoodle's expression soured immediately. "Not really."

"That good, huh? Do tell," prodded Domino.

"Better yet, I'll show you." Flufferdoodle hoisted himself up again and headed toward the house. Domino followed. They passed alongside the building and through the front yard. Where his territory gave way to the road, Flufferdoodle stopped and sat on the edge of the curb. "Sit, sit," he said as Domino came alongside him.

Domino sat. Before them, the pavement glistened in the morning sun as the remnants of the previous day's snow melted and evaporated. Winter would soon become spring, and the ground everywhere was soft with melt. Up above, trees were just beginning to bud while birds fussed and carried on in the branches, excited at the prospect of another nesting season. All seemed normal. Finally, Domino leaned toward Flufferdoodle. "What are we looking at?" he asked in a low voice.

"Oh, you'll see." Flufferdoodle remained focused on the street in front of them, so Domino did the same. It was the day the big, noisy truck would come by to collect garbage. All along the street, trash cans and bins stood waiting at the ends of driveways. The people had departed their homes for the day, and the truck had not yet arrived. All was quiet. Domino looked down the street to one side and drew in a sharp breath as one after another, three well-fed rats emerged from behind a trash can. They hopped into the rain gutter and began scurrying up the road. Domino looked at Flufferdoodle, but the orange tom simply sat still.

The rats remained on the far side of the street but showed no fear as they passed in front of the yard. "Good morning, Flufferdoodle," they called cheekily.

"*Good morning, Flufferdoodle?* How dare they?" Domino hissed. He gaped at Flufferdoodle in disbelief, but his friend kept his seat, following the rats with narrowed eyes.

Soon the rodents had passed by and began to talk among themselves. "Two houses up, boys—those people are totally sloppy. The garage door fits loose and we can get in there, and there's always some scraps to be found where they keep their trash cans.

Domino felt sick again. "So this is what it's like, now?" he meowed. "Rats parading in front of cats in broad daylight?"

From the direction the rats had come, a car approached. Domino saw the rats turn their heads when they heard it coming. They scurried to a nearby storm grate and vanished inside it until the vehicle had passed. Then they reemerged and proceeded on up the street.

"So they still fear people, anyway," Domino observed.

"Yes, but that's about it," replied Flufferdoodle. "Somehow, people still aren't very transcendent where rats are concerned."

"But the rats don't fear *you*?" Domino asked. "You certainly aren't their friend."

"Understatement of the year," Flufferdoodle huffed. "You won't catch one of them on my territory—or Meg's. It's the least I can do for her. But the constant patrol is killing me."

"I was going to say that your belly seemed slightly less impressive than usual."

"Ha, ha, yes, it is." Flufferdoodle's mood wasn't to be leavened.

"But you can't cross the street and get those rats?"

"Nope," Flufferdoodle said. "Oh, I could, I suppose. But then it would be war. I could be outdoors only at their pleasure, if at all. One or two rats, I can fight; gangs of rats, not so much. And when I would be indoors, my territory would become the new destination for every rat in the Neighborhood. Any time I tried to make a fuss, our old friend Max would be sure to stop by and set things straight. So we have a stalemate, of sorts."

"Ugh, how is that dog allowed to roam freely like this?" Domino growled. "Surely the people in his house could add a device to keep Socrates from opening the door."

"Oh, they think it's wonderful that Socrates can open the door," Flufferdoodle meowed. "I was talking to Mister a day or two ago. He said he had been near Socrates and Max's house, and he heard the people speaking with their neighbors. They think it's so funny that Socrates can open a door. They're so proud of him. 'Our cat is the smartest cat in the whole neighborhood,' they say. And the other people just laugh." He glanced back across the road. "Plus, if you ask me, it relieves them of having to walk that dog and pick up his poop. People can be so lazy sometimes." He grimaced in disgust.

"I see," said Domino. "So, what if you want to go off your territory? Do Socrates and company have a problem with that?"

"Oh, I'm free to go where I like," Flufferdoodle explained. "But once I leave my territory and set paw on the common ground, I am subject to their rules. I can forget about being a cat."

"Hmm, somehow I can't see you strolling about the Neighborhood, meowing cheerful hellos to cats and rats and birds and dogs alike."

"Yeah, probably not going to happen."

"And so here you sit."

"Here I sit."

The toms sat side by side awhile longer. Occasionally another rat or two would make an appearance. Domino noticed they stayed on the far side of the street from Flufferdoodle as they went about their business, visiting trash cans and dragging rotting scraps of food about and generally fouling the place. "I see they still don't trust you completely," he observed.

"Whatever we've said about rats, we've never said they were stupid," Flufferdoodle answered.

"True." Domino watched as a female rat, trailed by five nearly grown ratlings, appeared from the shrubbery between two houses. "I see they've been busy, these rats."

"Oh, yes. Not hard to do when all of one's natural predators have become too enlightened to hunt them anymore."

Domino glanced back up at the treetops. "And yet, the birds seem to be staying off the ground. Don't they know these are *transcendent* rats?"

"Much like rats, birds aren't stupid, either."

"Hey, Flufferdoodle! How's it going?" Both cats' ears flicked at the screechy, coarse rat voice. A large male rat was almost directly across the street from them. He was flanked by two other males who were busy gnawing at a chicken bone they had pulled from a trash can. "What's up, cat?" taunted the one who had spoken. He gave an exaggerated wave.

"Friend of yours?" asked Domino.

"Hardly," sniffed Flufferdoodle. "He calls himself Silky-Rat. Let's just say he makes the most of the new protections the rats have in these parts."

"What, not going to say hello?" Silky-Rat called. "What's the matter, cat got your tongue?" All three of the male rats laughed. The cats sat and glared. Then Silky-Rat abruptly adopted a confrontational posture and came to the edge of the opposite curb. "Hey, cat, I'm talking to you," he screeched. His two friends made obnoxious noises behind him.

Silky-Rat jumped into the street and came halfway across. He bobbed his head up and down and bared his teeth. "What's the matter? You don't want your *mate* to see you talking to a rat?"

"Oh, boy," breathed Domino.

"Now you see why I spend most of my time in the *back*yard," muttered Flufferdoodle.

They watched impassively as Silky-Rat made an aggressive lunge in their direction, running out into the street and halting after a few steps. Then the pavement around the rodent darkened and a hawk crashed onto him, grasping him in its talons. The cats watched open-mouthed as the huge bird rose to a bare tree limb, where it perched about a dozen feet above them. They could see Silky-Rat struggling in its claws and they could hear his pathetic squealing. The hawk gave them a warning glance then lowered its beak and quickly separated Silky-Rat's head from his body.

"Whoa," breathed Flufferdoodle.

"Outstanding," meowed Domino.

Across the street, the rest of the rats had vanished. The cats watched the hawk devour several shreds of Silky-Rat before it flew off to finish its meal somewhere more private. Then the garbage truck began its clamorous journey up the road.

Domino turned to his friend. "Well, I guess I'll carry on with my mission. Sure you don't want to come?"

"Nah, thanks." Flufferdoodle stood and stretched, arching his back high as a hill and yawning with his cavernous mouth.

"The damage you could do ..." said Domino, admiring his teeth.

"...is no longer appreciated in these parts," said Flufferdoodle as he returned to his normal posture.

"And you just accept that?" wondered Domino.

"I don't just *accept* that, but nonetheless, that is the way it *is*." Flufferdoodle sounded annoyed.

"Sorry, I didn't mean that the way it sounded."

"I know you didn't. Sorry for snapping at you. It's just

hard to stay cheerful lately." He butted his friend's shoulder lightly. "Let me know how your little sojourn goes on your way back."

"Will do." Domino paused to make sure the garbage truck was far enough away not to run him over. Then he was off, trotting across the street and bearing southward over the brown lawns.

Two houses down, Domino headed away from the street and into the woodlands alongside the Gully. As the trees closed around him, he felt damp leaves and twigs beneath his paw pads and heard birds whistling up above. The woods never changed. No amount of overthinking could rewrite the rules here. And although the patch of woods alongside the Gully was relatively small and hemmed in by houses, Domino took a deep breath and felt a little better.

He found Cricket dozing on top of a rock in a stray patch of sunlight near her den. He leaped up beside her and meowed a greeting.

"Hey, Domino," she meowed lazily. "What brings you here?"

"Just visiting. Checking in with old friends, having a bit of a roam. What's new?"

"Oh, not much." Cricket rose to her feet and arched into a deep stretch. Once again, her protruding ribs were an alarming sight.

"Cricket, please tell me you have enough to eat," Domino said.

"Of course I do, silly," she said. "I got a new benefactor, a nice man in a house not far from here. He leaves a bowl of food outside his door every day." She seemed melancholy for a moment. "Or at least, he did at first. Now he doesn't always fill it. I guess he forgets sometimes."

Domino had a pretty good idea why the bowl was empty sometimes, but he said nothing.

"Anyway," continued Cricket, "I had a pretty good winter, but I'm glad it'll be spring soon. The cold bothered me a bit more this year. Ha, guess I'm getting old," she laughed.

"A little meat on your bones wouldn't hurt, either," Domino chided.

"Yeah, sure." Cricket sat abruptly and brought up a rear leg to scratch vigorously at her ear. Domino noticed it was red and looked irritated.

"Whoa, maybe you should take it easy on that ear," he advised.

"Yeah, I know. I try, but it just itches so much that I forget sometimes." Cricket took a few bites at her midsection then smiled at him. "Itches there, too." She stood and leaped lightly off the rock. "I think I'll finish my nap in my den. Sun's not really warm, yet." She began to pad away.

Domino followed. "Going so soon?" he asked. He had hoped to chat with her awhile and get more information.

"Yeah, sorry. I just don't have a lot of energy today. Food bowl was empty this morning."

It was painful for Domino to see his friend in her diminished state. Cricket had always been the first to greet him when he came to visit. She always had a friendly purr and was quick to groom the back of his head. Now she shambled along, filling her days with meaningless pastimes and trying to keep warm as best she could in the absence of proper nutrition. "I really do wish you'd hunt when you need to, Cricket," he meowed gently.

"No one *needs* to hunt," she recited in a listless voice. They arrived at the entrance hole beneath the uprooted tree. "Okay, see you later, Domino. Thanks for visiting."

"My pleasure. It was nice to see you," he answered. They touched noses and Cricket turned to wiggle into the hole.

"Pardon me, coming through." Something brushed past Domino's legs and beneath his belly. He leaped high in the air and landed on point, fur raised, in time to see a scruffy-looking rat vanish into Cricket's den entrance.

As soon as he recovered from his surprise, Domino followed, squirming his head and shoulders into the space. In the dim light inside the den, he could just see the rat scurry alongside Cricket and lie down beside her. "Great Cats, Cricket, there's a rat in here!" he meowed.

Cricket lifted her head to look at him. "Oh, yeah, this is Daffodil. Daffy, this is Domino."

"Pleased to meet you," screeched the rodent.

Domino was at an utter loss. "Cricket, there's a *rat* in here," he repeated.

"Yeah, you just said that." Cricket chuckled humorlessly. "Daffy needed someplace warm to stay for the winter, and Socrates suggested I take her in," she explained. "I thought, why not? I got plenty of room. And it was nice to have a warm body in here."

"Yes, but it's a *rat's* warm body," protested Domino.

Cricket looked exhausted. "Domino, you got to get over that. That kind of thinking is the reason these poor rats need our help. You want Daffy to die out in the cold? She's with kittens, for goodness sake."

The sick feeling surged in Domino's belly. He backed quickly out of the den, spun, and scampered down the bank to the bottom of the Gully. A thin stream of clear snowmelt was running and he drank deeply. The frigid water soothed the heat of rage and confusion that burned in his gut, but it couldn't stop his head from spinning.

He finished drinking and began a fast walk back up the bank, away from Cricket's den. "Kittens?" he meowed. "*Kittens?* Rats do not have *kittens*, Cricket. They have more *rats*," he fumed at his absent friend. "Great Cats, Cricket, what has happened to you? Unless I miss my guess, *you* are carrying kittens. You need to take care of yourself, starting with eating that disgusting rat." He shook his head violently, but the dizzy sense of horror would not leave him.

He could see pavement up ahead through the trees. The garbage truck had already passed along this road, and the emptied cans were lying on their sides at the ends of driveways. Just his side of the tree line, Domino spotted a young rat making its way along the road. He went into a crouch and stalked up to the rodent. At the last minute, it made a turn into the woods and came right up to him, stopping short when it saw him. Surprised, Domino froze.

"Oh, hello," squeaked the rat.

Domino hesitated for a second at the oddness of the rat's behavior before remembering that the rats in the Neighborhood didn't fear cats. Then he fell upon the small beast, tearing out its throat before it had a chance to squeal. He glanced around quickly to assure himself no one had witnessed his transgression. All was clear. He picked up the carcass and crept back behind a fallen tree to eat in peace.

Not long after, Domino walked out of the woods and onto the paved road. The kill had refreshed him. His resolve had returned. He noted that he was now at the Prowl meeting place, and he sauntered slowly along the road. Before long, he spotted Mister and Tiger, lying in the dead grass in the middle of a lawn. Their heads were low, mimicking the stealth technique of the Great Cats, but their swishing tails gave them away. As usual, they were only playing. Meowing a greeting, Domino trotted up the lawn to them.

The two cats sat at attention as he approached. "Hey, Domino," they meowed.

Domino lightly touched noses with them and sat as well. "How are you both?" he began.

The two tabbies glanced at one another before Mister answered. "We're fine. How are you?"

"Doing great," Domino meowed.

"Did your leg heal?" asked Tiger.

"Does it look like I can't walk?" answered Domino.

"No, of course not," said Mister. The tabbies chuckled politely, but the conversation felt stilted and uncomfortable. Domino needed to loosen them up and get them talking. It was surprisingly difficult to think of things they had in common. "You guys ready for spring?" he finally meowed. "Got any big plans?"

"Oh, yeah, we're looking forward to the warmer weather," Tiger said. "We're hoping to stay out all night once or twice."

"If I can sneak past my people and get out after supper," added Mister.

"Wow, you guys are wild," purred Domino. "I'll try to come by when we get a warm night in case you're out. Hey, do you think there'll be a Prowl soon?"

"Not sure," said Mister.

"Yeah, Prowls aren't really a *thing* so much," added Tiger. "We have more of a meet-up now."

"What's a meet-up?"

"Well, it's like a Prowl but sort of friendlier," explained Tiger.

"More open," said Mister.

"Open to all creatures, I assume," said Domino.

"Yeah, of course," said Mister.

"Not all the cats show up, but there are more rats, so it's actually bigger," said Tiger.

Domino mentally reminded himself of his mission and kept his voice friendly. "And what do you guys do at these meet-ups?" he asked.

"Oh, lots of stuff. Talk, walk around, smell stuff," said Tiger. "The rats show us what they like to do, and sometimes we go for a scrabble with them."

"A scrabble?" Domino wondered. He gave no outward sign of the revulsion eating away at his innards.

"Oh, yeah, it's actually sort of fun," said Tiger. "Of course, rats can get into smaller spaces, so we can't go everywhere they go."

"There's also usually some storytelling," said Mister. "The rats have lots of crazy stories from living in the city. The street cats there sound just brutal. Really makes you think."

Tiger nodded. "Yeah. Really backward stuff."

"Oh, I'd love to hear some of those stories," meowed Domino.

Mister and Tiger glanced at each other again. Tiger was the braver cat. He met Domino's eyes. "Well, do you think you can try a little harder to be nice this time?"

"You were kind of disruptive at the last meet-up," said Mister quietly.

Domino looked down contritely. "I know, and I feel real bad about that," he said. "I've been thinking about how hard everyone here is working to be better creatures, and in retrospect I wasn't very open-minded." He looked up hopefully. "In fact, I was kind of hoping Socrates was around. I'd like to apologize to him."

He sensed the tension falling away from the two tabbies. "Yeah, sure, I bet he'd like that," meowed Mister.

"That would be great," said Tiger.

"Any idea where I can find him?" asked Domino.

"Nah, he comes and goes at all different times of the day."

"What about at night?" Domino asked. "The sun is just setting. Does he go home to eat supper? Most housecats keep similar schedules to their people, right?"

"Yeah, probably," said Mister.

"So maybe I can catch him at his house. Do you know where it is?"

"Yeah, you just go up this hill," Tiger said. He nodded at the rising slope behind them. "Pass through this yard and the one behind it and you'll come to another street. Head north and you'll see a white house with a blue door. There are some big clay pots on the front steps. That's his house."

"Great, thanks, guys."

"Wait, now that you're here, want to play?" asked Tiger.

"Yeah," meowed Mister. He went into a crouch.

"Maybe on my way ba—*Hey!*" Domino staggered back as Mister pounced on him. The tabby wrapped his paws around Domino's neck and tried to roll him. Domino recovered quickly and pushed back with his impressive strength. His healing leg was still slightly weaker so he compensated with the other rear leg, hugging Mister's neck and forcing him back and over. Domino pinned him long enough to assert mastery then stepped back, hissing dramatically over him.

Mister lay on his back, laughing and showing Domino his belly. "Come on, I'll destroy you. Fight me, you coward."

"Yeah, yeah," meowed Domino. He gave Mister a playful swat. "Okay, I'm going to go see if I can catch Socrates."

Mister rolled to his feet and butted Domino's shoulder. "Okay, good seeing you."

"Yeah, good to see you," agreed Tiger.

"Good to see you guys, too," said Domino, and part of him meant it. He turned and headed up the hill. He passed the house, went through the backyard, a small stand of trees, another yard, and soon found himself at a street, just as Tiger had said. But Domino didn't walk out onto the pavement. Instead, he stole through the brush between the yard and the street. The sun was now down for the night and the shadows were deep. He proceeded stealthily past two houses, breaking cover only to cross driveways. He was working his way through a privet hedge when he started picking up voices.

A helpful northwesterly blew Domino's scent behind him, even as it carried snatches of conversation to him from the creatures ahead. He could make out the mellifluous tones of a Siamese cat and the screechy accents of rats.

Drawing on every ounce of stalking skill he possessed, he crept forward, utterly silent, until he caught sight of the creatures through the sheltering privet branches. They were sitting in a small group on the lawn, halfway between the hedge and the next driveway. A streetlight on the far side of the road provided enough illumination that Domino could see them clearly. It was definitely Socrates, sitting and facing five or six rats. The rats had their backs to Domino, but the breeze blew their words to his pricked ears.

"And then the hawk took poor Silky-Rat and flew away with him," one of the rats was lamenting.

Socrates shook his head sadly. "That is just barbaric," he meowed. "We've got to figure out a way to get through to the birds."

"Or get rid of them," squeaked another rat.

"Hopefully there's no need to go that far, Cloud," said Socrates sagely.

"Yeah, but what if we can never make them see?" worried another rat. Domino recognized the scratchy voice; it was Sunflower Seed. "I mean, I want to be able to trust them, but I don't know if I ever could. It's easy for you to take that chance —you're a cat. But for someone my size, I don't know if I could ever really be safe around a bird of prey."

Socrates gave a patronizing little laugh. "I'll bet most of the rats here once said the same thing about cats," he said.

"But cats are different," insisted Cloud. "You guys have fur, like us. You're not as cold as birds. And you're smarter; you can think about things. You can see how things could be and should be, not just how things are."

"Well, that's true," concurred the Siamese.

"But birds," said another rat. "I just don't think they can ever do that. I don't think they have the capability."

"I'm afraid Chipper is right," moaned Sunflower Seed. "I just think about all the beautiful things you've accomplished here, Socrates; how hard you've worked and how safe and easy you've made life for all creatures. But I just think that as long as we have to worry about hawks and things, we can never truly have peace here."

"Patience, my friends. One thing at a time. I believe there are still one or two recalcitrant cats who don't get what we're trying to do. Let's worry about them first."

"Yeah, the whole reason Silky-Rat got eaten today is because that Flufferdoodle cat wouldn't let him on his territory," said Chipper.

Domino sucked in a breath, barely remembering to stay quiet.

"You're kidding," meowed Socrates.

"I wish I were," whined Chipper. "It was awful. Silky-Rat was trapped out in the middle of the road with no cover, no hiding place. We all saw the hawk circling. 'Run, Silky-Rat,' I yelled at him. 'Get out of the road!' Poor Silky-Rat was panicking. He tried to dash into the long grass at the front of Flufferdoodle's territory. But Flufferdoodle and that Domino cat just hissed at him and turned him back."

"Domino was there, too?" Socrates sounded surprised.

"Oh, yeah. So anyway, Silky-Rat had no choice but to try to get back to our side of the street. But he didn't make it." Chipper's voice broke as he finished his tale of woe.

"I'm so sorry, Chipper." Socrates lowered his head and clenched his eyes shut as an apparent wave of emotion overcame him. "Cats can be so stupid sometimes," he wailed. Then, in a quieter voice, he said, "Right now, I'm ashamed to even *be* a cat."

In the privet hedge, Domino's lips curled back in disgust. But out on the lawn, the rats drew closer to Socrates and sought to comfort him in their creaky voices.

"No, Socrates, don't feel that way."

"You're a *good* cat, Socrates."

"I wish all cats could be like you, Socrates."

Socrates kept his head bowed low, and several of the rats began licking the back of his neck obsequiously, as though they were cats grooming another cat. Seeing this, Domino was dangerously close to getting sick. He felt he would heave so violently, rats would hear him a mile away. He quickly averted his eyes from the nauseating sight and instead concentrated on the words he could hear.

Sunflower Seed was talking. "You've always been a great cat," he told Socrates.

"Great cat," Domino muttered. "As if."

"I think the best thing that ever happened to me—maybe to all of ratdom—was the day I first saw you through the air vent in your apartment. I watched you for a while, you know, before I tried to talk to you. I saw how open-minded you were with your dog. I heard how intelligent you were when you spoke. I thought to myself, *Now there's a cat I just have to meet*."

At last, Socrates lifted his head from his downcast posture of guilt. "I remember," he said to Sunflower Seed. "I remember the first time I heard your voice coming from the vent on the wall in the bathroom, and the first words you said to me."

"Me, too," squeaked Sunflower Seed. He turned to the other rats. "I said, 'Now *you* look like a cat I could get to be friends with.'"

"And you were right," meowed Socrates.

Sunflower Seed shrugged. "Like I said, I'd been watching you. I came across a few cats before I met you, you know. I could see you were different. You were the most intelligent cat I'd ever seen. You just have such a superior mind to every other cat—heck, every other creature—I think any of us have met." Socrates sat still, basking in the rodent's praise. "I have to say, meeting you was a gift to me and to my kind," finished Sunflower Seed.

Across the lawn, the front door of the house opened. The rats all froze. A long rectangle of yellow light fell across the lawn, stopping short of the animals. The black silhouette of a woman stepped out of the bright doorway and onto the small porch. "Socrates," she called. "Here, kitty, kitty."

"I have to go," the Siamese whispered. "See you guys in the morning."

The rats said good-bye in low voices.

"I'm coming," meowed Socrates. He sauntered lazily across the lawn.

"Here, Socrates," called the woman.

"What are you, deaf?" meowed Socrates. "I told you I was coming, you imbecile."

The woman finally heard his deep meows, even if she didn't understand them. "Oh, there you are. Come in! It's going to be too cold tonight for you to stay out. You'll get sick," she cooed.

She bent to pick up the cat, but Socrates went from a walk to a dash to get past her. "And my food better be in my bowl already. I can't stand it when you waste my time," he complained as he disappeared into the house. Then the woman closed the door.

The rats burst into raucous laughter.

"Wow, what a tough guy," scoffed Chipper.

"And you," laughed Cloud, pointing at Sunflower Seed. "'Oh, Socrates, you're so smart! You're soooo much more intelligent than any other creature ever to walk the entire earth,'" he said in a syrupy imitation of Sunflower Seed's voice.

The rats laughed again. "Hey, nice job blaming Silky-Rat on that fluff ball and his buddy," said Sunflower Seed to Chipper. "Did you see how ashamed that genius, Socrates, was?" More laughter.

"Yeah, that was amazing. He won't rest now until he can get those cats to do what he says, or just get rid of them. They're a blot on his perfect new creature society," said Chipper.

"And getting rid of them is nothing but good for us," nodded Sunflower Seed.

"I gotta hand it to you, Sunflower Seed," said Cloud. "You were absolutely right about that cat. I mean, he really is smart, anyone can see that. So how did you get him to be such a sucker?"

"I tell you, I seen cats like him before," explained Sunflower Seed. "When it comes to the highly intelligent ones, all you gotta do is tell them how *smart* they are, and they turn into total idiots."

"Really?"

"Works every time," said Sunflower Seed, chortling.

The rats were still laughing as they scurried over the curb and into the gutter. Domino held his breath as he heard them run past him not four feet away. The breeze protected him by blowing his scent away across the lawn, and the rats never noticed him in their haste.

"Well, this was a trip worth taking," Domino said to himself, once the rats were gone. Flufferdoodle's words about Socrates from several weeks earlier came back to him: *Just because he's highly intelligent, doesn't mean he's very smart.* Domino grinned. "How right you are, my friend."

It was time to make his way back home, which would take the better part of the evening. He would make sure to pass through Flufferdoodle's yard, so he could tell the big tom what he had seen and heard. But first he left the shelter of the hedge and worked his way around the yard, spraying every object he came across. After he had marked the territory thoroughly, he stalked off, laughing to himself. "That'll keep Socrates and Max busy tomorrow."

SIX

A sliver of moon had risen by the time Domino got back to Flufferdoodle's territory. There was no sign of the big tom in front of the house, so Domino crept around to the backyard. Still no Flufferdoodle. He sat up, squirrel-like, to look across the lawn and into the windows. He could see right through a darkened room to the next one. In there, it was light. A large TV was playing, and Domino could even make out the images of people moving about on the screen. *At least it's not an animal show*, he thought, *so maybe Flufferdoodle isn't really watching.*

He moved close to the house and called his friend's name loudly. He had to repeat it two more times before Flufferdoodle emerged from the cat door and trotted over.

The giant ginger cat touched noses with his black-and-white friend. "Hey, Dom, how'd it go?"

"Wait'll you hear this," Domino meowed. He told Flufferdoodle what he had heard, emphasizing the part where the rats manipulated Socrates to work him against Flufferdoodle and himself. Then they both had a good laugh when Domino described the rats mocking Socrates after he had gone inside.

"That cat has his head so far up in the air, he can't even see what's going on around him," snickered Flufferdoodle.

"Exactly," said Domino. Then he grew serious. "But Flufferdoodle, whatever Socrates sees or doesn't see, this is still bad news for us. Especially for you, since your territory is surrounded by Socrates's rat-friendly zone."

"Ah, he can't do anything on my territory," Flufferdoodle said in a powerful meow. He arched his back and seemed to double in size.

"I don't think Socrates *will* do anything on your territory," agreed Domino. "You certainly are too big for him to challenge. Anyway, a dainty cat like Socrates doesn't want to get his paws dirty. It's the rats I'm worried about."

Flufferdoodle laughed. "Let a rat come and try something on my territory," he scoffed.

"I doubt it would be just one single rat, though," Domino worried. "Remember that dead rabbit I told you about? These aren't your average instinct-driven field rats. These rats are organized. They've figured out how to alter their behavior so they can hunt and fight together, in a pack, like coyotes or something. They can hurt animals bigger than themselves."

"Ah, let 'em try it."

Domino became alarmed at his friend's lack of concern. "And what about Max?" he added.

At last, Flufferdoodle deflated and sat down. "Yeah, I'd rather not have to fight him. But if he came on my territory, my people would call animal control and have him carted off."

"Only if Socrates is dumb enough to bring him here when your people are around," said Domino. "But your people leave the house all day and they sleep all night. In fact, most of the time, Max could come here and challenge you."

"So what do you want me to do about it, Domino?" Flufferdoodle meowed crossly.

"I'm not sure. That's why I'm telling you what I heard, so we can come up with some sort of plan."

"What plan?"

"I—I don't know. But you've got to do something."

Flufferdoodle glanced away in annoyance. Then he looked at his friend. "You know, Domino, this is easy for you to say. You live away through the woods, across the road, and on a nice, big territory surrounded by woods and fields. You have people who expect you to keep that territory free of vermin. You have Celine to help you. You have everyone on your side. But here in the Neighborhood, I have no one. You have no idea how hard it is for me."

"I do, Flufferdoodle. I really do. If I think about it too much, I get sick for you."

"Well, you getting sick over on your fancy cat-friendly estate doesn't do me any good over here."

"Well, maybe you could come hang out on my territory during the day?"

"And leave my territory unprotected all day? And Meg's, for that matter." His ears flattened and his lips pulled back to reveal imposing fangs. "That is one thing I will not tolerate. I will not have Meg stuck indoors, with only a window to see the entire wide world, and have her sit there, watching rats scamper freely over her yard."

"No, of course not," agreed Domino. They sat together quietly and watched the skinny moon weave through the bare hickory branches overhead. At last, Domino said, "Well, let me know if I can do anything to help." He gently pushed his forehead against Flufferdoodle's enormous flank.

"Okay. Thanks for stopping by with the intel." Flufferdoodle turned his head to push his face against Domino's shoulder. Then the spotted cat stood and headed for the back of the yard.

Domino's mind kept working the whole way back to the barn. Try as he might, he couldn't figure out a solution to Flufferdoodle's impending problem. And it was surely going to be a problem. Socrates and his associates weren't going to tolerate any dissent from their vision of a rat-friendly world. Flufferdoodle controlled a tiny island of feline freedom for the time being, but Domino knew he couldn't hold it much longer.

And when Flufferdoodle's territory finally fell, there would be nothing holding the rats back from festering and flourishing in the entire Neighborhood. Rats were voracious breeders that devoured everything vaguely edible: trash, seeds, insects, bird eggs, worms, and other small creatures. It would only be a matter of weeks, months at best, before they began expanding their feeding grounds—and their authority—across the road to the Brown property. Even now, Domino was certain they had scouts setting up colonies in the north woods that bordered it.

It was only a matter of time before Socrates and his rats would be coming for Domino's territory. He and Celine could kill rats all day and all night, but the rats would keep breeding in the safe, fertile Neighborhood, and they would keep coming until the cats were overwhelmed and the Brown property was added to the rat-friendly domain. And that would be the end of Domino and Celine, because in his heart, Domino knew that *rat-friendly* really meant *rat-controlled*, and there was no place for cats in a world run by rats.

. . .

CELINE WAS out doing her rounds and Domino had been up nearly all night, so he spent most of the day napping in the loft. When Celine reappeared at dusk, he moved over so she had room in the nest. She curled beside him and he threw a paw over her shoulder, bathing her ears fondly.

"How did the recon mission go?" she asked in a drowsy voice.

Domino gave her a description of his activities the previous night. "So you can see the problem," he summarized. "What we need is a solution."

"I do see the problem, and I don't see an immediate solution. And frankly, I'm too tired now to come up with one," she murmured.

"Well, sleep on it and we'll see what we come up with in the morning. But also, tomorrow, please plan on helping me check the north woods for rats. We'll probably have to do some cleanup up there."

"Sure thing," Celine purred. "I always enjoy a target-rich environment." Then she was asleep.

Domino left the nest once for night patrol, but the territory remained quiet. In the morning, he and Celine did another quick round of the yard and outbuildings before heading for the north woods. But first they detoured to the back porch to fortify themselves with a bowl of kibble.

Just as the cats bent their heads to their breakfast, Mrs. Brown came out of the house. "Hello, kitties," she said in the pleasant voice she used when addressing them. They grunted in reply without looking up from the bowl. Quickly and smoothly, Mrs. Brown picked up Celine and popped her into the pet carrier. Then she hoisted the carrier and walked to the car.

"Domino, what's happening?" cried Celine.

Domino tagged along at Mrs. Brown's heels. "It's okay, Celine," he meowed.

"Domino, you said I could trust them," Celine wailed through the door of the carrier.

"You can! She's just taking you to the vet," he called back.

Mrs. Brown looked down at him. "Domino, would you like to come keep Licorice company?"

"*Licorice?*" spat Celine.

"I guess they gave you a name," explained Domino. "That's good. It means they care for you."

"Okay, hop in," said Mrs. Brown. She held the rear car door open for Domino. He leaped up onto the seat and turned to look for Celine. Mrs. Brown placed the carrier on the seat beside him, turning it so he and Celine could see one another through the cage door.

The slam of the car door made Celine spin around frantically in the carrier. "Ow! My ears," she complained.

"That was just the door closing. There will be one more," Domino explained. As Mrs. Brown settled herself in the driver's seat, he said, "Here it comes now."

Celine was ready for the slam this time. Then the engine started and the car began to roll forward. Celine's back went up and her tail bristled out. "What's happening?" she howled.

"We're moving," Domino said in a soothing meow. "The car will take us very far very fast, much farther and faster than you or I could possibly run." Domino had never ridden in the car without being confined in the carrier. He turned his head to look out the front window. "Great Cats, I wish you could see this, Celine."

"What?" Celine could only look out the door of the carrier, which Mrs. Brown had left facing Domino.

"We are running so fast. It's amazing. This must be what

it's like to be a cheetah." Domino breathed the name of the Big Cat in a reverent tone.

Still jumpy, Celine watched Domino's face as he looked forward. "I wish I could see," she said. "But wait, you haven't told me what a vet is."

Domino returned his attention to her. "A vet is a person who knows how to care for animals' bodies. He will examine you to make sure you're healthy."

"Of course I'm healthy," Celine snapped.

"Right," concurred Domino. "But then, sorry, there's no nice way to say this; he's going to stab you with needles."

"*What?*"

"The needles put medicine inside you," Domino explained hastily. "It keeps you from getting sick. You can't get rabies if you get stabbed with the needles." He touched her nose through the bars in an effort to reassure her. "If you can, try listening to the people talk while you're in there. They explain everything that's happening."

"Okay, I'll try," Celine said. Her voice was low and hollow with fear. Domino wished he could do more to soothe her.

Presently the car stopped, and Mrs. Brown came and got the carrier. "You stay here and be a good boy," she told Domino.

"Yes, *Myu*," he said sarcastically.

"Good-bye, Domino," called Celine, her tone verging on frantic.

"Relax, Celine. You'll be fine," he meowed after her. Mrs. Brown slammed the door and carried her away. Domino placed his forepaws on the door and stood up to look out the window. He watched them cross the parking lot and go into the low brown brick building.

Half an hour passed before the two females returned. Mrs.

Brown opened the door and placed the carrier on the seat, again facing Domino. "Here you go," she said in a cheery voice. As soon as she had closed the door, Domino went to the carrier and touched noses with Celine.

"Well? How was it?" he asked.

"Eh, no big deal," said Celine. She lifted a paw and cleaned it nonchalantly.

"What? Didn't they stab you with the needles?" Domino asked.

She regarded him briefly. "*Stab* is such a dramatic word," she said. She returned to her bath, speaking between licks. "It was more like a poke, like when we play fight and one of your claws catches me by accident."

Domino said nothing. His own memories of getting shots were not nearly so mild.

As if reading his thoughts, Celine added, "If you just relax and hold still, the vet is very gentle and you hardly feel it."

"You are something else, Celine."

Back at the house, Mrs. Brown leaned into the car. Holding Domino firmly, she touched the back of his neck with a small object. "Take it easy, big guy, it's just your flea medicine," she murmured. Domino flattened his ears but held still as the greasy liquid hit his neck. As soon as the woman released him, he made a show of leaping angrily from the car and running a short distance before turning to glare at her.

Mrs. Brown paid no notice. She gently removed Celine from the carrier and treated her as well. "Okay, Licorice, you are all set." She lifted the cat from the car and cradled her for a moment, stroking her head. Then she placed Celine on the ground. The cat butted her head into Mrs. Brown's hand as the woman patted her. "You were such a good girl," she crooned.

"Oh, brother," muttered Domino. Celine shot him a smug look.

"Wait here a minute," said Mrs. Brown. She went up the porch steps and disappeared into the house, returning a moment later with a small dish. "Here, Licorice," she called. A strong scent reached the cats' noses at the same time.

"Great Cats, what is that?" asked Celine. "I think it's the best thing I've ever smelled." She dashed up the steps with Domino right behind her.

"It's tuna. It's a kind of fish from the ocean," explained Domino. He strode briskly to Mrs. Brown and butted her legs, yowling. Celine came forward and sat demurely before the woman, looking up at her.

"Here you go, Licorice. Here's a treat for being such a good girl today." Mrs. Brown placed the dish in front of Celine. "You could use a good meal, anyway."

Domino immediately came to the bowl and pushed Celine out of the way. "Oh, no, you don't," said Mrs. Brown. She picked him up and held him, absentmindedly stroking his head while she watched Celine enjoy the rare dish.

"Put me down," commanded Domino. He squirmed and wriggled until Mrs. Brown lost patience. By then, Celine had wolfed down almost all the tuna.

"Okay, here you go," the woman said as she placed Domino on the ground. "Licorice, why don't you let Domino have a bite?"

Domino butted Celine's petite head from the dish just in time to lap up the last morsel. She sat back and watched him lick every trace of tuna from the dish. "My paws, you'd think you hadn't already gobbled up a field mouse this morning," she commented.

As it was chilly and Celine's backside was sore from the

shots, the two cats decided a nap was in order. "Any rats in the woods this morning will still be there this afternoon," Domino reasoned. They made their way up to the den in the loft and went inside. Domino wrapped his long body around the black curl of cat, placed a warming paw across her shoulders, and gave her a soothing bath. Purring filled the converted cooler as the two settled into the comfortable fleece nest.

"Domino?" asked Celine. "What's *spaying*?"

Domino stiffened. "It's something they do to female cats to keep them from having kittens. Why? Did Dr. Mundy spay you?"

"No. He told Mrs. Brown they'd have to do it another time because it was already too late. What does that mean?"

Domino flushed with a strange, warm feeling. "My tail, I can't believe what a bunny I am. I noticed it right away when I saw Cricket, but I didn't even see it in you."

"See what?"

"Celine, you're carrying kittens," Domino said.

"Kittens? Oh, my ..."

Domino's paw tightened protectively over her silken shoulder. Great rumbles of purring filled the interior of the converted cooler, and it was quite a while before the excited mates succumbed to the sleepiness that is a huge part of every cat's life.

SEVEN

L ate afternoon sun slanted across the two cats as they stalked over the brown meadow grasses. Ahead of them, the north woods loomed dark and dense. Domino updated Celine as they approached.

"This woodland is nowhere near as big as your woods," he explained. "If you ran straight through it, you'd come to another house and yard before you'd get very tired."

"Sounds pretty tame."

"Yeah. The only impressive thing I've ever seen here is an owl," he said. "So, here's what I was thinking: I head alongside the woods to the road while you go straight in and set up somewhere hidden, just inside the line of trees, where you can't see the meadow anymore. When I reach the road, I'll head into the woods the same distance, to where I lose sight of the meadow. Then I'll come east and drive anything I see ahead of me. When we get to you, take the first rat that comes by. I'll finish off the rest."

"Do you think there will be a lot of them?"

"I honestly don't know. There might just be a few at this

point, or there might be more than we can handle." That last option gave him pause as he thought about the kits in Celine's belly. "Are you sure you feel up to this?" he asked.

She gave him a look.

"Okay, okay. Let's get into position."

"Wait a minute." Celine lifted her head and sniffed. "The wind's shifting around."

Domino raised his nose. "So it is. It's coming from the west now. Maybe I shouldn't approach from the road?"

"Well, if we were going for a stealth approach, I'd agree with you," Celine reasoned. "But since you want to flush and drive the prey, this actually works in our favor. They'll smell you and start moving into the trap by themselves, and they won't smell me."

"Excellent. Let's get started." Domino left Celine to head west. The black female continued straight until she vanished silently amid the dark trunks. When Domino had almost reached the pavement, he turned and headed into the woods himself.

He proceeded just to the point where he couldn't catch sight of the brown meadow when he looked back. Then he paused and took some time to sniff and listen. The wind was very light, barely a breeze. The air had been warming for the past couple of days, and the woods had softened. Small pockets of snow remained nestled against the north sides of the trunks, but everywhere else the ground was bare. Domino smelled and heard many fine things; birds fussing in the branches and foraging on the ground, early spring shoots emerging from soil and twig, and heightened activity everywhere as the world shook off the dormancy of winter.

He began to move cautiously eastward, keeping the meadow just out of sight through the trees. The litter of leaves and twigs was damp with melt and absorbed any sound his paws made. Since stealth wasn't the plan anyway, Domino focused on gathering information as he went. The bustle of diverse small creatures all around told him the woods were healthy and hadn't yet been overwhelmed by a plague of rats.

But he also found disturbing signs. Before too long, he scented rat and began to follow a trail. The odor wasn't fresh but it hadn't been left too long ago, either. The route he was following showed signs of being in regular use; the soil was flattened, the litter cleared, and there were rat pellets every few paces. Curling his lip back over his fangs, Domino picked up his pace.

The rat path was easy enough to follow. Every once in a while a lesser trail branched off, generally toward the meadow (*and the Brown territory beyond,* thought Domino). The main path continued eastward, and so did Domino. At one point, he paused to examine something gray and furry just off to the side. It was a dry ball of fur, fallen open to reveal a collection of bones and teeth: an owl pellet. Domino glanced up nervously but saw nothing to alarm him. They still had another hour or so before night hunters became active, anyway. He sniffed at the pellet again. It had definitely been a rat at one point. Domino remembered Silky-Rat's demise in the talons of the hawk the other day and grinned as he resumed his course.

He continued to find signs that rats had been there, but everything was at least a day or two old. His pace quickened to a brisk walk as he abandoned the idea of hunting anything today. He turned his head to one side to mark the flight of a cardinal as it dropped to the forest floor. At the same instant, something hit him hard, knocking him onto his side in a shower of dead leaves and loose soil. Domino was up in an instant, back high, fur up, and teeth bared as he spun to face his attacker. But he saw only Celine, sitting back and laughing.

"Really funny," he groused. As his fur deflated, he shook himself off and inspected himself. "You know, you hit really hard for a cat your size," he grumbled. "I think you reinjured my leg."

Celine finally stopped laughing and stepped closer to him. "Oh, boohoo," she purred. "Here, let me take a look at it."

"No, thank you, you've done enough already." He danced in a circle, keeping her from reaching his hind leg but forgetting to limp in the process. "I don't need your pity," he said.

Celine only purred louder and touched noses with him. "So, what did you find? Any good intel?"

Domino sat. "Lots of evidence that rats come through here on a regular basis, but no rats. And no sign that any have been here for a day or two, anyway." He paused to yawn as his body wound down from its ready stance. "How about you?"

"Well, I stayed in one place mostly," Celine recounted. "I realized that the spot we're sitting on is actually a rat trail."

"Yeah, I noticed it, too. I followed it up here from the west end of the woods."

"Makes sense, if they're coming from the Neighborhood," Celine said. "So anyway, I set up alongside the trail, right here." She showed Domino the mossy, rotting fallen tree she had hidden beneath. He saw how easily she must have become invisible in the deep shadow alongside the trunk. "But I didn't see anything noteworthy," Celine continued, "until this big, muscular, fearless tom came strutting up the trail."

"Where?" Domino's hair rose up again as he stood quickly and looked around.

"Oh, my tail, I'm talking about *you*," Celine meowed.

"Yes, of course you are. I was being funny, that's all."

Celine watched him with fond amusement. "So, what are your conclusions, Commander?"

Domino sat again. "Well, we were right that the rats are beginning to set up operations in this patch of woods. The trails are well established. But I wonder where they all are? Why aren't they here today?"

"That's a good question," agreed Celine. "They must be up to something else. If they're not here, where do you think they are instead?"

A flash of alarm overcame Domino. "Flufferdoodle," he meowed.

AFTER A BRIEF DISCUSSION, the cats decided Celine would head back to the barn and keep an eye on the Brown territory. She said she was ready for a nap, anyway. "It turns out that making new cats is actually rather tiring," she explained.

Domino didn't fancy the idea of her being in harm's way, and he encouraged her to go. He watched her pick her way through the darkening woods toward the meadow, nearly unde-tectable against the shadowy soil, rocks, and trunks. Then he doubled back down the rat trail, checked for cars before crossing the road, and soon arrived in the euonymus hedge at the back of Flufferdoodle's territory. He saw nothing moving, but the soft westerly bore the scent of many creatures.

Domino emerged from the cover, crossed the backyard, and trotted past the house. As he rounded the corner, he came to a sudden halt at the sight before him.

Dusk was deepening but there was ample illumination from houses and streetlights and a high moon in a clear sky. The front yard was empty, too, except at the farthest edge of the territory, where grass gave way to curb, sat Flufferdoodle. His back was to Domino, who could see the great orange tail twitching in the grass. Arrayed across the street, facing Flufferdoodle, were legions of rats. They ran back and forth from yard to yard, calling raucously to one another in their abrasive, screechy voices. Some tussled over food scraps that had been dragged from unsecured trash cans in poorly sealed garages. Domino watched with disgust as a group of rodents fought and scratched one another over the remains of a dead bird that had been lying in the gutter. The sight of so many rats frolicking openly on lawn and pavement was simply unfathomable to him. What had become of the Neighborhood?

Domino tried briefly to calm himself, but it was impossible. He drew a deep breath and stalked across the lawn to sit beside his oldest friend. "Evening," he said.

Flufferdoodle startled at his sudden appearance before returning his glare to the scene before him. "Evening." Then he merely continued to sit.

Domino was close enough to notice that the great cat was trembling. "So this is how it is now?" he asked softly.

"Yep." Flufferdoodle said the word through clenched teeth. "They're here all day and all night. Oh, they creep into their sewers and crannies in the mornings and evenings, when people are active. I run inside and catch a few hours' sleep at those times. But as soon as the coast is clear, out comes the riffraff, and I have to get out here and hold the line again."

"And the people around here still haven't caught on?"

"Do you see any people out here?"

Domino saw nothing moving in any direction except myriad rats. "Nope."

"Exactly. As soon as the sun is down, they all sit indoors,

watching televisions and whatnot. They have no idea what is going on out here."

"I see. And how long *has* this been going on?"

"Since the day after that business with Silky-Rat."

"Silky-Rat... heh, heh."

"It's not funny," snapped Flufferdoodle. "Like you said, the exact details of what happened have been misreported. Not that I *would* have let that scumbag onto my territory, mind you, but he got himself killed. I had nothing to do with it."

"You don't have to tell me."

"Yeah, I know." Flufferdoodle sighed deeply and miserably. "Anyway, the next morning, I was catching some early spring sun on the front walk, and as soon as the kids were on the bus and the grownups had driven away, rats started showing up. All day and all night, they parade around and scream at me and tell me how horrible I am, and that my territory is their territory now, and that I should just get my tail inside my house because they can't stand the sight of me."

"Pleasant creatures."

"Yeah."

"Have any of them tried to get on your territory?"

"Oh, every now and then a brave one will make a dash for the hedges in front of Meg's house. I run over there and chase it back into the street. The rest of them hoot and holler and carry on, and I patrol back and forth until it settles down again. Not sure how much longer I can keep it up, though."

"Well, I can certainly help."

"And you're a great friend, Domino. But you've got your own territory to maintain and even with you here sometimes, we can't hold them off forever."

"Well, we certainly can't allow them to take over your territory. That's a revolting thought."

Flufferdoodle said nothing, so the two cats simply sat side by side, glaring. In yards up and down the street, as far as they could see, rats cavorted in a festive atmosphere. Occasionally, a group of brave young ones would march onto the pavement toward the cats, jeering and taunting.

"You're no better than us!"

"Rats have rights, too!"

"Your days are numbered, cats."

"Hunters are evil!"

"Hunters are evil?" wondered Domino. "*Hunters are evil?* Since when?"

"Where have you been?" Flufferdoodle mimicked a sophisticated meow. "Everyone knows that."

"I see."

Domino looked down the street and his spirits crashed as he spotted cats: Socrates, of course, but flanked by Lily and several others he didn't know very well. And loping around them like an idiot was Max.

Flufferdoodle's shoulders sagged. "Scat. I was hoping this wouldn't happen."

A crushing sense of hopelessness overtook Domino. How could they fight this? Overwhelmed, he could only sit beside Flufferdoodle and watch the delegation come up the street.

Socrates greeted many rats by name as he passed among them, and they fell in with him and the other cats. By the time they approached Domino and Flufferdoodle, the group was very large indeed. Domino gamed out numerous assaults in his mind and couldn't think of a single one where he and Flufferdoodle could defeat so many. But he was ready to try, and his body tensed to the consistency of steel as it prepared.

With the smuggest of smiles, Socrates arrived in front of them. "Greetings, fellow creatures," he meowed loudly. He sat up in his annoying way, like some demented prairie dog, and the other cats around him did the same. But Domino and Flufferdoodle were large cats sitting on the elevated curb, so the new arrivals were barely at eyelevel, even in their preposterous affected poses. Domino was cheered momentarily.

Then Max came to sit behind the group, and he was undeniably the largest animal. He gave Domino an evil grin. "Nice to see you again, cat."

"Wish I could say the same." Every muscle in Domino's body was taut with potential energy. His heart raced and hot blood coursed furiously through his veins. But he sat as still as a stone, moving only his eyes from one enemy to the next. The cats facing him seemed relaxed and confident. They did not seem poised to fight. Max was clearly itching for a rematch from their last meeting, however. And then there were the rats: dozens of them among the seated house pets, scurrying, scratching, sitting up, twitching, staring at him with beady eyes, grinning lips pulled back from sharp yellow teeth. Domino looked away from the disturbing sight. In his mind, he saw the shredded rabbit in the meadow. The hair on his neck began to rise, but he willed it to flatten again.

Socrates stepped close to Domino and smoothly thrust his face toward the black-and-white barn cat. Already coiled tense as a spring, Domino jumped back, hissing.

Socrates feigned offense. "My paws, Domino. When first we met, you informed me that around here, cats greet one another by touching noses. Is this no longer the case?"

"Apparently not," Domino said in a controlled yowl.

"I see," said Socrates, reverting to his sitting-up-high posture. "So you say customs have changed around here."

Domino didn't like where this was going.

Socrates turned slightly to look at the big orange cat.

"Flufferdoodle, Domino tells me that times are changing here in the Neighborhood. Therefore, I have come to you with a simple, reasonable, neighborly request."

Flufferdoodle briefly met Socrates's eyes but did not reply. The Siamese continued. "Flufferdoodle, I notice that there are some bird feeders on poles alongside your people's house there." He gestured behind Flufferdoodle to indicate the feeders. "Our friends have observed that birds go there to feed but for every seed they eat, they scatter two or three on the ground."

"What of it?" interrupted Domino. "It's Flufferdoodle's yard. He can run it as he sees fit."

Socrates did not acknowledge Domino's outburst. "Flufferdoodle," he meowed, "Do you plan to eat those fallen seeds?"

"*Pfft*," Flufferdoodle exhaled. "Of course not. Cats don't eat seeds."

"Exactly," exclaimed Socrates. "*Cats don't eat seeds*. But do you know who does eat seeds?

"Um, birds?"

"Well, yes, but as we've just discussed, they waste more than they eat." Socrates turned to look behind himself. "Is Ivy here? Ah, there you are. Ivy, come here, sweetie." He waited patiently while a large female rat came forward. Behind her followed seven ratlings. She came before the cats and sat up awkwardly with her offspring gathered around her.

The rat family was the epitome of rampant infestation and Domino longed to obliterate it. But in unison, the female cats gathered around Socrates said, "Awwww." The Siamese placed a friendly paw on Ivy's withers and looked imploringly at Flufferdoodle. "My dear fellow creature, Ivy here eats seeds. And as you can see, she must eat a great deal right now, because she is nursing a pawful of kittens."

"They're not *kittens*, they're ratlings," interjected Domino in an angry yowl. He noticed that Flufferdoodle flinched at his words but even worse, the cats gathered in front of him glared disdainfully and hissed.

"Domino, how could you?" chided Lily.

The barn cat was at a loss. "What is wrong with you all?" he meowed.

Again, Socrates ignored him and continued to address Flufferdoodle. "Now, Flufferdoodle, I'm not asking you to do anything. I'm not even asking you to lift a paw. In fact, I am asking you *not* to lift a paw. Ivy would like to take her kittens—"

"You mean ratlings," meowed Domino.

"—onto the grass here—"

"You mean Flufferdoodle's territory."

"—and clean up those seeds that are just rotting and going to waste otherwise." Socrates paused to let his words sink in. "Now, can you think of anything wrong with that?"

Flufferdoodle sat silently, looking into the space above Socrates's head

"I can think of something wrong with that," snapped Domino.

Socrates at last turned to acknowledge him, a look of barely suppressed amusement on his face. "Why am I not surprised?" he meowed. The cats, dog, and rats around him bellowed with laughter. "Domino, do tell all of us what could possibly be wrong with allowing a young myu to eat some unclaimed seeds that Flufferdoodle can't possibly use?"

An infuriating fluster settled over Domino, strangling his ability to think clearly. He struggled to put his feelings into words. "There's nothing obvious wrong it, of course," he sputtered. "It's the principle of the thing."

"The *principle*?" mocked Socrates. "You mean the principle of a myu feeding her kits is somehow offensive to you?"

"No, of course not. It's the whole principle of cats tolerating rats that's wrong," Domino stammered.

"Really?" meowed Socrates. "And who says that's wrong?"

"Cats say so." Hisses from the gathered crowd. "Well, cats did say so, at least until you came here and addled their brains."

"Addled their brains?" Socrates put on an expression of righteous offense. "Maybe I came here and taught them to *use* their brains. Maybe you're the one whose brain is addled and atrophied with old-fashioned gobbledygook." The crowd snickered and Domino sank further into a confused rage. "Tell me, Domino, why rats should not be tolerated. Go on, I'm giving you a chance to defend your beliefs. Go on, tell us all." He smirked expectantly.

"I'm telling you, it's no use," muttered Flufferdoodle. Domino startled; he had forgotten the big tom was there.

"I'm not letting them do this to you, Fluff," Domino whispered back. He thought for a moment then addressed the gathering in the street. "Rats should not be tolerated because they are nasty, destructive creatures. Wherever they thrive, so do disease and filth."

The reaction from the crowd was startling and virulent. Rats cried out in righteous outrage, their screechy voices painful to the tom's sensitive ears. Max growled menacingly. The cats meowed censoriously. Domino could only make out a few words above the clamor.

"Did you hear what he said about us?"

"Who does he think he is?"

"My tail, I didn't know anyone was still capable of that kind of thinking," squealed the rats.

Lily glared at him coldly. "Really, Domino. Way to make cats look like backward slugs," she scolded.

Domino could only sit back with his mouth hanging open.

Socrates coolly waited for the noise to die down before speaking in a loud, clear meow. "Well, Domino, it seems we have a consensus; your theory has been disproven. All around me are clean, healthy, friendly rats, and the Neighborhood is alive with creatures of all sorts. More creatures of more sorts than ever before!"

The crowd meowed, squeaked, and barked its approval.

"As you yourself were just telling me, customs have changed around here," continued Socrates. "And guess what? You don't get to be the only one who decides which customs change and which ones don't. As of now, the outdated custom of cats killing rats has been replaced with the smarter, more modern custom of all creatures not just tolerating one another but embracing one another in a new society where all creatures benefit."

Now the crowd cheered noisily, a sound that went on uncomfortably long, during which Socrates never blinked. He smiled smugly and stared into Domino's face with his cold, pale eyes. Because his eyes were a little crossed, Domino got the hair-raising sensation that Socrates wasn't really seeing him, not as a cat anyway, but rather as an object to be removed or an obstacle to overcome. Domino felt panic rising in him. He knew this was how the rabbit in the meadow must have felt, as rats—probably some of these very rats before him—attacked en masse and shredded the life from it. Not the normal, mortal terror that is part of the natural order when a predator takes its prey, but a sheer bewildering confusion, the horror of the world gone awry, a nonsensical distortion wrenching the life from the healthy, for no reason except the aggrandizement of its own power. Domino longed with every individual hair in his pelt to fight this suffocating threat even as his brain understood there was no way to scratch and bite a poisonous idea. His mind scrambled for an action to take, like a drowning cat clawing at anything, *anything* to save it. And still before him were Socrates's eyes—cold, merciless, colorless, bloodless—the eyes of a ghost, a foul spirit, a madness that had taken hold of every cat and turned each one into a shambling, mindless creature indistinct from any other, still shaped like a cat but having lost everything about itself that made it a cat.

As the sound died down, Domino realized he was now trembling as well. Socrates gave him one last grin before turning to the big orange tom. "And now, Flufferdoodle, if you would be so kind as to stand aside, Ivy and her kits are going to go and feed." Without waiting for an answer, Socrates bent down and nuzzled (*nuzzled!*) the brash female rat, pushing her gently toward the curb. Behind him, Max stepped a little closer.

Domino sat paralyzed. The rat climbed up onto the curb between the two cats. She glanced up at Flufferdoodle with a sly smile before signaling back to her spawn to follow.

Domino looked at Flufferdoodle in desperation. The orange giant sat motionless, his fur vibrating with tremors of exhaustion and stress, staring yet into the air above the gathering in the street. "Great Cats, Fluff, you're not going to let them do this, are you?" howled Domino.

Flufferdoodle would not look at him. He only meowed softly, "I'm sorry, Domino, I'm just so tired ..."

Domino lost the battle to control himself. He flew at Flufferdoodle, ramming the cat harder than he had ever hit anything in his life, knocking him onto his back. He clamped his jaws to the thick throat and held on, claws like razors into

Flufferdoodle's shoulders, hind legs raking along the massive belly. A great roar issued from the orange tom as Domino held on a moment longer. Then he leaped back from Flufferdoodle, back high, eyes wide, ears flat, mouth open to vent an agonized yowl.

Flufferdoodle rolled to his feet and stood, head low, glaring back at Domino. Then he turned and slunk quickly across the brown grass to the rear of his house, where his cat door was. Domino watched him retreat into the darkness. Dead leaves and debris clung to the magnificent orange fur from Flufferdoodle's recent roll on the ground. Domino had put them there. He turned and fled to the rear of the yard, dashed through the euonymus hedge, flew through the woods, and raced right in front of a car on the road. He shot past Thor so fast the dog barely had time to glance up in confusion. The barn door was ajar and Domino tore inside, only stopping when he realized there was no other place left to run. This was it. His home.

EIGHT

The interior of the barn was illuminated by errant moonbeams when Celine awakened from her nap and padded down the steps from the loft. She found Domino in an agitated state. He was pacing the perimeter of the barn floor and halting every few steps to lick compulsively at the site of the old injury on his back leg. He barely looked up as she walked toward him. She sat and watched him. After she had seen him go through his pace-lick-pace routine a few times, she spoke in her soft, lilting meow. "I guess it didn't go well at Flufferdoodle's place."

Domino stopped moving to look at her. "It did not," he confirmed. Then the pacing began again.

Celine watched awhile longer. "Well, since you have all that nervous energy to burn off, perhaps you'd like to accompany me for a late evening patrol? We haven't exactly kept an eye on the place today."

"Yeah, okay." He forced himself to hold still until his mate reached him, and they strolled out of the barn together.

Celine took point as they went. Silent and invisible, she

was a deadly shadow moving among the structures and objects of the grounds. Near the children's clubhouse, Domino heard the frantic screeching of a field mouse and trotted toward the commotion. He reached Celine as she finished dispatching the creature. She growled around the morsel in her mouth, delivering a hearty swat to Domino's face when he got too near. In his morbid state of mind, Domino welcomed the physical rebuff. He hissed and raised his fur high, but he held his position as Celine growled again. Very well, she would take the meat. The kittens—*his* kittens—needed it.

He watched as she tore the mouse and swallowed the scraps. Soon his stomach began to rumble. When she finished, he said, "How about coming to the porch with me? I could use a bite, too."

Soon, Celine was chasing down the mouse with mouthfuls of dry cat food before finally pausing to watch Domino eat. She waited patiently until he had his fill. Then she leaped heavily to the wide porch rail. Domino licked the crumbs from his whiskers before joining her. They lay on their stomachs, heads together, resting and digesting their suppers. Celine sensed that the evening spent pacing, the patrol, and the full belly were at last having a calming effect on Domino. His tail stopped twitching and he settled into a more comfortable position. She immediately began grooming his ears and head. Domino closed his eyes and eventually purred.

"Ready to tell me what happened?" she meowed gently between licks.

The purring ceased. "I guess." She waited. "Well, don't stop grooming me."

"Oh, sorry." She restarted the soothing, stroking motions. Domino sighed as the last bit of tension left him. Then he told her, in short, tight meows, what had transpired at Fluffer-doodle's.

Celine stopped grooming before Domino finished his story. "My tail," and "My paws," she exclaimed at different points in the story. When he shamefacedly described his attack on Flufferdoodle, she mewed in sympathy and butted her head into his chest, near where his heart was.

"Well, that's the most incredible story I ever heard," she meowed when he had finished. She rolled onto her side to accommodate her large abdomen more comfortably. "I mean, really. I have just never heard anything like that before."

"I know. Me neither." Domino laid his head on his paws in misery. "It's not like I'm surprised to see rats being crafty and devious to get their way and gain access to food and safe, warm places. That's what rats do. I just can't get over those cats, though. I've known some of them my whole life. What's gotten into them?"

"Well, try not to be too hard on them," Celine said. "I don't think they really understand what's happening. After all, there isn't one of them who really *needs* to rely on hunting for anything. Their food comes from boxes and cans that people open for them. They live in houses where people keep out vermin. They don't have any kittens to protect." She paused to put her thoughts together. "Maybe this is what happens when cats get too comfortable, too far removed from the natural order of things. They don't understand why things have always been done a certain way, so they don't see the need for it. The customary ways just aren't important to them anymore."

"And that's fine, I can even understand that," meowed Domino. "If a cat chooses for himself that he can't be bothered to hunt, if he even decides he'd like to hang out with rats or mice or rabbits or slugs—whatever. That's his business. He'll get ticks and fleas and diseases, but that's his business." Domino's green eyes glowed intensely in the moonlight. "What I don't get is this insistence that everyone else make the same choices. I mean, what do they care if Flufferdoodle wants to keep his territory free of vermin? So what?"

"Right."

"Or Cricket. She really needs to hunt. She's starving on her feet. But they impose on her kind nature, and they make her feel so bad about hunting that she won't do it. They don't care that she's being hurt by their stupid ideas."

"Yes, that is worrisome."

"Yes, it is. They say they want all kinds of animals to live together in peace, but on the other paw, they only want the *same* kind of all kinds of animals, if that makes sense."

Celine nodded. "It does."

Domino stared into her eyes, needing the confirmation that someone else understood. Celine looked back at him with her calm, golden gaze. Then she leaned forward to touch noses with him. Domino closed his eyes, letting the garbled feelings leave him and focusing only on his mate's touch. *Thank the Great Cats for her,* he thought.

The kitchen door swung open and Mr. Brown emerged onto the porch. He spotted the cats on the moonlit railing. "Aw, now if that ain't the sweetest thing," he said. "And how are you two this evening?" The cats eyed him suspiciously. "You taking good care of my place, Domino?"

"Of course I am," the tom meowed indignantly. A large, rough hand scratched behind his ears and he purred loudly in spite of himself.

The hand moved to Celine and she blinked and purred at the unexpected neck rub. "You better take good care of your lady, too," Mr. Brown admonished. "She's a sweet little thing."

"Oh, yes, sir," Domino sneered.

"Shh, don't insult the man. He knows what he's talking about," purred Celine.

Mr. Brown sat on the bench and pulled out a pipe. The cats watched as he put a flame to it, and the scent of burning tobacco began to waft over them. "Lovely evening," the man said between puffs. "Nice that it's finally warm enough to sit outside a bit, even if I have to wear a jacket."

"Yes, very nice, except that there is a massive rat infestation over in the Neighborhood, and they're going to come here soon, too," meowed Domino.

"Yeah, I know, you always have a nice, warm, fur jacket on," Mr. Brown answered.

Domino looked away and sighed loudly. "If only they could understand us," he muttered.

"That would certainly change things," agreed Celine. She wrinkled her nose. "Domino, I don't care for that smoke in my face. I'm going back to the loft."

"I'll join you."

"Now where are you two going?" complained Mr. Brown as the cats leaped to the deck and descended the steps into the yard. "Okay, then, have a good night." The cats didn't look back as they crossed the yard and went into the barn.

IN THE FOLLOWING DAYS, Domino tried to put the horrors of the transformed Neighborhood behind him. He focused on his territory instead.

Celine declared herself too low on energy to work her woods. Rather, she agreed to patrol the area from the barn to the stone wall, freeing Domino to take the territory across the yard and long grass to the north woods. This he patrolled daily, scratching up rat trails, thoroughly marking the area with his scent, and dispatching the occasional vermin when he found one.

The rats were hulking and bold, far different from the rare rodent he used to come across, back before Socrates had arrived. They went about their business craftily, seeming to work together for a common goal, each knowing what it had to do and proceeding with a sort of calculated malice. When Domino leaped upon one, its face would register the usual surprise and terror of apprehended prey. But there was also something else: defiance, a sense of entitlement, as though the rat believed it somehow had a right to the territory, and it was Domino who was trespassing.

Besides this newfound arrogance, the rats were also heavy and strong. They were clearly well fed, which Domino did not find surprising—after all, they had the run of a plentiful Neighborhood of people and pets. This health and abundance lent them unprecedented vigor, and they fought back heartily. More than once, Domino sustained minor injuries while terminating one. He responded by becoming wilier, quicker, quieter, and more lethal.

And yet the rats kept coming. They yielded plentiful meat, but Domino's revulsion at the invasion soon tainted his taste for rat. That, combined with the sheer number of rodent kills, led him to stop eating the beasts altogether. His stomach rebelled at the sight of a fresh kill; his gag reflex threatened at the thought of the greasy, stringy meat sliding down his throat. Instead, he strewed the corpses along the edge of the woods by the roadside as a warning to the next ones.

But they kept coming. Daily patrols of the north woods were now a necessity.

When Domino wasn't paying attention and sternly disciplining his thoughts, when he was bathing himself at the end of the day or just before he drifted off to sleep alongside Celine in the cooler-den, he would think about Flufferdoodle. How must the big tom be getting on in his new reality? Did he actually sit in his yard as rats fed at the bird feeders? How could he stand the sight of them? Or did he stop coming outside altogether? A shudder would course through Domino as he tried to imagine what the Neighborhood was like now.

Nor could he think about Flufferdoodle without pain and shame welling up within him. Even when he was able to direct his conscious thoughts away from his old friend, the pain was always with him, a dull, nagging ache like the scarred muscle in his rear flank. He missed the big orange tom terribly, but he could never face him again. His own behavior at the lowest point in his friend's life was just too awful.

And yet, Domino's territory was good. The silly, clucking hens were laying again, now that the sun warmed the earth for a longer time each day. Rain had replaced snow and there were clear puddles from which to lap water. The children were back in the clubhouse, installing fresh captives in the terrarium for the cats to stare at. Mrs. Brown kept the food bowl full of dry cat food and added the occasional bit of chicken or tuna. ("That's for Licorice," she admonished him when he tried to eat the treats.) The new leaves adorning the branches were good. The sun-warmed patches of dust were good. The kits in Celine's belly were good.

After falling asleep to the sound of rain on the roof, Domino awoke to a bright morning and an empty place beside him. He padded down the steps, meowing for his mate. From the far wall of the barn, behind the dusty jeeps, he heard a soft answer. In a dim corner next to the shelving, nestled into a box of old rags, Celine lay on her side, nursing three tiny kittens.

Domino's mouth hung open in awe. When he could meow again, he stammered, "Celine! Why didn't you call me?"

She smiled broadly. "Why would I disturb you? Were you going to help somehow?"

"I—I don't know. Are you okay?"

"I'm fine."

And then he was lost in the kittens. He lowered his head so that his nose nearly touched them. A completely novel scent filled his senses. The kittens trembled and fidgeted and threw off heat. Their fluffy pelts already showed their markings—an all-black male, a spotted male, and a spotted female. For an unknown amount of time, Domino simply watched them. He watched Celine as she settled them down, smoothed their tousled heads, and set them to napping again. Then she looked up at him and blinked lazily. Domino stepped closer and touched noses with her. The drone of contented purring hung over the family like a swarm of hovering bees.

Domino looked again at the sleeping kits. They were so small! Their paws were nearly as tiny as those of a field mouse. Their sides rose and fell with rapid breaths. Even as Domino gazed on them, powerful new feelings appeared and began to install themselves in his heart. They did not replace his other concerns entirely but simply moved them aside and took up the majority of the space. And yet, it seemed Domino's heart swelled to take them all in.

So he was a pawpaw now. His responsibilities had just expanded to include, above all, the safety of these tiny creatures. He must watch over them, guide them, and protect them as they crept toward maturity, someday to work territories of their own. He greedily anticipated every moment.

Domino and Celine basked in the sight of their first litter.

And as they gazed, the world became an entirely different place.

BY THE FOLLOWING MORNING, the cats had established a routine. Celine would nurse the kits until they fell asleep. Domino then watched over them while she went to the food bowl. She returned to the nest to nap along with the kits. Domino spent these quiet times either patrolling or up in the cooler, catching up on his sleep. And he needed more rest than ever, since the entire territory was his to patrol now, including the ratty north woods.

Mrs. Brown brought the children to visit the kittens. She made them sit several feet away from the rag box and told them to speak quietly. Celine lay with the kits, watching them, and Domino sat up straight alongside the box, his chest out, smiling a big cat smile at his people. "Well, what do you think? Have you ever seen such a beautiful litter?" he meowed.

The Browns oohed and aahed appreciatively. After a while, Mrs. Brown herded the children away.

Several weeks passed, and the kittens opened their eyes. They moved around on shaky legs and emitted adorable, high-pitched mews. Domino spent more time than he should sitting by the box and admiring them.

"I think we should call the black one Marble," purred Celine.

"What's marble?" asked Domino. He nudged the kitten in question with his snout, knocking him over. He smiled as the tiny cat popped up again and raised a paw, ready to go.

"I remember from when I was a kitten and lived with my people that the boy had these round, smooth, shiny stones he played with. He called them marbles. They were mostly solid colors, and one of them was all black. I used to think it was so beautiful."

Domino considered the fluffy black kitten in the box. He was a far cry from smooth and shiny but since he had obviously inherited his mother's coat, Domino was sure he would be one day. "Very well, Marble it is."

The black-and-white spotted male mewed and took a wobbly step toward his parents before tripping over his brother.

"What about him?" asked Domino.

"Well, he seems to be the leader of the pack so far," Celine said thoughtfully. "And he has your wonderful spots. He reminds me of that time of year when the snow is melting and interchanges with patches of bare ground."

"He's going to be a fine tom," Domino meowed.

"I agree. I've even been calling him Tam to myself," said Celine, pronouncing the word *tom* with a kittenish inflection.

"Tam works," agreed Domino. He turned his attention to the spotty female, who had been watching them both the whole time. "And what about this one?"

"I'm not sure." Celine tilted her head and considered her female kitten. "She seems to be similar in disposition to Tam, brave and ready to lead and explore. And she has the same spotty coat."

"But she's delicate, like you."

"I hardly think of myself as delicate."

"Well, you know what I mean—finely wrought. And she seems more ready to watch and learn than Tam, a little more curious and introspective. She's a lovely example of what makes cats so splendid." Domino tried to think of a name that represented the female feline ideal. "Catlyn!" he exclaimed suddenly.

The tiny female kitten mewed.

"That's a beautiful name," said Celine. "Catlyn it is."

"Come here, Catlyn," said Domino. The kitten came quickly on rubbery legs, mewing to her pawpaw.

"I guess they can understand what we're saying now," observed Celine.

"I guess so." Domino bent to touch noses with Catlyn. Then he pushed her back with his head. She sprang forward, and he bowed his head and shoved her back. She came at him again, and they played the new game. "And they should start meowing words soon, right?" Domino asked Celine between shoves. "I can't wait to hear what they have to say."

A WEEK LATER, Domino watched the kits one morning while Celine did a quick patrol and went to get breakfast on the porch. Tam and Marble were old enough to wrestle and were already larger in size than their sister, although none of the kittens were big or sturdy enough to do any real damage yet. Catlyn divided her time between taking on her brothers and shadowing her father. There was less wobble in the kittens' steps today, and Domino felt nothing but quiet happiness as he watched them.

But soon they were back in the rag box for a nap, and he had no distractions. He stood over their sleeping forms protectively, watching their fuzzy sides rise and fall and trying to keep his thoughts in the present time and place.

"Why don't you go see him today?"

Domino jumped at the sound of Celine's voice. Having kittens had done nothing to diminish her stealth. "Who?" he barked. But they both knew whom she meant. Domino hung his head. "I can't."

Celine didn't argue. Instead she came to him and rubbed

her cheek against his. Domino closed his eyes and let her soft purrs wash over him. Celine moved past him into the rag box and settled into a dark crescent around the sleeping kits. She blinked up at her mate. "Well, I'm ready for a nap, so you're off-duty for the time being. Go do something useful." She winked and laid her head on her paws.

"Fine, I will. It's time for a rat patrol, anyway." Domino indulged himself with one last view of his family before turning away and leaving the barn.

Celine's question stayed with him as he trotted across the greening grasses toward the north woods. It buzzed him like an annoying fly. *Why don't you go see him today?* His own lame answer hung in the air as well: *I can't.*

Could he ever face Flufferdoodle again? He missed his great friend terribly. Sometimes he even pictured himself going to the big cat's territory, coming humbly before him, and apologizing. But then the Flufferdoodle of his imagination transformed within the fantasy. At first, he would be his usual self, sitting tall and proud, the lord of his yard. But then he would shrink down and hang his head, and his feline posture would crumple into a lowly slouch. Flufferdoodle would not look at Domino, and Domino realized Flufferdoodle would not look at anything. His yard was no longer his own. It was a playground for rats, a territory belonging to no one and everyone, with no borders or demarcations, simply another location within one big Neighborhood, where all went where they pleased. No cat could claim a territory ever again, and so a vast part of a cat's life and purpose was gone forever. And Domino knew Flufferdoodle would not look at him out of shame, which was ridiculous, since it was Domino who should be ashamed. But he also knew that there was yet a tiny part of himself that *was* ashamed of Flufferdoodle, even as he knew the orange tom had no other real choice.

Domino leaped over a large tussock and shook his head; what a mess it all was.

Still brooding, he slaughtered two rats as he worked the woods. He followed a well-used trail eastward until it came out of the trees and dissipated into the larger meadow. Domino could not follow any one path here; there was rat scat everywhere, in all directions. He pondered what it meant and had to conclude that there were enough rats coming through the woods to scatter in numerous directions and complete who-knew-what missions. He didn't care for it.

After searching through the meadow grasses for a while, he came up with nothing new. And still he was filled with nervous energy. Without allowing himself to stop and think, he passed back through the woods and crossed the road.

As he moved through the sparse forest on the other side of the pavement, Domino encountered rat paths and pellets, but he didn't find any of the creatures. He moved with stealth nonetheless, very much wanting to see without being seen.

With a lump in his throat, he crept into the euonymus hedge, ready to catch a glimpse of his friend, but then he froze. Screechy, unpleasant voices stung his ears. He remained concealed behind a leafy branch and moved only his head ever so slightly so he could see. Two rats were just ahead, bickering among themselves.

"Maybe *I* want to go for a scrabble. Does that ever occur to you?"

"Frankly, I don't care what you do, sow. I'm outta here."

"Ha! Of course you are. Off you go, never a thought about me or what I want. Always you, you, you."

"So, go! Who's stopping you? My scat, you always have to make it into a big 'poor me' session."

"And who will keep an eye on the ratlings if we're both out?"

At this point, Domino noticed that a rough nest of leaves and grass was partially concealed beneath a low branch just behind the quarreling rodents. He could even see naked, squirming rat babies bobbing about in it. He felt like gagging.

"For scat's sake, they're okay by themselves for a while, you stupid pelt."

"Watch what you call me, bunghole." Then the female rat stopped screeching and looked down at the nest. "Yeah, I guess you're right, though. It's not like they're big enough to crawl around or anything yet. They'll be fine." She looked at her mate with a toothy grin. "Come on, let's go."

"Yeah, that's my girl." With a course laugh, the male rat turned and scuttled out from beneath the hedge, the female just behind him.

"Parents of the Year," Domino muttered when they had gone. He was upon the nest in a trice. There were eleven baby rats in a mound, hairless, eyeless, and writhing like a mass of gray maggots. Domino pulled his lips back from his teeth and laid his ears flat. "Let's see," he said to himself, "I think I'll juggle them for a while first. Toss them like a salad. Then I can open them up and scatter them around for all the rats to see. Yes, that sounds about right."

Oblivious, the ratlings fidgeted and squeaked. Domino lifted his paw to begin scooping them, but something caught his eye. He looked up as flashes of color came through the network of leaves and branches. Out on the green lawn, sunlight glanced off bright fur as Flufferdoodle strolled across the back-yard. The ratlings were forgotten and the lump was back in

Domino's throat. Suddenly, his heart was thudding painfully against his ribs. He summoned all his stealth and moved forward, not noticing he was stepping on the squirming nest. When he got as close to Flufferdoodle as he could without being seen, Domino sat and watched.

The rats who had just left the hedge were scrabbling for seeds with two other rats beneath the bird feeders. Another pair of rats scurried alongside the house until they came to the cellar doors. Domino watched them as they examined the structure, trying to find a way in.

Although the ratty side of the yard was the sunniest, Flufferdoodle headed the other way. His stomach hung so close to the ground, its lower reaches were hidden in the grass, and his once powerful strut had become a defeated waddle. *Spending a bit too much time indoors, old boy?* Domino wondered to himself.

Flufferdoodle seemed not to see the rats at all. He came to a halt in a flickering scrap of sunlight and sat, facing away at an oblique angle to the rats. He lowered his head and began nibbling at the spring grass shoots. He looked to be making an attempt at normal cat behavior, as though there were no vermin just yards away. The lump in Domino's throat made swallowing difficult.

Domino and Flufferdoodle had spent many a pleasant afternoon in the sunny yard where rats now scurried and foraged. They had lolled in the warmth, batted at the nodding flowers in the garden, and just dozed if they felt like it. But now Flufferdoodle was making do with a fleeting patch of sunshine in the shady, cold part of the yard. He lowered his bulk onto his belly and blinked drowsily a few times.

The rats by the feeders had stopped eating. They watched Flufferdoodle and whispered among themselves. Then the male from the hedge squeaked out, "Hey, neighbor! How's it going?"

Flufferdoodle rolled onto his side, showing the rats nothing but his back, and looked as though he were asleep. But Domino noticed his ears flicking back as the rats cackled before going back to their feeding.

Muted squeaks came from behind Domino and he remembered the nest. He pictured himself merrily flinging the ratlings into the air, swatting and clawing and snapping his jaws. But he continued to sit and watch the parents out on the lawn. When Silky-Rat had been killed near Flufferdoodle, it hadn't gone well for the big tom. Great Cats only knew what kind of a racket the rat parents would raise if they came back and found a pile of tiny corpses. Domino sighed. He could practically feel the warm, soft nuggets in his claws, but the last thing he wanted to do was bring a new furor down on Flufferdoodle's head.

Tail twitching, he turned and moved silently along the hedge. Soon he was behind Meg's house. Now that the weather had warmed up, the windows were open. He could see Meg's panther-like shape on a ledge, her nose pressed to the screen, her remarkable blue eyes peering out of her dark face. Domino swallowed hard. She was looking for Flufferdoodle. A crispy dead leaf made the tiniest crackle as he stepped on it, and the Siamese in the window snapped her head in his direction. Domino froze.

"Hello?" Meg called. "Hello? Is anyone out there?"

Domino stayed hidden but smiled wanly to himself. Hearing Meg's raspy voice was as pleasing as letting a warm ray of sunlight wash over him.

Three rats scurried around the corner of Meg's house and came into the yard. Domino watched them scavenge around the patio table for dropped bits of food. Meg saw them, too. Even at a distance, Domino could see the worry in her lovely eyes. She was trapped indoors, and Flufferdoodle had always taken care of her territory as a sign of his affection. Now he was missing and there were rats in her yard, in broad daylight. Domino realized that Flufferdoodle hadn't been able to face Meg and tell her the truth about what was going on. Instead, he was simply avoiding her. Poor Meg must be beside herself. And Flufferdoodle... well, Domino could only imagine what kind of self-loathing the big tom must be feeling.

He had seen enough. Once again, he was on the move through the hedge. When he had put enough distance between himself and Flufferdoodle's former territory, he worked his way through a heavily landscaped yard and across the street to the Gully.

Among the trees again, Domino relaxed but didn't lower his guard all the way. He covered ground quickly but kept his tread quiet. The woods seemed eerie and unnatural and it took him a moment to figure out what was wrong; it was too quiet.

Ordinarily, at this time of year, there would be birds every-where. They should be foraging among the litter, calling out the boundaries of their territories, fussing over nestlings, and making a din with their incessant socializing. It didn't seem like spring without the noise. Domino walked on grimly. He had an idea why there were no birds in the woods. Eggs and nestlings are prime meals for rodents. He doubted that rats would ever be so *transcendent* as to give up their predatory feeding habits, even as they demanded that cats give up their own.

At last, he caught sight of Cricket. She sat in a sunny spot near the mouth of her den, carefully licking at two scrawny kittens. Domino trotted up to her with tail high and ears forward. "Cricket," he meowed. "You have kittens! Congratulations."

The calico cat stopped grooming and looked up. "Domino! How's it going?" She stood a little stiffly and stepped forward to touch noses with him.

Domino bent to sniff at the kits. "And who do we have here?"

"Oh, these are some of my kittens. This is Stone and this is Rock."

Struck by the warm expression that lit her face, Domino momentarily stopped noticing that her fur was coarse and dry, and that her body looked thin and frail. "I can see why you named them that, with those solid-gray coats." *Just like Rudy,* he thought. *That dog.* Aloud he said, "What a handsome pair of little toms."

"Thanks, Domino," purred Cricket. "Hey, come inside and see the girls. They're napping." She turned and crept into the den before he had a chance to say anything.

Domino glanced at the two gray kits. As befit their youth, they seemed curious and mischievous, but to a lesser degree than his own kits. They were also a good deal smaller, even smaller than Catlyn. "Now, you toms stay right here," he admonished. Then he squeezed in behind Cricket.

In the dim light, he saw her nudging two little kittens to stand up. "Go say hi, kits," she instructed. The diminutive cats, one calico and one gray, wobbled to their feet and let him touch their noses. "These are Dapple and Pebble," beamed Cricket.

"Hi, cuties," said Domino. They mewed sweetly.

And then Domino noticed that there were two rats packed into the den.

"Hey," squeaked one of the bloated rodents. The other one ignored him and nibbled at an itchy spot near its paw. Alongside the two rats, clusters of hairless ratlings writhed and shoved one another.

A black film seemed to cover the scene before Domino as primal rage flooded his muscles. He had to get out of there before he did something violent and brought the wrath of the Neighborhood down on Cricket and her kits. He meowed quickly and mechanically, "Cricket, your kits are simply beautiful. I'm glad I could stop by, but I have to get back to Celine now." He turned and fled the den.

"Send Rock and Stone in, would you?" Cricket called after him. "They need a nap."

Outside again, a shaking Domino faced the skinny kittens. They looked up at him with dull eyes. "Okay, you two, go see your myu," he told them. "She says it's time for a rest."

They remained silent instead of complaining, as his own kits would have done. In the instant before they turned to go, a breeze moved a branch somewhere in just such a way that the afternoon sun threw a bright ray across their tiny faces. In that moment of illumination, Domino caught miniscule movements. Even as his brain told him he didn't want to see, his eyes focused in. Fleas scurried across the bridge of each little nose, around the gummy eyes, and in the delicate folds of the ears. The benighted kittens were crawling with them.

Domino didn't stay to watch them go inside. He raced out of the Gully.

NINE

Domino tore across the yard just out of Thor's reach. The German shepherd was busy gnawing on a new rawhide toy, but he looked up briefly. "Crazy cat," he muttered to himself before going back to his chewing.

Domino tried to skirt the garden near the barn, but Mrs. Brown caught sight of him. "There you are, Domino," she called in a stern voice. "Where have you been? Someone's been in my garden. Look at this."

In spite of his churning emotions, Domino paused to look her way. "What happened?" he meowed.

"Someone's been nibbling my pea shoots right down to the root. They're ruined. And look at this." She pointed angrily to a row of holes. "Every time I put seeds in, someone comes and digs them out and eats them. Domino, I expect you to do something about this. This is your job."

Domino was stricken. "Indeed, it is." He stepped over the loose soil to sniff the offending holes in the ground. A faint odor of rat clung to the ground. "I can't believe this. How are they doing this? I patrol as much as I can between here and the north woods." He looked up at the woman's frowning face. "I'm sure we'll get back on top of things once Celine can go back to full patrol duties," he explained.

"Yeah, yeah, go tell it to someone who cares," Mrs. Brown grumbled. Then she smiled ruefully and squatted alongside the cat. A gentle hand scratched behind his ears and rubbed the tense muscles in his neck. "I'm sorry, Domino. I know you have a family to look after now." The cat rumbled in appreciation. "Just see if you can keep an eye on this garden a little better, okay?" She stood up and sighed. "Guess I'll drive over to the nursery and see if I can get some seedlings."

Dismissed, Domino resumed his urgent pace to the barn. The sight of Cricket's scrawny, flea-infested kits lingered behind his eyes, and he longed to push his face into his own kittens' fluffy coats and smell their healthy scent.

Inside the barn, Mr. Brown and the two bigger children were working on the motor on the back of the boat. There was a lot of banging and strong smells of oil and chemicals. The oldest child spotted Domino. "Uh oh, here he comes," said the boy.

"You mind your business and I'll mind mine," meowed Domino. He passed the nearest child and ran under the boat trailer. But when he came out the other side, the rag box—and his family—were missing. He turned on the people, who had put down their tools and encircled him. "Where are they?" he howled. "What have you done with them?"

"Now, take it easy, big guy," soothed Mr. Brown. "Licorice didn't care for our racket, so she moved the kittens upstairs."

"We made them a nice new box with warm blankets and everything," added the girl. "They even have their own litter box up there, and food and toys and everything."

"Most spoiled barn cats I ever saw," muttered Mr. Brown.

"Come on, we'll show you," said the boy.

He scooped Domino up and carried him to the narrow stairs at the back of the barn. The girl followed her brother, while Mr. Brown went back to work on the motor. As Domino's head emerged above the floor on the second level, he began to wriggle in the boy's arms. "I'm perfectly capable of walking, thank you. Put me down."

"Geez, okay," said the boy. He loosened his grip and allowed Domino to jump to the floor.

From a luxurious new box full of fluffy blankets against the far wall, Celine looked up and meowed a greeting. She stood, stretched, and walked over to touch noses with her mate. "What do you think of the new nest, Domino?"

He looked over her shoulder at the plush bed. "Very nice," he commented briefly. "Where are the kits?"

Celine registered his anxiety. "They're right over there, see? They're fine. How was the hunting?"

"Got two rats. Then I went over to the Neighborhood to see how our friends are getting on." He shook his head sadly.

"Oh dear. How was it?" meowed Celine. Before Domino could answer, the girl picked the black cat up and held her, stroking her fur and murmuring to her affectionately. Celine went limp in her arms and bent her head back so the girl could scratch under her chin.

Domino could hear Celine purring. "Okay, guess we'll catch up later," he said. At last, he turned to watch his kittens. They were in a loose group halfway between the new nest and the open loft door. The two younger children were playing with them. The girl had a felt mouse on a string, which she trawled past Marble repeatedly while the kitten worked on his pouncing technique. The boy had another toy mouse dangling from the end of a fishing rod. He raised the rod and hurled the mouse across the room. Then he cranked the handle on the reel and the mouse raced back toward him. Tam and Catlyn tumbled over one another, trying to apprehend the faux rodent. Watching them, the boy laughed so hard his whole body shook. When the mouse and kittens all piled up at his feet, he raised the rod and repeated the process.

Domino sat and watched the proceedings. The gnawing anxiety he had carried since his visit to the Neighborhood began to melt away. His kittens were strong and healthy and full of energy. His home was safe and secure. Presently, Celine came and sat beside him. "You're doing a great job with those kits," he told her.

Celine purred in acknowledgment. "So, how was Fluffer-doodle? Did you talk to him?" she asked.

Domino's ears flattened then stood forward again. "No. I only saw him through the branches of the hedge." He glanced down at the floor. "Celine, there are rats nesting in the hedge. They have free reign of Flufferdoodle's territory. I saw him come out of the house and try to ignore them. But you can tell he spends most of his time indoors now."

"Did the rats see you?"

"No. I was going to wipe out a nest full of ratlings, but then I thought better of it. I didn't want to get Flufferdoodle into any more trouble."

Celine said nothing. Domino could tell her mind was deeply troubled, but apparently she couldn't come up with a solution to the situation, either. He went on to tell her about Cricket's kits, the rat nests inside Cricket's den, and the flea infestation.

Celine's golden eyes went wide and shone with a mixture of pity and horror. "Oh, poor Cricket," she meowed softly. They sat and watched their own healthy kittens at play in silence. "Domino," Celine said, "I'm glad I met you. I'm glad I'm with you in this good, safe place while we raise our kits."

Domino purred noisily and leaned against her warm flank. "I'm glad, too."

The felt mouse flew past them and began its return to the boy with the fishing rod. Quick and lethal looking for such a young kit, Catlyn timed a pounce flawlessly and landed on the toy. An instant later, her much larger brother rammed into her and knocked her onto her side. The toy was his and he clung to it with his sharp kitten claws and teeth. Catlyn got to her feet, a look of frustration on her tiny face. Tam had full possession of the toy now, and she didn't try to take it back from him. Instead she hopped over to her parents and looked up. Celine bent to touch noses. Catlyn rolled onto her back in front of Domino with a paw raised, inviting him to tussle. The big cat laughed. "You want to take *me* on?" He rumbled with purrs and went into a crouch. Then he easily flipped the kitten onto her other side so that she faced away from him. She jumped up and spun to try again. Laughing, Domino sparred with her until she tired of the game and wobbled off to visit Marble.

Domino watched Tam with the felt mouse. The little tom gripped the toy and flipped onto his side, bringing his hind paws up to rake at it. The young father purred with pride. "Tam will have a big, fine territory someday," he meowed.

"Tam will have an awful lot of work to do and many enemies someday," said Celine.

"*Humph*," snorted Domino. "There's nothing wrong with being big and strong."

"Indeed not," agreed Celine. "I wish I had more size myself. But being big and strong isn't everything. I just hope Tam develops his mind as well as his muscles."

"I'm sure he will. He's your kit, isn't he?"

More purring.

DOMINO SPENT much of the night on patrol. This time, he stayed closer to the buildings. He centered his operations on guarding Mrs. Brown's garden and went on short sorties from there. He saw no creatures on the ground, only a barred owl gliding overhead on silent wings. Dawn found him fast asleep in the old cooler by the hayloft door.

"Mew?" A tiny voice rang into the snug space. His back to the door, Domino ignored it and tried to stay asleep. Soon there were whiskers tickling the inside of his ear, which vibrated with kitten purrs.

"Go see your myu," he mumbled, clinging to the last vestiges of sleep. The tickly whiskers left his ear and were replaced by tiny paws traversing his ribs. Domino flicked his tail in annoyance. That was a mistake. The purring stopped as an all-out assault opened up. Domino gave up, lifted his head, and drew a cavernous yawn. He stood and stretched, and Catlyn tumbled off of him. As she got to her feet, he gently closed his teeth on the back of her neck and lifted her by the scruff.

He emerged from the den into late morning sunlight slanting into the loft. He carried the wriggling kitten across the plank floor to where Celine sat in front of the new cat bed, watching Marble and Tam as they played. She mewed a greeting as her mate approached. Domino deposited Catlyn at her feet and said, "I believe this is yours." The kitten immediately sprang up onto her hind legs, paws raised and ready for battle. Domino ignored her and leaned forward to touch noses with Celine.

"How was night watch? Did you see anything interesting?" she asked.

"No. Very quiet." He sat and yawned again.

"Well, if you can watch the kits for a little while, I'll take a turn around the chickens and over to the stone wall."

"Very well."

Domino spent the next hour alternately dozing and batting kittens off himself. Eventually the two smaller Brown children came up into the loft and began playing with the kits. Domino lay in the cat bed and tried to go back to sleep, but he was antsy. Presently Celine returned and joined him. She had a serious air about her and seemed shaken.

"What?" he asked.

"It's the middle of the day, right?"

"Yes."

"And yet, I just got a big rat alongside the hen house."

"Huh, I don't care for that." *Must be a Neighborhood rat for sure,* Domino concluded. "Remember the day I first saw you?" he asked. "The same thing happened—a rat in the hen house in the middle of the day. A big one, too."

"And very arrogant. Yes, I remember."

"Well, did you take care of it?"

She shivered. "I did, but it wasn't easy. Domino, this thing was huge."

"Yes, but so was the one you got last fall."

"Yeah, but I was in much better shape then."

"Of course you were. You were living in the woods. You'd have been dead if you weren't."

"I've gotten soft."

"Nonsense. You're simply doing brilliantly at something else right now." He stood and stretched, then came to sit beside her. "Look over there." He nodded with his chin.

Celine lifted her downcast eyes to where he was looking. She saw three sturdy, fuzzy kittens tumbling and leaping at toys wielded by the children.

"See that?" asked Domino.

"Yes, I see." Celine began to purr in spite of her bad mood.

"Right now, this is the number one thing you're supposed to be doing. And you're doing the best job ever. I can run the patrols for a while."

"Thanks," Celine purred. "But I hate to see you running yourself ragged, taking over my watch as well as your own."

"Whatever did I do before you were here?" he meowed melodramatically.

Celine gave a small laugh. "Yes, but you weren't fending off a full-scale rat invasion single-handedly," she pointed out.

"And I'm not doing it single-handedly now, either. You've been adding longer rounds back into your schedule every day."

"I know, but it's not enough. Mrs. Brown is still upset about her garden."

"I'm already handling it," Domino soothed. "I spent the whole night watching and all was quiet. I wouldn't be surprised if that rat you got today was the problem."

"Let's hope."

"Yes, let's. And in the meantime, don't be so hard on yourself." Domino pushed his face against hers and down her neck, purring. A faint rat smell lingered on her fur but beneath it was Celine's own honest scent of health and fresh air. He indulged in resting his head on her back and breathing her in for a moment longer before sitting up straight again. He sighed deeply. "Guess I'll head out for a while," he meowed.

"What's the plan for today?"

Domino smiled at her eager tone. "Don't worry, those

kittens will be on their own by summer. You'll have plenty of time to get back in the game."

"I know. I was just wondering. I like to hear about it, even if I'm not doing it right now."

"Well, I thought I'd head up to the north woods and spend an hour or two cleaning them out. I assume that's where your feisty rat came from."

"So that's the way they're coming from the Neighborhood?"

"It certainly seems to be. I can't go up there without finding at least one or two. And there are trails everywhere."

Celine stood and arched her back into a stretch, then reached forward and flexed her forelegs. When she sat again, she said, "I bet I can completely take over the southern part of the territory again in a week or so."

"Heck, we can probably start training these kits in a week or so," added Domino.

"They're already well on their way." Celine and Domino paused to watch the young hunters practicing on the toy mice. Sensing their parents' attention, the kittens lost interest in the game and came over, mewing loudly about how hungry and tired they were.

Celine looked up at her mate. "Guess I'll feed them and have a rest. I'm a little worn out myself. That rat put up a serious fight."

She never complained, but Domino knew that nursing the growing kits was exhausting. "Fine. Just take it easy this afternoon. I'll be back in time for you to have an evening patrol, if you're up for it."

"I'm sure I will be." Another nose touch. "Happy hunting." With the kittens hopping and tripping about her, Celine stepped into the padded nest, followed by her offspring.

. . .

TEN MINUTES LATER, Domino was at the far end of the meadow, working the edge of the forest. A strong wind blew fitfully from the east, carrying portents of bad weather. *Maybe Celine will want to skip that evening patrol, after all,* thought Domino. The wind whipped the long grass around his legs and agitated the new leaves on the trees and shrubs, filling the air with a cacophony of shushing sounds. Broken sunlight flickered through the dancing branches, creating the illusion of movement everywhere Domino looked. "Lousy conditions for hunting," he grumbled to himself.

Suddenly, a big, grizzled cat stood before him. Domino halted and blew up to twice his size before he recognized the stranger. "Great Cats, Rudy, you scared me." He had to meow loudly to be heard over the noisy breeze, so he stepped closer to the visitor. "This stinking easterly," he grumbled. "Can't smell or hear a thing coming from your direction."

"Domino, I have to talk to you," Rudy meowed. Now Domino noticed that the tough feral tom seemed to be on edge. He was panting and his pupils were dilated in his wide eyes. His normal swagger was gone, replaced by a jumpy demeanor comprised of equal parts anger and fear. It was unnerving to see the seasoned, self-assured tom in such a state of distress.

"Of course, old friend. What is it?"

Rudy took a moment to look behind himself carefully. Satisfied that no other creature approached, he turned his attention back to Domino. "Those *rats*," he began, pronouncing the word *rats* with contempt. "They're not who they say they are. I knew them, back in the city. Well, I knew *of* them. I never actually associated with rats, of course."

"Of course," meowed Domino.

"That rat who calls himself Sunflower Seed—his real name is Rip. He was a big pack leader back in the meatpacking district. He took on more than he could handle, though. Got into it with the street cats there. Big mistake."

Domino took in the new information. "I knew there was something off about that whole thing."

"Yeah. Anyway, the cats went after him and his pack. He holed up in an apartment building for a long time. But that got exterminated, and he and that female and a few others were the only rats to escape with their lives.

"And her name ain't Meadow, either, by the way," he added. "She was called Shredder back in the district. Real nasty piece of work."

"Shredder. Huh, sounds like a real sweetie."

Rudy had more. "The building they lived in? That was where Rip and Shredder first found Socrates. Smart as a person, that cat, but also completely innocent. Lived in an apartment his whole life, no idea how the streets work. Anyway, Rip knew a stooge when he saw one." Rudy's breathing had evened out by now, but his words kept coming fast, as though he thought he might run out of time at any moment. He paused to look behind himself again.

Domino nodded. "I heard them talking about it one time. I was hiding in the hedge in front of Socrates's house. Socrates was talking to those rats. Sunflower Se—I mean, Rip—was describing the time he first saw Socrates through an air vent in the wall. I guess they started talking then, and Socrates totally had no problem being friends with a rat."

"Like I said, he was completely innocent. No idea how things worked or that there was really anything wrong with rats." Rudy looked profoundly sad. "*Was* innocent. I'm not so sure he is now."

"I don't think so. I think he's pretty thoroughly corrupted by now," agreed Domino. "But when I was watching them that time, after Socrates went back inside the house, the rats started laughing at him. They were talking about how stupid he was, and how they could use him to do whatever they wanted him to do."

"Yeah, that's the situation. Socrates is totally fooling himself. They don't care about him. Rip hates cats, after they handed him his tail back in the city. But I guess when he was holed up in that apartment building, he had time to think. He must've been able to watch Socrates and put his plan together and figure out a way to beat cats."

"Or maybe he just figured out what kind of cats he could beat," mused Domino. "I bet that's what happened. I can see it now. Rip and his rats eavesdropping in the walls while Socrates and Max's people planned their move to the Neighborhood. But how did the rats get all the way out here? I doubt the people would have brought them. People hate rats."

"Oh, the people must have brought them, but they probably didn't *know* they were bringing them," Rudy meowed. "I've seen people move in and out of houses in the Neighborhood. A big truck comes, full of boxes and furniture and things. Lots of places for rats to stow away."

"That's true. I've seen that, too." Domino stared at the blowing grasses as he thought about it. It made sense.

"There's a disgusting, filthy house with territory that abuts the back of Socrates's territory. The people in that house leave garbage all over the yard, and the building is in poor repair, with plenty of crannies and places for rats to nest. They've been busy there all winter."

"Oh, yes. Many rats now." Domino nodded his head toward the woods beside them. "I was just coming up here to do my daily clean up. There are rats in these woods pretty much all the time now. The Neighborhood is overflowing."

"Yes, but anyway, I came to ask you a favor." Rudy's meows were clipped with barely suppressed rage.

"What is it?" asked Domino.

"It's Cricket. She has kits now."

"I know. I went to visit her, and I met them. Handsome lot, by the way."

"Thanks." Pride and worry shone in Rudy's eyes. "So, if you were over there, you know the, ah, *situation* in which Cricket lives."

A dull pain contracted Domino's heart as he thought about Rudy's worry. "Yeah," he meowed sadly.

"I tried to get her to leave." Rudy was practically wailing now. "I told her the Neighborhood was no place for a cat no more. But she laughed. She thought it was some kind of joke. 'Rudy,' she says, 'the Neighborhood is a better place for cats than it ever was. And better for *all* creatures.'" He stared into Domino's face plaintively.

The barn cat nodded. "I know. I tried to tell her she should stop listening to that garbage. She was way too thin when I saw her. But Flufferdoodle told me that there's nothing you can do with these brainwashed cats."

Rudy seemed irritated. "Flufferdoodle. *Pfft!* He was taken in, too."

"Flufferdoodle was *not* taken in. He had no choice." Domino's back went high and his ears laid back.

Rudy noted his reaction and backed off. "Yeah, I guess he didn't. But anyway, I couldn't talk any sense into Cricket."

"Me neither." Domino settled down again. "But what can I do to help? You said you had a favor to ask."

"Right, right." Asking for things does not come easily to a

street cat, but Rudy's expression was honest and humble. "Do you think Cricket and her kits could come here somewhere? On your territory? If I could talk some sense into her, do you think they could come live here somewhere?"

Domino saw the pain in Rudy's eyes and felt his own throat tighten. He swallowed and meowed, "Sure, Rudy. It's a big territory. There's plenty of room." He laughed roughly. "I could use some help keeping the rats out of here, too. You think Cricket would hunt again?"

Rudy shook his head. "I honestly don't know."

He couldn't meet Domino's eyes, and Domino knew why. Rudy was asking him not only to share his territory with five more cats, but also to provide for them, as they would not be feeding themselves. It must be killing Rudy to ask this of him. "No worries," Domino meowed briskly. "I could tell just from looking at them that those kits will be killers. We'll get them trained up right. Like I said, I could use some help around here."

Rudy could look at him again, and the gratitude in the old tom's eyes made the lump swell in Domino's throat. He managed a bracing smile for his troubled friend.

"And Domino, there's more," meowed Rudy. "Socrates and those rats, they're not content with taking over the Neighborhood. It really, really bothers them that you're over here in your own territory, free to do what you want. That you hunt and kill and act like a cat, basically. They can't stand that."

"Great Cats, what do they care?" Domino exclaimed.

Rudy's wild, fearful expression was back. "I don't understand it, either, but they're putting something together, some kind of plot against you. I hear them talk about it when I'm prowling, and I get what information I can, but I can't get all of it. But Domino, they're serious about coming here and taking over your territory. And they'll do whatever it takes to control you."

Fear struck like a cold stone in the pit of Domino's stomach. His body went into fight-or-flight mode, dumping adrenaline into his blood stream. His muscles tightened and his fur stood on end. And Domino realized with sinking horror that his reaction wasn't simply in response to Rudy's chilling words, but in fact a huge, tan form had burst from the wind-tossed ground cover just behind the gray tom. Domino barely had time to cry, "Dog!" before Max was upon them.

Before he had drawn his next breath, Domino was up the nearest tree and looking down from a safe height. Down below, Max had clamped onto the older, slower tom before he could escape. Domino could only watch as the growling cur shook the life from the gray cat.

He clung to the sapling with every claw rived into the bark. The urgent spring wind rushed all around him, roaring in his ears and shaking leaves and branches. His heart pounded and he panted in horror. He was unable to close his eyes or look away from the murder below. *At least Rudy's neck must've snapped right away,* his mind tried to comfort him. *That cat was dead immediately. He's gone now; he's not feeling any of this.*

Max roared loud, angry sounds of hate from deep in his throat as he shook and tossed the lifeless body. As Domino watched, a smaller creature emerged from the woods, ghostly pale and eerily calm. It was Socrates, trailing along behind Max to see that Rudy was properly dispatched. Domino's fur bristled so hard it made his skin hurt. Socrates sat and watched with cold eyes as Max finished with the body and dropped it, eventually lost interest, and sniffed his way to a nearby tussock, lifting his leg to urinate on it.

Socrates was innocent, Domino remembered Rudy saying. *But certainly not now,* he thought. *That cat is as evil and corrupt as the meanest rat ever born.*

Socrates turned his cold eyes up to Domino and stared at the larger cat clinging to the upper branches. Domino could feel the Siamese's mind calculating, wondering if he could get his enemy down from the tree for the dog to handle.

"Try it, you rabid freak," Domino raged. "You better figure out what you'd do without that dog because I will shred him, if you want me to come down there."

Socrates smirked but said nothing. Domino pictured himself flying down from the tree like an avenging hawk and tearing the smug Siamese into tiny scraps of meat. He would transform himself into a ball of whirling rage and destroy the vile creature so thoroughly there would be nothing left but tufts of fur and a putrid stain in the soft, spring soil.

But his instincts bound him safely to the tree. Socrates stared at him a minute longer. Then he looked around for his dog and called loudly enough for Domino to hear, "Come on, Max. Let's go home. That's enough good work for one day."

The yellow dog looked up dully from where he was chewing on some deer pellets he had found. "Yeah, okay," he woofed. He bounded over the clumps of meadow grass and past the Siamese as he headed toward the road. Without looking back, Socrates turned and followed.

TEN

The spring gale rushed around the old barn all night. It set the ancient wooden building to creaking and groaning, while rain pounded a staccato rhythm on the roof.

In the den by the hayloft door, Domino writhed and turned. He spent the long night hunting for sleep but found no relief.

Eventually, the constant drumming of rain eased off. Domino sighed and shifted his position yet again. He dozed briefly until yesterday afternoon's scene replayed itself in his mind. Only this time, it was Tam whose neck was snapped while Domino watched helpless, clinging to the bucking sapling.

Domino snapped awake, groaned, and rolled onto his back. The quality of the darkness in the den had shifted ever so slightly, signaling that sunrise wasn't far off. Domino listened; the roaring wind had finally dissipated. All was still.

He emerged from the den and paused for a long, deep stretch before sitting at the edge of the open door and surveying the yard in the waning dimness. Nothing moved.

Thor still slept in his doghouse, where he had been spending his nights since the weather had warmed. No lights shone from the house.

Domino knew that no amount of craning his neck would allow him to see Mrs. Brown's garden to one side or the chicken coop to the other. Though his eyes burned from lack of sleep, his body was tense and full of restless energy. He turned and padded silently toward the stairs at the back of the barn.

Halfway across the floor he was met by a black-and-white spotted, diminutive image of himself. "Where are you going?" mewed Catlyn.

"Shh, kitten, don't wake the others." He bent to rub his face along her head and shoulder. "I'm going for a patrol, now that the weather has settled down."

"Pawpaw, I'm ready to start patrolling. Take me with you! You can start teaching me." Her earnest eyes, yellow like her myu's, looked into his without blinking.

Domino could not refuse her. "Okay, you can start by getting to the stairs without making any noise." He followed her closely as the kitten got low and went at a shaky stalking pace to the back of the barn. He suppressed a smile lest she turn unexpectedly and see him. At the top step, Catlyn paused and contemplated what was, to her, a great height. She attempted a leap down to the next level, but her landing was less than graceful and she bumped her nose. Domino waited while she stood and attempted the next step. This time, she managed a controlled fall but didn't land much better than the first time. Domino sighed. She would have her myu's slight size as well as her golden eyes. He joined her on the step and whispered to her, "Do you know the secret of climbing down from a height without tumbling head over tail?"

"No, Pawpaw."

"Try letting your tail lead the way."

Catlyn thought for a moment then maneuvered her back-side to the edge of the step. She reached down as far as she could with one long back leg but couldn't touch the next riser. She paused then brought the other hind leg down, too. Her body dropped and she clung to the wood with her front claws. Before she fell completely, her back feet were standing securely on the step beneath. Her wide eyes met her father's and he smiled at her, nodding encouragement.

Catlyn turned and brought her forepaws down to stand easily on the lower step. She repeated the process, more fluidly each time, until she had reached the ground floor of the barn, under full control of herself.

"Very good, Catlyn," purred Domino.

Catlyn looked around the large space. "I haven't been here in so long," she said. "I hardly remember it."

"Hasn't changed." Domino shifted his feet as his nervous energy surged again.

"What's the matter, Pawpaw?"

"Well, I should really check on the yard now. But I'm a little worried about taking you with me. I'm not sure you're big enough to go outside the nice, safe barn yet."

"Pawpaw, of course I am. Did you see how fast I learned to climb down?"

"I did indeed."

"And you'll be with me, right?"

"Of course I will, kitten."

"Then I'll be safe."

"You argue as well as your myu. Come on, then. But stay at whiskertouch."

Domino passed through the cat door. Outside, he paused to sniff and listen warily. All seemed safe and quiet. Soon Catlyn stood beside him. "Let's go, Pawpaw," she whispered. Her excitement matched his anxiety in intensity.

Domino again managed to suppress the smile that wanted to light up his face. He maintained a serious demeanor and hissed softly, "First we'll patrol by the chicken coop." *And I hope we don't meet one of those big rats, or your myu will kill me,* he thought.

The chicken coop proved to be secure and the area around it free of vermin. Domino assessed Catlyn, and she seemed to be ready for more adventure. "What now, Pawpaw?" she mewed.

He looked around. Thirty feet away, near Celine's woods, was the old shed the children used as a clubhouse. He remembered that mice sometimes frequented the place. Something small like that might be a good introduction to hunting for the kitten and the risks were minimal, especially if he stunned the small rodent before letting Catlyn work it over. "Let's check on the shed," he whispered. "Come on."

Side by side, the tom and the kitten made their way over the rough lawn to the building. Domino showed her how the door didn't close all the way, so cats—and mice—could always get inside. Domino never understood why Mr. Brown didn't fix the door, but he was glad of it. He enjoyed visiting the place.

Once inside, he showed Catlyn how to freeze and become essentially invisible. In this position, they waited to see if any creature would reveal itself through its movement. Sure enough, there was a muffled fluttering noise from the window above the old wooden worktable. Domino moved silently to the table and Catlyn copied his movements. "Wait here," Domino breathed. He leaped gracefully to the tabletop and froze again.

The sky outside remained near black as a bright sliver of moon wavered down to the horizon. Inside the window, an early season moth beat its wings against the panes, seeking the light source. Domino grinned.

He turned to glance back down. Catlyn looked up at him with a rapt expression. He calculated quickly and knew she couldn't make the leap. "Catlyn, go over to the corner of the table," he instructed.

She did as he said. "Oh!" she mewed, understanding his direction. She sized up the splintery old table leg, leaped as high as she could, clung to it with her sharp little claws, and scrambled the rest of the way up.

At the sight of the struggling moth, Catlyn dropped into a crouch and froze. Domino saw her eyes had locked onto the prey and her body was doing everything it was supposed to, so he did not interfere. She took a stalking step toward the moth and froze again, ascertaining that it had not seen her. Then she took another. Domino sat still and watched as his kitten put weeks of practice with toys to use. And for the first time since witnessing Rudy's horrific end, he felt hopeful and happy again.

DOMINO HAD to carry the kitten back up the barn steps by the scruff of her neck, and she did not relinquish her hold on the vanquished moth the entire time. When they emerged on the second floor, Domino set her down, lifted his head proudly, and meowed in a loud voice, "Someone made her first kill."

Celine, Tam, and Marble all stopped their various activities and looked up. Catlyn struck a heroic pose and held her kill up high for everyone to see.

Celine came over first, followed closely by Marble, with Tam trailing at a distance. "Oh, Catlyn, that is wonderful! I am so proud of you." The sleek black female bent to rub her face along the top of her kitten's head as deafening purrs came off her in waves.

Marble came up to the moth and sniffed at it. Catlyn politely placed it on the ground and sat back so her sibling might paw at the creature and try out some of his moves.

Celine came to sit beside Domino so they could enjoy the sight of their kitten's first kill together. "So, where did the moth come from?" she meowed softly. "Downstairs?"

"No, actually. We got it in the shed."

Celine turned to stare incredulously into his face. "You took a four-week-old kitten outside? Past a chicken coop that attracts huge rats and over to an unsecured shed? At the edge of the *woods*? At *peak* predator time?"

Domino gave her a confident smile. "She was fine. She knows how to handle herself." Celine's mouth dropped open in disbelief. "Besides," he added, "she was with me. I wouldn't let anything happen to her."

"I hope not. Because whatever would happen to her would happen to you, too, but a lot worse."

Domino touched his nose to hers. "Relax, Celine," he purred. "This is actually pretty funny, coming from the six-pound cat who spent her youth living like a wild cat in those woods."

"I sure didn't try it when I was four weeks old."

"Okay, point taken. But, really, I was very careful with her. I checked for problems before I took her outside and again when we got into the shed. I kept her beside me. It was a very controlled trip. And besides, just look at her. She's already got hunting in the blood. See how happy she is?"

They stopped talking to watch again as Catlyn and Marble took turns stalking and swatting the dead moth, which was rapidly degrading into more of an oversized bug as its wings were shredded off bit by bit.

Domino closed his eyes and breathed deeply, grateful for the peace and safety he had in this place. Then he opened them again to watch the kits some more. The only thing that detracted from his pleasure was Tam, who sat off to the side. The young tom did not come over and congratulate his sister, but sat watching his siblings with cold eyes full of anger and envy.

BECAUSE DOMINO HAD SPENT the night tossing and turning, the midday sun on the blanket in front of the loft window proved too much for him. He stretched out on his back and let the heating rays go to work on his belly. Soon he was joined by Celine.

"The kittens are asleep?" he murmured drowsily.

"Yes, and they're getting so big, there's hardly room for them and me in that nest. Mind if I join you here?"

Domino rolled onto his side in answer. Celine lay along the length of him, doubling the warmth in which he basked. Purring, he was about to drift off when Celine spoke again.

"Have you decided what to do about Cricket yet?"

"No. I mean, I *want* to honor Rudy's last request. I want her to bring her kits over here somewhere. But I'm not sure she would do it, even if we begged her. And anyway, I don't think it's safe to go over there to talk to her. Like I told you, Socrates would have had Max kill me, too, if he could have."

"I agree; it's very dangerous. But Max is probably the dumbest dog I've ever seen. And Socrates is an apartment pussy. He has no outdoor skills. I could stalk right in front of him in broad daylight and he wouldn't even see me."

Domino chuckled. "That's true."

"So, I had an idea. How about if I go over there and try to talk some sense into Cricket? Myu to myu. I bet I could make her think of what's best for the kits."

"You will do no such thing. It's much too dangerous."

"Says the tom who thinks it's okay for a four-week-old kitten to be prowling outdoors at daybreak."

Domino sighed and flipped onto his other side so he faced Celine. He laid a big paw protectively across her withers and cracked open his sleepy green eyes to look into her serious yellow ones. "Celine, I knew that awful dog was nowhere near here when I took Catlyn outside. Thor may be a loudmouthed moron, but he's good for some things, and alerting us to the presence of other animals is one of them."

"You couldn't know whether an owl or a fox or a weasel or a raccoon would be prowling out of the woods near the shed."

Domino's eyes slipped shut again. "I knew I would kill any such creature before it got near my kit."

"Is that so? You could kill a bobcat or a coyote?"

"If it threatened my kit, yes."

Celine fell silent and Domino began to doze off. But then she gave a deep, sad sigh.

"What is it?" Domino murmured.

"It's Cricket's kits. I can't stop thinking about them. They're growing up in filthy and unnatural conditions, and they won't know any better. They'll grow up thinking it's right, that that's the way life is supposed to be. They're sick and hungry. And worse, they're missing out on their growing time. Poor Cricket is starving on her feet. She can't feed them enough. You said they're about half the size of our kits. Domino, they'll never get a second chance to achieve full size."

Domino could hardly speak as drowsiness pulled him

under. "You're small, and you do okay," he mumbled semi-coherently.

"I have you."

And then Domino was asleep. He took a good, long nap until the sun had moved enough to leave him in the cooling shade, and the pattering sounds of kittens playing nearby woke him.

Celine was gone.

ELEVEN

Tam tumbled over Domino's tail and the big tom jumped a foot into the air. He spun and pinned the kitten under a powerful paw. "Did your myu say when she was coming back?" he demanded.

The kitten rolled his eyes. "For the fourth time, *no*."

Domino released him and Tam sprang to his feet. "Hey, I know what we can do while we're waiting. Why don't you take me out for a patrol?"

"For the *fifth* time, no."

Tam went into a crouch and hissed. At a stern look from his pawpaw, he gave up any idea of a tussle and galloped off to play with his littermates.

Domino went back to scanning the landscape outside the barn window. The sun was so close to the horizon that a ten-foot tree cast a 100-foot shadow. His head whipped to the left at a flicker of movement in the corner of his eye, but it was just a couple of hens making haste to the safety of the coop for the night.

A banging noise drew his attention to the house directly

across the yard. He watched as Mrs. Brown came out on the back porch and scraped something from a dinner plate into his food bowl. Domino's stomach immediately chimed in with a noisy growl. "Shut up," he grumbled at it.

Over to the right, Thor was lying in front of his doghouse and gnawing on some disgusting sloppy rawhide fake bone that the oldest child had given him that afternoon. Domino glared at him while the simple beast chewed and chewed, oblivious to his surveillance. *Amazing how something as stupid as a fake bone will occupy a dog's attention for an entire afternoon,* mused the cat. Then he saw Thor's head go up as the dog stopped gnawing and pricked his ears forward. Domino followed his gaze to see what the dog was looking at.

From the deep shadow along the bank of hydrangea emerged a slender black form. "Oh, thank the Great Cats," exclaimed Domino as he recognized his mate.

Celine skirted Thor's territory and crossed a small open space. Even at this distance, Domino could see that she was moving in a nervous quick-slink. A small, white butterfly flushed up from the grass in front of her and Celine jumped three feet in the air. Then she doubled her pace and soon disappeared at the edge of the barn, out of Domino's line of sight. He took a moment to compose himself, turned, and sauntered toward the back of the loft. He was sitting and waiting when Celine crested the top step and came onto the planked floor.

"And where have you been?" Domino asked in a throaty growl. He deployed his best glare of admonishment, but Celine was not fazed in the least.

"I went over to see Cricket and try to talk some sense into her." She stepped up to Domino and tried to touch noses.

Since his righteous anger hadn't affected her, Domino

slumped his shoulders in frustration and turned his face to the side. "Not so fast, Celine. I specifically told you it was too dangerous to go over there. And you yourself have been complaining that you aren't in great shape."

Now Celine became frustrated. "Well, you weren't going to do anything about it," she meowed.

The kittens came swarming, mewing and complaining that they had missed their afternoon snack. "Hang on, give me a few minutes," meowed Celine. She turned her attention to the kits. "Come on, then," she said and led the way to the nest.

Domino paced the floor, back and forth from the top of the stairs to the hayloft door, while he waited. The sun vanished and dusk deepened to twilight before Celine met him as he came back toward the stairs.

"I don't know about you, but I'm starving," said Domino.

"I'm not just starving, I'm exhausted, too," answered Celine. The skittishness was gone, and now she seemed simply worn out.

Domino lifted his head to call to the drowsy kittens dozing in the nest. "You guys stay here. Your myu and I are going to go get something to eat. We'll be back in a little while. Do *not* leave this area."

"They never have," murmured Celine in a low voice only he could hear.

"But they will try it any day now," he answered her. "Tam especially. He is crazy to get outside, ever since his sister got first kill." He started walking to the stairs with Celine just behind him.

The leftovers in the food bowl turned out to be scraps of chicken that had been cooked with very little seasoning and were thus quite palatable to the cats. Domino was happily gobbling it up when his ravenous mate shoved him aside and wolfed down three large mouthfuls in quick succession. Domino watched her feed in admiration for a moment before shoving her head away from the bowl and taking another bite. A second later, Celine's delicate head displaced his again.

"Wow, you really are hungry," he observed.

She made a small growling noise around another mouthful in reply.

"Fine, I'll just pick at this stale old cat food," he said. He chewed sulkily at the pellets until Celine had emptied the leftovers bowl and sat licking her chops to get the last bits off her whiskers. She blinked at him drowsily before taking a few steps toward the porch railing and leaping up lightly. Domino followed her and soon they were lying on their sides, heads together, watching a pale crescent moon rise above the barn roof.

Finally, Celine looked at Domino until he looked back. "I was very, very careful," she said, pronouncing each word distinctly.

Domino sighed. "I know you were. And I know you're not stupid. I just... I don't know. I wish you had let me do it, or at least let me come with you or something."

Celine gave a small purr and leaned forward, and this time Domino let her touch noses with him. Then he drew back and said, "So tell me what happened. I watched you coming back across the yard. You seemed as jumpy as a long-tailed cat in a room full of rocking chairs."

Celine almost smiled but then a grim expression took hold of her features. She glanced away into the yard. "It's as bad as you described it over there. In the middle of the day, when all the people are at school or work, the rats totally run the place. They are out in broad daylight, and what few cats are around either don't give them a second look or they actually talk to them. Like they're friends or something." She shuddered. "It's disgusting."

Domino said nothing and waited for her to talk at her own pace.

"Cricket looks so bad," Celine continued. "Her fur is completely rough and dry and even falling out in places. I could see every rib through her hide. She was sitting out in front of her den when I got there. Just sitting. Her head was hanging down, like she simply didn't have the strength to hold it up anymore. It was the saddest thing I've ever seen." The black cat stopped talking again as the painful scene replayed in her mind.

"I know," Domino meowed softly.

"I didn't know what to say. I tried to act normal. I asked if I could meet her kits and she just nodded for me to go in the den." A choking sound cut off her narrative for a moment. "Domino, you were right. They were so tiny. And they were as skinny and frail as their myu. They hardly looked up to see who I was."

Domino nodded.

"And there were two great big rats lying there, in the same den, surrounded by their nasty little maggots, more of them than I could count." In the dim moonlight, Celine was visibly shaking.

"So did you have any luck talking to her?"

"Domino, it's even worse than what I just told you. I came out of the den and tried to say how handsome her kits were, but Cricket just cut me off and started mewling. She said that the rats had told her... the rats were... ugh, it's so awful, I can't even say it."

Domino rubbed his face against hers to encourage her.

The words poured out of Celine in a rush. "She said the rats were making her feed their babies, too."

Profound sickness struck Domino's gut like a physical blow. A stream of drool flowed from his mouth onto the wooden rail as he fought back the nausea. "Dear Cats!" he sputtered when he could draw a breath again.

Celine's story was gushing out of her now, as though she needed to get the words out fast before their meaning could sink in and attack her brain. "That's how I felt, too. I told her it was unacceptable. I got so sick and furious, I felt like I was crazy. I told her, absolutely not. She needed to feed her kits and nothing else, period.

"She said the rats told her that Socrates said she had to, because cats had always been so horrible to rats, and it was their fault that rats had such a bad life or something. I told her it was physically impossible for a cat as skinny as her to care for all those babies.

"And Domino, she actually agreed with me. She said I was right and that she didn't want to feed the ratlings, but whenever she lay down to feed her own kits, the ratlings swarmed her and pushed her kits away, and she was so weak, and there were just too many of them to fight off. I told her Socrates had no right to order her around. Cats don't take orders from anyone, especially vermin.

"Finally, she even seemed to get a little angry. It was so good to see her get mad instead of just resigned and despairing. And she said she wanted to tell Socrates that she couldn't feed ratlings as well as her kits, but she was afraid. So I told her I'd go with her—"

"You *what*?"

"I told her I'd go with her."

"Oh, my tail, you could have been killed."

Celine's eyes were intense in the dim light. "I told you, I wasn't myself. I felt like I was crazy, I was so angry. So, I marched with Celine right up to the street where she said Socrates hangs out in the daytime, and we found him."

"Was the dog there?"

"No. Cricket assured me that he's locked in the house when the people are at work during the day. Except on *weak enz* or something?"

"Weekends. The two days that people stay home instead of going to work or school," Domino explained.

"Oh, right. So anyway, no. No dog today. And so, we went right up to that smug cat. He was sitting there with that awful Lily cat and one or two others whose names I forget, and also a lot of rats. It was revolting. But we went right up to him, and then, all of a sudden, Cricket sort of froze and didn't say anything."

Domino nodded. "I told you, they've gotten to her. They've really gotten to her."

"I know, but I had to try," Celine continued. "Meanwhile, Socrates acted all pleasant, like he was happy to see me or something. 'Why, my dear Celine! To what do we owe the pleasure?' and so forth. I just brushed it off and said, 'Cricket has something she wants to say to you.' But Cricket just sort of hung her head and looked at the ground and didn't say anything. I could see that she was shaking. 'Well?' Socrates asked, in this phony, solicitous sort of voice, like he knew Cricket could never say anything against him. Like he was almost tormenting her or something. All the other cats and the rats were sort of snickering. It was so upsetting."

Domino's heart pounded in rage at the scene Celine described. "So, what happened?"

"I finally spoke up," answered Celine. "I told Socrates that

Cricket would not be feeding any ratlings anymore. Then Socrates ignored me and asked Cricket if this was truly what she wanted. What she wanted! As if a starving myu would ever choose to feed ratlings along with her own kits!

"And Cricket looked up at him all meek and started stuttering. She said something like, it wasn't that she didn't *want* to feed the ratlings, it was just that she didn't have enough for all the babies.

"And then Socrates got all contrite and considerate-like, and he said that of course, she was right, and that no cat could be expected to feed kittens *and* ratlings at the same time. Then he said he would take care of it." She looked into Domino's face and he saw that her eyes were deeply disturbed. "Domino, I didn't care for the way he said that—he would *take care of it*. He was acting all nice and everything, but somehow it gave me the creeps.

"But Cricket was happy and grateful. She licked the back of his head for him and said 'thank you' about a zillion times. Finally, I said, 'Let's get back to your kits, Cricket.' And I walked her back to her den."

"Did you ever talk to her about moving over to our territory?"

"I did talk about it on the way back to her den. I didn't mention Rudy or anything because it sounds like she had already disregarded his advice. Also, I didn't want her to start asking me if I had seen him lately or anything."

"Right, good point."

"Anyway, I told her she was welcome over here, that there was plenty of food and no rats to take anything from her or her kits."

"And?"

"It looked like she might actually be interested. She told me she would think about it. I guess starvation is an awful lot to *transcend*." Celine winked. "So, I told her we would come over and help her move the kits. I told her we would come in a day or two, and she could come back with us if she wanted. Domino, I think she's really considering it."

Domino was quiet for a moment, thinking of all that Celine had told him. He could never have imagined such an array of horrors as now existed on a daily basis over in the Neighborhood. He leaned forward and butted his forehead against Celine's. "I'm proud of you," he purred. "I mean, I'm still really mad at you, but I so admire your courage and your heart. You're a good cat."

Celine purred back. "I'm sorry to have worried you," she meowed softly.

"That's okay. You were right; someone needed to go help Cricket." Domino doubted he could have done what she did. He didn't think he possessed enough self-control not to attack Socrates the next time he saw the ridiculous Siamese without his canine guard. He could only hope to get the chance someday. That cat had to go.

TWELVE

Woof! Woof! Woof!

"Great Cats, shut up, Thor," murmured Domino. *Woof! Woof! Woof!*

Without opening his eyes, Domino rolled onto his other side. He clung to the blessed oblivion of sleep with every bit of will he had.

Then another sound pierced the night. Eerie and chilling, it began as a high keen and morphed into a drawn-out, guttural wail. Domino's eyes sprang wide open and his fur stood at full length. Beside him, Celine had shot directly from sleep to her feet, her back arched to the barn ceiling and her eyes wide to the darkness. Even Thor stopped his incessant barking.

The horrible sound repeated itself, closer this time. Domino judged it had originated somewhere in the meadow beyond the driveway. The sound was so loud and unnerving that he involuntarily jumped up and spun to face the hayloft door.

"Domino, what was that?" Celine's voice shook and her teeth chattered.

"I have no idea."

Silence reigned for a moment before Thor resumed a subdued barking.

Once again, the terrifying yowl pierced the night, and once again it seemed closer. Thor kept barking this time, and Domino and Celine crept to the door and looked out.

Thor did not strain at the end of his tether as he normally would have but instead remained near the safety of his doghouse while sounding the alarm. Then he stopped barking and watched the darkness. The cats watched with him.

Another minute passed, and the horrible sound came once again. It was at the very edge of Thor's territory now, just behind the bank of hydrangea bushes. In the moonlight, the cats could see the shrubs trembling as some deranged creature crashed through. Thor's fur stood at the nape of his neck and he backed fearfully to the entrance of his doghouse. Interior lights came on in the main house, followed by bright exterior lights that flooded the yard. Undistracted, the cats kept a razor focus on the edge of the bushes.

The creature burst forth. It was much smaller than the cats had expected, judging from the volume and fearsomeness of its cry. Neither did it appear muscular or threatening in any physical way. Rather, a wretched skeleton of a thing slipped from the covering branches and pelted heedless across Thor's territory and toward the yard between the house and the barn.

The cats traced it with their eyes as it tore across the open ground. As it passed just beneath them, it gave another heart-stopping cry before fleeing into the darkness toward the children's clubhouse.

Domino turned to Celine, who returned his wide-eyed look. "Great Cats, that was Cricket," she uttered.

Before Domino could answer, Thor raised a fresh round of

barking. The cats turned quickly to see what it was. A much larger and heavier feline form, covered in dense orange fur, hesitated in front of the hydrangea at the edge of Thor's territory.

"Good grief, that's Flufferdoodle," exclaimed Domino.

Celine squinted. "Is it? My tail, I hardly recognize him."

"Yeah, he's put on a little weight since last you saw him. Spending too much time indoors." He kept his eyes locked on the barking dog and the big cat. "What in the world is going on?" he wondered aloud.

Thor continued to bark furiously as the cat held his ground. Finally, the porch door banged open and Mr. Brown stomped down the steps and over to the dog. He was carrying a rifle in one hand and a flashlight in the other. "What is it, boy?" the cats heard him say. He shone the flashlight around the yard until it reflected back at him from Flufferdoodle's eyes. "Oh, for Pete's sake, it's just a cat, Thor." The big shepherd looked up at him expectantly and wagged his tail. Then he went back to barking at the visitor.

"Okay, that's enough, Thor. Tell you what; you come inside for the night, okay? You can sleep in your bed in the kitchen. I have to get some sleep. I gotta work tomorrow." He detached the tether and grasped the dog's collar, leading him toward the porch. "Come on, now. Good boy." Soon the door closed behind them, the lights went out, and stillness finally returned to the yard.

"I'm going down to see what's going on," said Domino.

"Myu? Pawpaw? What's happening?" came tiny voices from the nest by the wall.

Celine was already heading in that direction. "If you're not back soon, I'm coming down there," she called over her shoulder.

"Don't worry, I'll be fine." Domino vanished down the stairs.

When he came out of the barn, Domino found Flufferdoodle standing there, waiting. For a long moment, the two toms only stood and looked at one another. Finally confronted with his shameful behavior the last time he had been with Flufferdoodle, Domino found that he could not speak.

Flufferdoodle broke the silence. "You're not going to hit me again, are you?" His much-missed basso profundo meow was sweet to Domino's ears.

"Probably not, but don't push it."

Flufferdoodle sighed heavily, and Domino noticed that the big cat was still catching his breath. Clearly the hefty tom hadn't made such a long journey in quite a while. "May I?" asked Flufferdoodle. Without waiting for an answer, he allowed his hindquarters to slam onto the ground so he could sit and rest.

Domino didn't know where to begin. "Lovely evening to go visiting," he tried.

"Yeah, I saw that moon and thought, 'Wow, I simply must go for a ramble,'" Flufferdoodle meowed sarcastically.

Domino nodded in the direction Cricket had run. "Do you know anything about that?"

Flufferdoodle sighed again and looked at the ground as though gathering strength to tell his story. Domino knew it wasn't going to be a good one.

"I understand your mate was in the Neighborhood yesterday?" began the visitor.

"How did you know that? She's very stealthy."

"Not when she marches up the street and challenges Socrates the Great," explained Flufferdoodle.

"Oh, yeah. That."

"Yeah, that." Flufferdoodle lifted his chin. "Not that she wasn't absolutely right, mind you. Look, not all the cats in the Neighborhood are happy with things, you know. They're just too scared to do anything about it. But a lot of them come talk to me during times of high people activity, when the rats aren't around to see what they do. They tell me things."

"So you're the only dissenter who's out in the open? I wonder why Socrates and his rats allow you to do that?"

Flufferdoodle gave him a look. "What are they going to do, kill me? The day those rats or that dog attacks a treasured Neighborhood pet like yours truly in his own yard is the day the people open their eyes and see what's going on. In other words, it's the day the exterminator is called to finish the rats, and the dog gets hauled in by Animal Control for being off-leash."

"You always did have a head for law and order," meowed Domino with admiration.

"Yeah, so anyway, all the cats knew what was going on with Cricket and her poor kits and those awful rats in her den. A lot of cats weren't happy about it, but no one wanted to speak up, either. They didn't want to be next, you see. So, when Celine went up to Socrates and challenged him, she was sort of a feline hero for the afternoon. A lot of cats were really happy someone was finally standing up to Socrates and his rats. And not being stupid, as we've discussed, Socrates realized this right away. So good old Socrates agreed that Cricket shouldn't be expected to feed kittens *and* ratlings, and he promised Cricket he would take care of it."

"That's right. That's exactly what Celine told me."

"Yeah, well, he took care of it, all right. After Celine left, nothing happened for a while, as the people were all coming home from work and the rats had to stay hidden. But once everyone had settled down for the night, apparently, a bunch of rats swarmed Cricket's den."

"Oh, Great Cats."

Flufferdoodle's head hung as he finished his awful tale. "Yeah, no more kittens. Poor Cricket fought tooth and claw, and I hear she took out more than one of those awful rats. But in the end, there were too many of them and they forced her out of the den and finished their evil business."

Domino didn't know what to say. He threw his head back and looked up at the empty sky. Stars danced in his vision, whether in the sky or in his mind, he couldn't tell. He felt the world spinning wildly. He wanted to sick up what he had heard, but it wasn't a physical malady and there wasn't an action to be taken. Finally, he looked back at his old friend, and his vision cleared. "Poor Cricket," he mewed sadly.

"Yes, the poor, poor creature," agreed Flufferdoodle. After a pause, he continued the story. "Anyway, you remember that sweet old cat, Ginger? She lives down past the Gully?"

"I think so."

"Yeah, well she found Cricket lying in a ditch a few hours later, all scratched up and writhing around like she'd been poisoned. Ginger tried to help her, but Cricket just kept getting more and more agitated. She wanted to go find Socrates and kill him, but Ginger knew that would be the end of her. She kept Cricket moving in the other direction and eventually, they wound up in my yard.

"I tried to make Cricket rest and eat something. She tried, for a while. I even got her to eat a morsel or two that I brought out from my bowl, and she let Ginger clean one or two of her wounds. That's probably the only reason she isn't dead yet.

"But those disgusting rats came into the yard. And, Domino, they are so evil. They saw Cricket and came right over to her. First, they started screaming at her that she had killed some rats, and that was against the way the Neighborhood works or something. Ginger reminded them that the deceased rats had been in the process of killing Cricket's kits, so then the awful rats started teasing Cricket. *Hey, Cricket, how are your kittens? Oh, that's right—you don't have any.* Like that."

"Ugh," hissed Domino.

"Finally, I swatted them away, but it was too late. Whatever was left of Cricket's mind snapped. She seemed like she was on fire. She chased down every rat in the yard and shredded it."

"Cricket did that?"

"Yes, Cricket."

A smile flickered across Domino's face. "Good for her. I'm so sorry it took something this horrible to wake her up, but I'm glad she at least remembered she's a cat."

"Oh, it was a glorious sight to behold, if one put the reason for it out of mind. She ran in bigger and bigger circles, rooting out more rats and just demolishing them, until there weren't any more to be found. She was howling and screaming and after a while, she was just running around like she was totally rabid, not even with any sort of goal in mind.

"Domino, she's in real bad shape. She's so skinny, I'm surprised she hasn't dropped dead, frankly. And she's loud and wounded and out in the open, and she stinks of blood. I followed at a distance, to keep an eye on her. Eventually, she made her way across the street and over here to your territory. And I followed to make sure she was safe."

And in spite of the sickness inside him from what he had heard, Domino was suffused with affection and gratitude for a good friend like Flufferdoodle. Part of him couldn't believe that the big tom was here, on his territory, talking to him again, as though he hadn't been a horrible traitor when Flufferdoodle was at his lowest.

"You did that for her? You hauled yourself all the way over here to keep Cricket safe?" he asked.

"Of course. I did it for you, once, too, as you may recall."

"Yes, I remember. And you watched for predators for Cricket, like you did for me?"

"I did."

"And what were you planning to do if one showed up? Sit on it?"

"Really?"

Domino gave his old friend the same grin as when they had been boon companions. Flufferdoodle made a show of becoming visibly irritated. "Look, I know I've put on a little weight, okay? Sorry I don't have a big, open territory like yours to run around in—"

"Yes, you do."

Flufferdoodle snapped his mouth shut as he met Domino's eyes. He nodded once in acknowledgment of the magnitude of the offer, coming from a tom as territorial as the barn cat. "Thank you, Domino. I just might come over every now and then."

"See to it that you do."

They sat in silence for a while, neither admitting it out loud, but both quietly joyful at the reunion. Then Flufferdoodle sighed once again and hauled his considerable hindquarters off the ground. "I guess we'd better go and see what became of that poor cat."

"I guess so." And Domino respectfully stepped back so that his guest could take point.

The trail of blood, terror, and rage was easy enough to

follow. At the end of her strength, Cricket had instinctively sought an enclosed space in which to collapse. The two toms found her wadded against a wall inside the clubhouse like a dirty sweatshirt one of the children had tossed there and forgotten. They approached gingerly, fighting pain at the sight of their demolished friend with every step.

"Cricket?" meowed Flufferdoodle. "It's me, Fluff."

No reply.

"Cricket, it's Domino. I'm here, too," said the barn cat in a soft meow. "You're okay now. It's safe here."

The toms glanced at one another before approaching the body and sniffing.

"She's alive," said Domino, sensing a pulse.

"She's breathing," said Flufferdoodle at the same instant.

The scrawny calico twitched a few times then shifted her position to stretch out. A stuttering groan escaped her but her eyes remained shut.

Flufferdoodle and Domino looked at each other in confusion. "Well?" asked the big orange cat. "Is she hurt bad?"

"I don't know," exclaimed Domino.

"Well, look."

"Okay." Domino sniffed at Cricket's prone form. He smelled plenty of blood, both feline and rodent. Prodding gently with his snout, he surveyed the multiple wounds to Cricket's head, legs, and body. After a moment, he lifted his head and looked at Flufferdoodle. "She has many cuts and bites and scratches, but I don't think any of them are very deep. It's just that there are so many of them."

"So, she's probably lost a bit of blood." Flufferdoodle exhaled angrily. "That and the fact that she's nothing but skin and bones, with no reserves to draw on to heal herself."

"And all the energy she expended running around and

fighting for the past few hours," Domino added. "So, what do we do?"

Flufferdoodle thought for a moment. "Well, she probably needs those wounds cleaned first. Any infection at this point would kill her pretty quick. Poor old girl," he added.

"Yes, that's right. And then we also need to make her eat something. But I can't imagine her getting up and walking over to the porch in her current state," continued Domino. Flufferdoodle said nothing, only nodding in agreement. There was a confused pause before the cats spoke again.

"Do you know anything about cleaning wounds?" asked Flufferdoodle.

"I'll go get Celine," Domino answered. "You keep an eye on Cricket."

"You got it."

Domino exited the clubhouse. Just behind him, Flufferdoodle lay himself across the threshold of the door, a great, orange barrier against any prowling creatures who smelled blood and thought they might get an easy meal.

But back in the barn, Celine was inconsolable.

"Great Cats, Domino, I should never have gone with her," she wailed. "I should have let her listen to her instincts, and her kits would be alive right now." Celine trembled with remorse and dismay.

Domino felt almost as much at a loss how to help Celine as he had Cricket. He butted his head against hers with such emotion that he inadvertently knocked his mate back onto her haunches. In her distraction, Celine didn't even notice.

"Celine, it was *not* your fault," he meowed firmly. "Those kittens were doomed either way." Celine didn't answer, so Domino pressed on. "Let's face it, they were starved and weak.

They would never have made the trek all the way over here, even if we could have convinced Cricket to move."

Celine didn't argue, and he kept talking. "The unfortunate truth is that their myu made some really bad decisions—"

"Oh, poor Cricket," wailed Celine. "She lost her kits! How can I ever face her again?"

Domino sighed in frustration. "Celine, listen, get a grip on yourself." A sharp hiss from his mate convinced Domino to moderate his tone. "Listen, it is not your fault that Cricket's kits are dead," he continued in a quietly urgent meow. "Do you really think those rats weren't about to gobble them up, anyway? Even if you hadn't been there? I'm sorry they may have used your visit as an excuse, but it was only a matter of time either way."

"The rats didn't use me as an excuse; that evil, despicable, traitorous cat did."

A surge of rage swept through Domino's body, tightening every muscle. "Yes, that's true. That... *cat*... ordered it. That's what Flufferdoodle said. And you even said you thought Socrates was up to something, when you got back from your trip."

"Yes, that's true." Grief and fury battled within Celine as she spoke. "*He* ordered the kittens killed. It wasn't my fault, right?"

"That's right. So please, please, please don't blame yourself. You only did something that Cricket should have done herself, for her kits, a long time ago."

Celine turned wide, shining eyes to him. "But, Domino, what if she blames me?"

"Then she blames you," he answered bluntly. "But the truth is, the only creatures actually responsible for killing her kits are the rats that did it. Worrying about how much of it is your fault and whether Cricket will blame you are not good excuses for not helping her now. And anyway, in her current state she won't be blaming anyone."

And so, Celine returned to the clubhouse with Domino. Flufferdoodle stood when he saw them approach, and he and Celine touched noses like old friends. Then the huge tom stepped aside so she could go in. Domino followed her.

Cricket hadn't moved from her deathly sprawl. Celine froze at the sight and smell of her, so Domino stepped forward. He lowered his muzzle near to Cricket's ear and meowed gently, "Cricket? It's me, Domino, again. I've brought Celine with me." Cricket's front paws twitched and he stopped talking. But the calico went still again after that, and he continued. "Celine has come to help you with your wounds," he explained. "You just lie still and keep resting, and she'll get you cleaned up so you don't get sick, okay?"

As there was no response, he backed away and looked to Celine. She took a deep breath and approached her unconscious friend. Like Domino had done, she murmured softly into Cricket's ear. "Hey, Cricket, it's me, Celine." She gulped and continued. "I am so sad about your kits. They were fine kits indeed." Her voice shook, so she stopped and stared at the wall for a moment. After drawing a bracing breath, she continued. "Cricket, you fought very hard and did everything you could. Now you need to rest and heal. I'm going to clean your wounds so your body can heal safely, okay?" And then she went to work.

THE EMACIATED calico spent the remainder of the night nearly motionless. Celine worked on her for hours until she was satisfied that Cricket's wounds were prepped to heal cleanly. Then she returned to her kits and the nest in the barn while the toms kept watch over the patient.

Flufferdoodle took his leave after the sun had just risen. "Should be safe to head back, now," he explained. "All the big prowlers will be back in their hidey holes for the day."

"It's good to see you again, Fluff," meowed Domino. With a nod, Flufferdoodle turned to go.

Domino went into the clubhouse to check on Cricket. Celine's ministrations and the hours of deathlike stillness seemed to have rejuvenated her body. Though she still slept, she had gathered herself into a more natural resting position for a cat. Her eyes remained shut, but as Domino watched, her legs twitched and kicked, and tiny, broken meows escaped her bared teeth.

Pity clawed at his heart and he went to her. "Good morning, Cricket," he meowed softly near her ear. "You are okay now. You're safe and your wounds have been cleaned. You have only to rest and get better now." He purred encouragingly and, remembering all the soothing baths Cricket had given him in the past, he set to grooming the back of her head and ears. Soon the calico cat became still again, resting in earnest.

But Domino feared for her, once consciousness returned fully. Her body would heal over time, but he did not know whether her mind or her heart could.

Cricket spent the day in a fitful, feverish state, meowing and fighting in her sleep. Celine and Domino took turns sitting with her. As the afternoon sun approached the horizon, they both happened to be in the room at the same time, talking in low voices.

"Her body is getting stronger, that much I can see," whispered Celine.

"Wait, what's she doing?" interrupted Domino.

Cricket's nose was twitching as though sniffing a scent that was actually present in the clubhouse, rather than the invisible demons she had spent the night and the day battling. Then her eyes sprang open and before the cats could react, she was on her feet.

"Cricket, you're awake," meowed Celine.

But the calico cat ignored her, wobbled past them, and leaped clumsily onto the top of the low bookshelf. She found what she was looking for—the fish tank in which one of the children kept a bevy of pollywogs—and began lapping water ravenously.

Celine turned to Domino. "Oh, thank goodness," she said.

Domino gave her an encouraging purr before turning to watch Cricket. The visitor gulped water for what seemed like an eternity. Then, licking droplets from her whiskers, she turned to survey the space. "Where am I?" she meowed.

"You're on our territory," meowed Domino. "And you're welcome here. You're safe here." Cricket turned poorly focused eyes on him. "Celine cleaned your wounds, and you've been asleep for a night and a day," he explained.

"My wounds?" A look of profound confusion crossed Cricket's features. She jumped down to the floor again, nearly collapsing on impact. Her wide eyes searched the cats' faces and found apprehension and pity. "My *wounds?*" she screamed. Then she let loose another demented yowl like the cries that had heralded her approach the previous night. In the confined space, it rang painfully in the cats' ears. Domino and Celine both flinched before moving toward Cricket.

"Cricket, please, take it easy," Celine pleaded. She butted her head along Cricket's neck and shoulder, but the calico jumped away from the contact. The barn cats watched help-lessly as she worked herself into a wretched state of terror and pain, finally collapsing into a shaking heap and lapsing into a feverish sort of fugue state.

Domino and Celine exchanged glances. "Well, at least she drank some water," Domino finally said.

"True," Celine answered. "I guess we should try to get her to eat something, too. The next time she's awake, I mean."

"Yes, good idea. I'll go see if there's anything in the food bowl."

"Okay, I'll keep an eye on Cricket while you do that." Celine watched her mate turn to go. "Hurry back," she added.

Domino returned a few minutes later and deposited a large mouthful of chicken scraps and kibble on the floor near Cricket's head. The cat was sleeping fitfully but as her hosts watched, they could see her nose begin twitching in the failing light. Soon it was simple, primal hunger that spurred her from oblivion. Cricket's eyes opened partway as her starving body crawled to the morsels and devoured them.

But the return of awareness also brought the return of unbearable, unquenchable pain. Cricket's eyes went wide once again as she whipped her head around, searching frantically for something. Realization crashed over her anew, and she rolled and spun on the floor like a rabbit in a snare.

"Oh!" exclaimed Celine, as empathetic sorrow struck her in the chest like a blow.

Domino stepped forward and stopped again, unsure what to do. "Now, Cricket, please try to take it easy," he meowed.

But the calico only writhed in increased agitation before leaping to her feet. She took one last, desperate look around before crashing through the barn cats, careening off the corner of the shelves, and dashing out the door. Domino and Celine glanced at one another before following. But by the time they emerged onto the lawn, Cricket had vanished into the gloaming. A moment passed, then they heard the stricken cat's mournful cry, once, at a great distance for the brief amount of time that had passed. Both cats shivered at the terrible noise.

"Sounds like she's way out in the meadow already," remarked Domino.

"Well, I guess we can't do much else for her right now," said Celine. "I guess I'd better go check on the kits."

"Yes, I'll come with you," Domino replied eagerly.

Both cats suddenly very much wanted to be with their plump, healthy kittens.

They did not see Cricket again.

THIRTEEN

The next morning, Domino set off to clear the north woods of rats. But before he even set paw within the tree line, he could smell blood and murder. He continued into the woods and immediately came across the remains of a rat. The rodent had been slain with uncommon savagery and partially devoured. Its innards were strewn across a good length of the trail, and Domino found more gore spattered up the trunk of a nearby tree.

Nor was this the only one. Fascinated, Domino methodically worked through the woods from the road at one end to where the trees gave way to meadow grasses at the other. He counted seven kills (more or less, as it was sometimes difficult to tell whether the feet and spleens and tails and ears came from one single rat or several different ones). After determining that the only rats in the area were very much deceased, he shook his head in amazement. "I guess Cricket has some hostility toward rodents to work out," he said to himself. "Well, that's fine by me. I've been needing some help with these woods since the kittens came." Tail high, he trotted across the long grasses, through the bank of hydrangea, along the perimeter of Thor's run, and back to his snug barn and bright-eyed family.

A string of peaceful days passed. The kits grew quickly. Celine regained her strength and increased her patrols. Between her expanded workload and Cricket's brutal enforcement in the north woods, Domino found himself able to lower his guard a bit and return to a semi-normal routine. He could complete his rounds, tumble on the barn floor with his kits, monitor the Brown children's activities, assist Mrs. Brown with digging in her garden, and still sneak in a decent nap or two. Flufferdoodle even made an appearance one day, ostensibly to follow up on Cricket, and the two toms spent a delightful afternoon chasing sparrows and rolling in sunny dust patches.

Up in the hayloft at night, after patrols had been completed and the kits were asleep, Domino relaxed on the blanket in front of the open window. Celine would lie beside him and settle into a purring crescent before dozing off. Relishing these moments, Domino let himself believe that everything was okay now, and he and his family might go on as before and live out their lives in peace, self-determination, and safety.

TAM NEVER STOPPED PRESSURING Domino to take him hunting, and soon Marble joined the choir. Eventually, even Catlyn, who never spoke back to her pawpaw, began to meow about it. "It's probably safe enough if we take them outside during the day," Celine said.

"Yes, there shouldn't be anyone dangerous prowling around at that time," agreed Domino.

He and Celine helped the kits down the stairs. Except for Catlyn, they were big enough to descend head first, if with a few stumbles. Soon they were blinking in the sunlight as they took their first steps outside. "Now stay close," Domino admonished them. "We're going to take advantage of whatever cover we can find."

"But why?" wondered Tam. "We're the biggest things out here right now. Why do we need to take cover?"

"Because we don't want our prey to see us coming," Catlyn explained.

Tam glowered at her. "I'm sure you were so *stealthy* when you caught that moth," he commented.

"Okay, that's enough," Celine said. "Marble, you come here with me. You have my coat. Let me teach you how to become a shadow."

As the spotted cats watched, she arranged herself at the base of the barn, where the high sun created a black line where wall met earth. Celine pricked her ears forward, lowered her carriage, and slipped along the strip of darkness toward the corner of the building. Just behind her, Marble mimicked her movements in kittenish bursts. His siblings watched in admiration as he became difficult to see indeed, considering that the yard was in full, hot daylight. "Whoa," they meowed.

"Yes, not bad at all," said Domino. He turned to the remaining kittens. "Now, can you two explain why that worked so well?"

Both kits shook their heads in bewilderment.

"It's because they took advantage of two things: their own appearance and the conditions on the ground."

Meows of comprehension.

"So, let's start by assessing ourselves," Domino instructed. "What do you guys look like?" He concealed a smile as the little cats twisted their heads about, trying to see every inch of themselves.

"We look like you, Pawpaw," said Tam. "Black-and-white spots."

"Correct. So, what kind of conditions—what kind of terrain —do you think would suit you best?"

"Terrain where the shadow and light is broken up into spots?" answered Catlyn.

"Correct again. So now what?"

"We should find that terrain?" ventured Tam.

"Very good," his pawpaw purred.

The kittens swiveled their heads around. Catlyn quickly located a suitable location. "Over there—under that tree," she meowed. "See how the leaves and the branches are breaking up the sunlight into spots?"

"Oh, yeah," said Tam. He was off, bounding through the grass.

Domino watched his fleeing kit in a panic. "Tam! Stop right now," he ordered.

The little tom did stop, after a few more bounds, and turned irritably to his father. "What?" he growled.

Domino was on him in an instant, delivering a mild swat to the kitten's hindquarters. "Number one, you *never* growl at me," he said.

Tam's belligerence faded at his pawpaw's tone. "Sorry," he muttered.

"That's a little better," said Domino. He stepped back and called to his other kit, who hesitated near the barn. "Catlyn, come here."

Once she reached them, Domino continued in stern meows. "Couple of things," he said. "First of all, you two are still very little and inexperienced. So for the time being, you stay next to me."

"Yes, Pawpaw."

"Now. Tam, you cannot simply go running into an area of high cover like that patch of rocks and long grass beneath that tree. There might be something bigger than you hiding there."

Tam's eyes widened. "I didn't even think of that."

"Well, you need to start thinking of that. You may be the biggest kit in the litter, but you are *not*, by a long shot, the biggest creature out here."

Tam nodded in understanding. "I'll try to remember to be careful," he meowed.

"Good. And there is also a second reason why you wouldn't simply gallop into a likely hunting area: you are *hunting*. You should not announce yourself to your prey, giving it time to run and hide in a secure place you can't reach."

"Oh." Comprehension dawned on the kits.

"So, we should stalk over to the hunting grounds?" Catlyn asked.

"Yes, but there is more to it than that," Domino said. He went on to explain to the kits about letting the wind bring them enlightening scents, swiveling their ears to listen for telltale rustlings, and using their sharp eyes to spot movement. Catlyn listened carefully and asked questions, but it wasn't long before Tam's eagerness to hunt began to distract him, and his attention wandered.

Finally, Domino began the stealthy approach to the likely hunting grounds, with his kits following and mimicking his movements. Once in the sunlight-dappled rough, he lay beside a fallen branch and watched as they worked the area. "Stay in the shade cast by the tree, where I can see you," he admonished them, and they mostly did. Only Tam strayed into the sun, once, as he chased and caught a small, white butterfly.

"I did it, I did it!" he exclaimed, accidentally releasing his quarry as he meowed triumphantly. But the battered insect wasn't able to fly very well, having lost a portion of a wing, and Tam soon re-apprehended it and brought it to his father for inspection.

"Great job, Tam," purred Domino. He butted heads with his kit with the force of pride, and Tam pushed back heartily. Catlyn came over to purr her congratulations and Tam butted her flank, his resentment of her moth kill a week earlier seemingly gone at last.

A pleasant while and several maimed insects later, Domino herded his kits back toward the barn. They had done well. Tam in particular had quickly become lethal, using his superior strength and size to great effect. His understandable dissatisfaction with catching mere flies and beetles was the reason for Domino's termination of the training session for the day. As they crossed the open space near the barn, Tam dropped into a crouch and froze. Following his predatory stare, Domino saw a blue jay pecking at something on the ground, perhaps ten yards away. He walked to his kitten's side. "Sorry, Tam, not today."

The kitten rolled onto his back in frustration. "Me-arghhh! But, Pawpaw, I can totally catch it. I'm ready!"

Domino shook his head. "You might even be able to stalk it, though that is questionable over open ground, but you are not ready to kill it. Toy mice and butterflies are good practice because they can't do much to you. But that bird there," and he nodded at the jay, "has sharp claws and a dangerous beak, and there is much it can do to you, once you catch up to it."

"Oh, come *on*," Tam hissed, earning himself another swat on the backside. Angry, the tiny tom dashed ahead of his family and disappeared through the cat door and into the barn.

Catlyn had watched the entire episode silently. Once Tam had gone, she turned to Domino. "Why is he so impatient?"

Domino sighed in frustration. "He's impatient because he's

good, and he knows it. And knowing how good he is makes it hard for him to see the things he *doesn't* know." Domino shook his head ruefully. "Okay, come on you. Inside. Your myu and Marble are probably already back."

Indeed they were, and Marble had a lovely dead dragonfly, riddled with tiny puncture wounds, to show off to his littermates. Catlyn made many mews of admiration, while Tam, still in a bad mood, meowed a curt, "Nice work," before going off to sulk in the corner where he hoarded toys.

"LET ME GO WITH YOU!"

"Not now, Tam. I'll be patrolling near the woods, and Great Cats know *what* can come out of there at any time."

The petulant kitten turned to Celine. "Myu, will you take me on patrol?"

Celine turned exasperated eyes to her mate before looking back at her kit. "Tam," she explained, "I know you feel ready to do big cat work. But the truth is that you are not as ready as you think."

"Oh, come *on*!"

"Watch the way you talk to your myu," hissed Domino.

"Tam, listen," Celine went on. "There are many hazards out there for a kitten. And, yes, you are good for your age, but a cat and a kitten together cannot stalk effectively. We would be seen."

Tam rolled his eyes.

"And finally, some of the rats we've been catching are bigger than you are—and they are very mean. So I'm sorry, but you simply aren't big enough yet. Period."

Tam growled rudely.

"Hey!" Domino meowed. But the young tom ran off to the

back of the loft, where he vanished among the boxes and outgrown toys the Browns stored there.

Domino shared a look with his mate. Then he turned to the other kits, who had been watching the entire scene. He spoke loudly enough so that even Tam could hear, hiding among the clutter. "Your myu and I are going to patrol now. You kittens are going to stay here, upstairs, in this loft. We'll be back soon and after a meal and a nap, we will take you guys out for practice."

"Oh, great, midday," Tam complained from his hiding place. "Like there's anything worth hunting out at that time."

"There is, too," protested Catlyn.

"Like what? Butterflies? Whoopee."

"Enough!" roared Celine. She turned to Domino. "Let's go." He followed her down the stairs.

They parted outside the barn. Celine peeled off to the north, slinking along the base of the barn as she headed for Mrs. Brown's garden and the grassy area around it. Domino went in the opposite direction, planning to inspect the coop and continue on to the children's clubhouse.

He stewed as he prowled along. He was proud of Tam, but his patience with the kit's arrogance was wearing thin. Tam was so sure of himself that he was regularly disrespectful to his parents, and he often acted imprudently in his eagerness to be a big cat. Domino shook his head; Tam needed to realize that no one could speed up time, not even he.

The hens lifted their heads from pecking at the ground to watch Domino as he passed among them. Though they knew he was their protector, they were still birds, and they stepped away nervously to make room for him. He didn't so much as glance at them, instead going directly to the coop to pace its perimeter and sniff at the corners.

The hens clucked reports at him.

"Saw a mouse last night."

"Nothing to see here now."

"No rats, but some rude starlings came early this morning and pecked at *our* seed."

Satisfied that no unwelcome creatures were around, he proceeded to the children's clubhouse. Inside, he inspected the floor for signs of intruders but found nothing. Even the sick-sorrowful scent of Cricket's brief convalescence had all but faded. Domino jumped up onto the worktable and stared out the grimy window. But he didn't really see anything as he continued to brood about Tam. That kit was going to get himself into real trouble if he didn't get his head on straight.

Satisfied that the building was secure, Domino left the shed and headed back toward the barn, head low and eyes locked on the view in front of him. Up ahead, he caught sight of movement. To his astonishment, Tam exited the barn through the cat door and stood glancing around. Domino's ears went back and his head and tail became perfectly level with his body. He picked up his pace to a trot. "Tam!" he meowed sternly, though the kit was too far away to hear him.

Meanwhile, Tam had settled on the shade-mottled rough under the big, old hickory as a destination. He lowered his carriage and began to cross the open space between the barn and the tree.

Domino's blood pounded in his ears, he was so angry. He was going to straighten that kit out when he reached him.

Tam was halfway across the yard. His form was impressive for his age, but he still wobbled a little as he stalked.

"If I can see you from way past the chicken coop, so can every prey," muttered Domino to himself. "And predator, for that matter." He was within hearing distance of the kit by now and meowed loudly, "Tam!"

This time the young tom heard him and froze. His head snapped in his pawpaw's direction. Domino quickened his trot toward the kit. He was close enough to see that Tam's eyes were wide with apprehension but narrowing fast in defiance. Then the ground all around the kit seemed to dim. The darkness tightened and began to take shape. "Tam!" Domino screamed, breaking into a full run. Confused and frightened, the kit remained frozen. In the next instant, the hawk crashed onto his back.

"Tam!" yowled Domino again. He was too many strides away from the kit and could only watch as the bird began its work. Domino simply couldn't move his legs fast enough. He felt as though he were stuck in swamp mud, moving like a slug, while the world sped on sickeningly before him.

When he was only a few strides away (*Oh dear Cats, no! It can still be all right. Oh, my kit!*), a black blur socked into the hawk from the side, knocking it onto the ground and off the limp kitten. Domino halted and watched for an opening as Celine spun with the deadly bird in a flurry of feathers and fur. Then Mrs. Brown appeared and swatted the hawk away with a broom. "Go on! Get out of here!" she yelled.

With three enemies besetting it, the hawk decided to leave while it still could. It lifted off the ground clumsily and fluttered above the scene as it checked itself for injury, then found its wings and rose rapidly away.

Celine was at her kit's side. "Tam," she mewed urgently. "Tam, are you okay?"

But Domino could see that he wasn't. The next hunting lesson he had intended to give the kits had just been demonstrated by the raptor with deadly precision: *Once you have your prey in your grasp, you kill it immediately so it can't get away. This is best done by severing the spine at the neck.* Poor Tam had learned the lesson for himself. As Domino watched, the kit's bright green eyes had already begun to mist over.

Mrs. Brown crouched beside Celine and saw the same thing Domino had seen. "Oh, no. Oh, Licorice, I am so sorry, sweetie." She stroked Celine's head and neck as the distraught myu pushed her snout into the kit's flank, nudging him to get up.

"Tam? Tam!" Each one of Celine's plaintive mews was an individual blow to Domino's devastated heart. He could sense that Mrs. Brown felt it, too. She kept stroking Celine's head and murmuring to her, and now she was also doing that odd thing humans do sometimes, where water comes out of their eyes. She seemed to understand that Celine needed some time to figure it out for herself, so she sat and comforted the cat as best she could. Numb and dazed, Domino simply stood and watched. His big, strong, tom kit—the pick of the litter!—was gone, and he had no idea what to do next. The world beyond the three forms in front of him dimmed and faded, and all sound was eerily muted. Nothing else *was.* So, he simply stood and watched.

Eventually, Celine's desperate meows and nudges faded into soft, sad whimpers. At last, the black cat looked up at Mrs. Brown and meowed, "Tam?"

The woman placed gentle hands on both sides of the cat's face and looked into her eyes, myu to myu. "Licorice, I am so sorry about your kitten. But you can't help him now, and I can't, either. Believe me, I would if I could." Her voice was firm and soothing at the same time. "You have two other good kittens upstairs in the barn. Why don't you go see that they are okay?" Mrs. Brown went on. "You're a very good mom. Please don't be too sad. Go take care of your other babies." She gave Celine some good, strong pats along her head and neck and down her back. Then she wiped the water off her face and sniffled. She turned to Domino and patted him, too. "I'm sorry about your kitten, Domino. He was a beauty."

Her touch seemed to wake Domino from the daze he had slipped into. He meowed up at her—more a sound of acknowledgement than any word in particular—and finally went to his fallen kit. He touched noses with the little tom and ran his cheek along the still neck and shoulder. Then he nuzzled his stricken mate.

Gently, Mrs. Brown put her hands beneath Tam's still form and lifted him. Then she stood, turned, and carried the kitten across the yard and into the house.

MARBLE AND CATLYN took the news of their littermate's demise in silence at first. Meanwhile, Celine was struggling, and Domino gave her space. She was unable to sit still, as the maternal instinct to protect still flooded her body. She patrolled the perimeter of the hayloft compulsively, mewing anxiously. Whenever she reached Tam's toy hoard or passed through his hiding place in the storage clutter, her meows became quite loud and heartrending.

Domino gathered the kits to him and crammed himself into the nest with them. It was a very tight fit, and Catlyn lay entirely on top of him while Marble was half on him and half in the bed. Soon, the questions started.

"Did the hawk eat Tam?" asked Marble.

"No, we chased the hawk away."

"Are you sure he was dead?"

"Yes."

"What exactly does *dead* mean?" Catlyn this time.

"It means that a creature no longer lives in his body."

"So Tam's not dead?"

Domino sighed. "Well, yes and no. His body is dead."

"What happened to his body?" asked Marble. "I thought you said the hawk didn't take it."

"It didn't. Your myu hit the hawk so hard, it was knocked halfway across the yard. Then Mrs. Brown came out and hit it with a broom—whack! whack! whack!—until the evil bird flew away. Then Mrs. Brown patted your myu and me and told us how sorry she was. Finally, she picked up Tam's body and took it inside the house."

The kits were working hard to understand all this. Domino could especially see Catlyn's little brain working away. At last, she asked, "So, where is Tam now?"

Domino took a moment to remember what he knew of the next life before he began speaking. "He went to be with the Great Cats."

"Whoa!" Both kittens' eyes were wide.

"But won't they eat him?" worried Marble.

"No, silly kit," said his pawpaw. "Tam is as big and strong as any of them now." He saw confusion on his kittens' faces. "When a cat dies," he explained, "he leaves his body here and goes to live in a beautiful place called Africa. Once he gets there, he becomes one of the Great Cats. He becomes large and powerful, and he rules over all the other creatures—even the dogs are smaller than the Great Cats in Africa."

"What is Africa like?" asked Marble.

"Oh, it's beautiful—vast and wild and full of long grasses and climbing trees and warm stones. And there are all sorts of strange creatures there for the Great Cats to hunt and eat. Some of the creatures are even bigger than the Cats, but the

Cats are so strong, they can kill them, too. And no creature can kill the Great Cats." He thought for a moment then added, "Tam is safe now."

"But, how do we know about Africa? Have you ever been there?" wondered Catlyn.

"No, I've never been there. Cats have always known about Africa and the Great Cats because we see it on televisions."

"What's televisions?"

"A box of light that shows what faraway things look like and sound like. All people have them in their houses," Domino explained. "When you start going on the back porch of the Browns' house, you can go up on the bench and look in the window, and you will see one inside the house."

Celine was approaching the nest after her ninth or tenth circumnavigation of the loft. Instead of passing her family blindly again, this time she seemed to see them. She uttered a loud meow of relief and joy at coming upon them and trotted the rest of the way. She touched noses with the kits and then Domino as though they had long been parted, meowing fretfully all the while. Then she attempted to join them in the nest, ultimately climbing on top of everyone and covering them up. Only the kittens' heads poked out from beneath her full-body embrace, and she purred loudly as she licked behind their ears.

Domino was, of course, the base of the cat pile. He didn't mind a bit.

THE FAMILY DOZED FITFULLY through the early afternoon. Celine woke frequently to anxiously check on each of the kits. Then she would look around for her missing third kit before remembering what had happened. She would utter a sad, stuttery meow, frantically lick Marble and Catlyn's heads for a few minutes, and doze off again. Domino's heart hurt every time she did it.

Eventually, the cats heard the slam of the porch door. Worried about Celine, Domino thought to use the occasion to distract her. "What do you suppose the Browns are up to?" he wondered aloud. "Shall we go see?"

"Sure, I guess," she mewed dully.

They stood and stretched, letting the kittens tumble off of them and onto the soft bed. Once they reached the open hayloft door, they sat and watched.

All four children were descending the back steps into the yard, their mother behind them. The oldest child (who had gotten as big as an adult this spring) carried a small cardboard box. The other boy carried a shovel. The two girls each carried odd-looking sticks. Mrs. Brown had an armful of flowers.

"What's this all about?" asked Domino.

"I'm not sure."

He saw Celine's interest waning as grief began to overtake her. "Perhaps we'd better go monitor the situation," he meowed briskly. Before she could demure, he added, "Come on!" He nudged her flank and with a heavy sigh, Celine rose and led the way to the steps.

They joined the Brown family as they were passing in front of the barn. "What's going on? Where are you going?" Domino meowed at them.

"Oh, look, here are Domino and Licorice," observed the smaller boy.

"That's so sad," said the older girl.

"Hey, cats," cooed Mrs. Brown. She stooped to scratch behind their ears as they rubbed her legs. "Come on, then," she said straightening. "You should probably be there for the funeral, after all."

"What's a *funeral?*" asked Celine.

Domino tried to remember what the strange word meant, but he hadn't really heard it enough to know. So he answered, "I guess we follow them and find out."

The little platoon processed past the chicken coop and the children's clubhouse, turned toward the big meadow, and finally came to a halt beneath the spreading oak near the old stone wall. With the afternoon sun slanting through fluttering leaves and the bright, scented meadow beyond, it was a lovely setting.

The younger boy set shovel to earth and began to dig while the rest of the people watched. Domino and Celine sat and watched with them. Soon, a sizable hole had been carved from the earth, the displaced soil neatly stacked beside it. The child stepped back and leaned on his shovel expectantly.

Now the oldest boy went to the hole and carefully placed the cardboard box inside it. He straightened and gazed down sadly. He cleared his throat and spoke.

"We are gathered here today to say farewell to Spot, the first-born of Licorice and Domino, and the pick of the litter."

Celine gasped. Domino's eyes widened with comprehension. "So that's what's in the box," he muttered. "And now we know what a *funeral* is," he added, a little louder.

"His name's not Spot. It's Tam," meowed Celine to the people.

Miraculously, they heard her. One of the smaller children mimicked her cry back to her, unknowingly doing a fair pronunciation of the deceased kitten's name. "Yes, that's right: Tam," said Celine. Somewhat soothed, she sat back down.

The oldest boy continued. "Spot was cruelly cut down in the springtime of his life, and now we will never get to see what kind of cat he would grow up to be."

Domino felt Celine shiver beside him. Once again, her pain helped him set his own aside. He turned his head to nuzzle her. When he looked up, he saw that the smallest girl's mouth was open and pulled down at the corners, and water was coming out of her eyes.

Mrs. Brown noticed it, too. "Okay, Billy, no need to make it *too* sad," she admonished. "Let's move it along."

The boy nodded and continued. "Let us pray," he said. All the people bowed their heads, so the cats did, too. "Our Father, who art in heaven ..." he began. The rest of the Brown family joined in, all apparently knowing the exact same words to say at the exact same time.

"How do they do that?" Celine meowed to Domino.

"I don't know, but it sounds really great all together like that," he added loudly, so she could hear him over the people. "Imagine if we could do that at a Prowl."

The smallest boy was watching them with a smile. When the family stopped reciting the prayer together, he pointed at the cats. "They was prayin', too!" he laughed.

"Yes, I heard them," said Mrs. Brown.

"Good cats," said the smallest girl. She got on her knees and patted them both. The cats accepted her affections with purrs. Then they swiveled their heads as a strange sound floated over the scene.

The oldest girl held a funny-looking stick to her mouth, blowing into it and working her fingers. Silvery music flowed forth as everyone else became still and simply listened. The sweet notes drifted on the breeze, accompanied only by the soft rustling sounds of the leaves above. The cats sat enchanted by the vibrations in their pricked-up ears. Somehow, as the music draped over them like a blanket, they were comforted.

When the girl stopped playing, everyone stood silently for

a moment. Then Mrs. Brown said, "Okay, kids, here you go." One at a time, starting with the smallest and going up to the biggest, the children went to their mother and received some flowers from the bunch she was holding. Domino recognized springtime blooms plucked from around the yard: lilac, tulip, daffodil, bridal veil, and cherry blossom. After taking some flowers, each child went to the hole and dropped them onto the box. When this was done, the younger boy took up his shovel and began replacing the dirt in the hole, covering bloom and box alike.

Panic flitted across Celine's face. "Great Cats, Domino, they're burying him. *They're burying him!*" She jumped up as though to go to the hole and dig up her kit.

Domino stepped in front of her and gently stayed her, nose to nose. "Shh, it's all right, Celine. It's the right thing to do," he purred encouragingly. "Tam's not in there. It's just his body, and he's not using it anymore. Would you rather they left it lying about, for any creature to see and pick at?"

The urgent energy left Celine and she sat still, hanging her head. "No, of course not. You're right, Domino."

Inside, part of Domino felt like crawling into the hole to be buried along with his kit. But the part that cared for Celine and the surviving kits was bigger and stronger, and he focused on that part of himself. He ran his cheek along his mate's and purred some more. "We'll see him in Africa someday, when we get there. He'll be a big, fine cat by then, and he'll have an enormous territory, full of meat-bearing creatures for us to hunt and eat."

At last, he heard a weak answering purr from his mate. "Yes, we will, and it will be splendid," she said.

When the hole had been filled, the biggest boy went over the stone wall and into the nearby woods a little way. He returned bearing an enormous stone, which he laid on top of the fresh dirt. The smaller girl stepped forward and planted two sticks, lashed together in the middle to form a cross, into the soft ground just behind the stone. At this point, the cats sensed that the *funeral* had concluded, and the Browns were simply milling about and preparing to walk back to their house, so they stood and headed back toward the barn. Behind them, they could hear the children begin asking their myu some of the same questions the kits had peppered Domino with earlier that day, as they had grieved together in a big cat pile in the nest.

That night, up in the loft, the cats slept as a family again. This time, they heaped themselves together on the pile of old blankets where Domino usually napped, near the open hayloft door. This was his favorite place to doze, as the opening in front of him allowed information to feed in from the territory outside, and he could fairly monitor the goings-on even in his sleep. Also, there was enough space on the old blankets for everyone to fit comfortably.

The kits fell asleep quickly, as kits do, leaving the adults to drowse. The afternoon breeze had died and a fractured, reddish moon hung low and heavy in the sky. It was an antsy night and more than once, they heard Cricket's mournful keen from way out across the meadow. Every time it drifted in, Domino clenched his teeth. He wished Celine didn't hear it, but he knew she did. He sensed her wakefulness beside him each time the sound came, and he could feel her trembling as her fur stood on end. He knew what was bothering her.

He lifted his head and touched his nose to hers. "Hey," he murmured, "listen; you are fine. You're sad and rightfully so, but you're also strong and healthy and surrounded by your family. You will not go mad like Cricket."

Celine let a pent-up breath escape in a shaky sigh. "Thank you," she said. "I needed to hear that." As the fragment of moon drifted toward the roof of the barn, Domino felt his mate relax. She touched his nose again, lowered her head to her paws, and exhaled deeply. Her eyes closed and she fell at last into a deep, healing slumber.

When she was finally peaceful, Domino was alone for the first time since losing his kit. He looked out at the night sky, but it was smudgy and opaque; no star was bright enough to pierce the mantle of high clouds. Only the murky crescent peeked through on occasion. Domino traced it until it was high over the barn and he could no longer see it. Then he stared once more into the oblivion. "Good night, Tam," he said softly. He laid his head down and let his grief drag him into a dreamless stupor.

FOURTEEN

After what seemed like no time, or maybe years, Domino was awakened. It was pitch dark now, and his family still lay sleeping alongside him. As his ears flicked in annoyance, Domino realized it was Thor's incessant barking that had woken him.

Or maybe it was the strange, strong scent that drifted over the cats. Domino took a deep sniff and his nose burned. Even before his mind had fully awakened, he was on his feet. His eyes, widened to take in any visual information available in the darkness, began to sting and water. "What in the world is going on?" he meowed.

Celine was on her feet now, too. "Domino, what is that smell?"

"I don't know. It smells familiar, though." He stood still, his muscles clenching, as he tried to remember where he had smelled it before. It seemed to be coming from the back of the building, so he oriented himself in that direction. Pricked forward, his ears began to pick up crackling sounds coming from somewhere below them in the barn. Domino flinched with recognition. "It's fire," he meowed urgently. "There's fire in the barn."

Celine gasped in alarm. "What do we do?" she asked.

"We have to get out of here."

"But the only way out is down the steps, and that's where the fire is." Celine's voice was tight with fear, but Domino didn't hear panic in it—yet.

He paced rapidly to the edge of the hayloft door and looked down. It was definitely too far to jump, even for a strong, mature cat like himself. There was no way the kits could handle it. Domino glanced out at the yard. Thor was at the end of his leash, barking uproariously at the barn, but no lights had come on yet in the house. As Domino watched, a dense cloud of smoke spread across the dark yard and hid Thor from view. The barking stopped abruptly, followed by a series of canine coughs. "Great, the one time we could use your racket," Domino muttered to himself.

He turned back to his family. Celine stood rigid, staring at him with wide, frightened eyes. The kits stirred in their sleep as the acrid smoke began to fill the loft. "I guess we have to go down the steps," Domino said.

Celine seemed relieved to have a course of action, even if it was a dangerous one. "We'll just have to be careful of the fire, that's all." She was fairly dancing with anxiety at this point, and Domino could hear the edge of panic creeping into her voice.

He drew in a breath to tell her to pick up Marble and he would take Catlyn, but the noxious air triggered a wracking coughing spasm. Clenching his burning eyes, Domino fell onto bent forelegs.

"Domino, come on," Celine urged. "We need to go now. I can't keep my eyes open another minute. I can't breathe."

"Myu? Pawpaw? What's happening?" came Catlyn's tiny voice.

Gasping, Domino got to his feet and swallowed hard several times to halt the spasm. "Okay, grab a kit and let's go," he rasped. He could barely make out Celine's form in the murk as she picked up Marble by the skin on the back of his neck. Domino bent to take Catlyn in his mouth. When he looked up, Celine had taken off toward the back of the barn. He followed at a blind run through the burning fog.

By the time he reached the top of the stairs, his eyes were streaming. Pain seared his nostrils as he drew heavy breaths through his nose. Blinded, he tumbled through the opening and landed badly on the second step, dropping his cargo. "Catlyn!" he roared, gagging from the smoke.

"Here, Pawpaw," came the frightened mew. The kitten had only fallen another step down, and Domino's whiskers quickly revealed her location. Without pausing to ask if she was hurt, he scooped her up again and descended the stairs.

Halfway down, the opacity of the atmosphere became complete. The fire was big now, roaring and snapping and lighting the fog with a hellish red glow. As he descended, Domino was relieved to see that the glow was off to the side, where the Browns worked on the motors of their jeeps and boat. *Right where our first nest was,* Domino realized with a chill.

The smoke was unbearable now. With each step, the urge to cough was more powerful. But Domino knew that if he coughed and dropped Catlyn again, he might never find her in the zero visibility.

He stepped off the last riser, dragging air through his burning nose, and bumped into Celine. For a moment, the smoke cleared enough for him to see her. Marble hung from her jaws, his hind feet just scraping the ground. Celine's eyes were perfectly round, the pupils enormous within them, as she scanned the black-red cloud for her mate. She was running on instinct and fear now but had still somehow made herself wait to make sure he was behind her. *Run! Go!* he screamed in his head, unable to talk around the kitten in his mouth.

Celine turned to run for the door but instead leaped sideways as something dashed between her feet. As it scuttled past Domino, he realized it was a rat, and a very large one. Before he could react, it had vanished into smoke. The filthy creatures had a much higher tolerance for contaminants of all kinds, Domino knew. The rodent had seemed right at home in this hellish environment, using the poisonous fog as cover to pass around the cats unseen. *We have to get out of here,* his mind raged.

In front of him, Celine had recovered and run for the door. Domino followed. One of the children must have left the large front door open, because the cats could sense the smoke interchanging with the night air, even if they couldn't see it in the murk. They pelted in that direction.

More than once, as he ran, Domino felt the scurrying rush of a rodent as it brushed past him, around his legs. He heard the prickly, screechy sound of their malevolent laughter. Once, he even felt something try to yank Catlyn from his grasp. He tightened his grip on the kit's neck and kept on. Soon he felt the concrete floor turn to loose gravel and soil beneath his paw pads and he knew they had left the barn. The smoke pouring forth from the open door was so dense and the night so dark that Domino still couldn't see anything. Then he crashed into Celine's backside and stopped short. A wisp of clarity divided the smog, and Domino saw that Celine had stopped at the sight of three massive rats baring needle-sharp teeth at her. Every instinct told her to hold onto her kit, but she couldn't fight with Marble in her mouth.

Domino came alongside her and stared back at the rats, also without letting go of his kit. Variable bands of smoke hid and showed the rodents; now there were only two, now there were five or more. The cats went back-to-back, fearful of being surrounded. Another bloom of smoke obliterated the view in front of Domino, and then it cleared briefly. Every hair on his body stood on end as Socrates materialized before him. The vile cat grinned smugly at his enemy. "Why, Domino, what's happened to your lovely barn?" he intoned.

The urge to kill had never been so strong in Domino. But before he could so much as put Catlyn down, he was once again enveloped in stinging, blinding fumes. He backed up a pace and jumped as another rat skimmed his leg, taking a nip of his flesh on the way past. His lust to kill morphed into hot panic as he realized he had been separated from Celine. Now he did drop Catlyn, making sure to keep her between his forepaws. "Celine!" he meowed as loudly as he could.

"Ouch! Pawpaw, something bit me," squealed Catlyn.

Domino clenched his eyes to keep himself from slipping into senseless flight. Then he felt the velvet softness of Celine brush his side. "Thank the Great Cats," he said. "Celine, stay at whiskertouch. Let's get out of this horrible smoke." He knew she couldn't answer, as she had never let go of Marble, so he lifted Catlyn and together, the cats dashed through the noxious smog.

After what seemed like an endless flight, they finally emerged from the smoke into clear air—and found them-selves standing at Thor's feet. In the panic and confusion, Domino had blundered well onto the dog's territory, leading his family to certain demise. Fear knocked him onto his haunches as the German shepherd loomed over the cats. Domino could only watch helplessly as the massive beast appraised the situation. Thor grinned triumphantly as he realized that at long last the cats had made a fatal mistake and had come barreling onto his turf—bearing their kittens, yet!—and with plenty of room to spare. Domino shuddered, his gaze locked with the dog's as he understood the big beast would be the last thing he would ever see. Thor opened his mouth, revealing long, sharp fangs and lowered his head toward Domino.

But instead of biting, Thor spoke in brief, clipped words. "Bring the kits in here," he said. He spun and took two paces before turning back to the cats. He was now in front of his doghouse, standing to the side of the doorway.

Stunned, Domino stared at the dog.

From the direction of the burning barn, he could whiff the stink of disaster, hear the roar of flames, and sense the scurrying of myriad rats come to spread destruction and to celebrate it. Sparks rode the night air all around like malignant fireflies, stinging where they landed. Domino could feel the heat of the conflagration warming his backside.

"Well, come on," barked Thor.

Celine looked at him and he nodded to her before trotting to the doghouse. With a quick, cautious glance at Thor, he darted past, into the safety of the small structure. When he reached the back wall, he turned and, at long last, released Catlyn from his aching jaws. Celine joined him immediately. She also turned to put her back to the wall before gently placing Marble on the ground between her forepaws. Her mouth hung open as she panted. Her enormous eyes were trained on the big dog standing just outside the entrance.

Thor bent to look into the doghouse once. The cat family

looked back at him apprehensively. Then he turned his back on them and sat to watch the proceedings in the yard.

For once in his life, Domino didn't care what was going on in the territory outside the shelter his family had found. By happy accident, a slight night breeze had kept the smoke from reaching this part of the yard, and the air in the doghouse was clear and breathable (even if it did stink of dog). He and Celine sat huddled together, shivering and coughing, their kits nestled between them so tight that only their little snouts could be seen poking out from between their parents' legs.

Muffled sounds made their way into the space: crackling and snapping, Mr. Brown's excited shouts, the distant wail of sirens coming closer, and eventually big tires crunching on the gravel driveway. At the loud noise and flashing lights, Thor finally scooted into the doghouse along with the cats, spinning excitedly to look back out through the door.

"Ouch! You stepped on my paw, you lumbering beast," hissed Domino.

"Domino, hush!" admonished Celine. "He didn't have to let us come in here at all."

Mrs. Brown appeared in front of the doghouse. The cats couldn't see her because Thor was blocking their view, but they heard her urgent voice. "Come on, Thor, you come inside the house now. There's too much activity out here." She pulled on the lead attached to the dog's collar.

But Thor planted his feet firmly, leaned back against her pull, and growled.

"Thor! Don't you growl at me. Come on, let's get you somewhere quieter." She gave the lead another yank.

Thor's growl erupted into a warning bark.

"Thor, what's got into you?"

"Leave him alone, Jen," came Mr. Brown's voice. "He's

probably just scared. If he feels safer in his house, then leave him be for now. He can't get hurt here; he's far enough from the fire."

"Okay, you're probably right about him being scared." Mrs. Brown's voice was quieter, indicating she had turned away to talk to her husband.

"I'm sure of it, and I don't want you to get bit for your trouble."

"You're sure he's safe here?"

"Yes, he'll be fine." The people's voices were fading as they began to walk away. "I just hope my cats are all right. I hope they got out of that barn." Soon the thrum of the big diesel engines on the fire trucks became the predominant sound. There were also indistinct shouted conversations in the distance as the firefighters went to work fighting the inferno that consumed the barn. At one point, there was an enormous splintering crash, immediately followed by shouts from the firefighters. In the morning, the animals would realize it had been the sound of the barn collapsing.

Once the cats had stopped trembling and coughing, they went to work licking the kits clean of soot and dust. The youngsters were soon curled around one another, asleep. Not long afterward, the physical and emotional toll of the previous day and night overcame the adult cats as well. They curved their bodies into a protective wall around their kits and lay their heads, cheek to cheek, on their paws. Then they fell into the profound slumber of exhaustion.

Thor continued to monitor the events outside, his large body in the doorway guarding against rat, cat, or any other danger entering the doghouse. Toward dawn, when the big trucks had rolled away and the yard at last fell quiet, even the German shepherd surrendered to the aftereffects of the night's excitement. He lay down, careful to keep his rump from settling onto the family of sleeping cats. He pointed his nose toward the yard, silently ordered it to alert him to any threatening new scents, closed his eyes, and slept.

THE CHILDREN'S loud exclamations in the yard woke Domino. The quality of light in the doghouse told him the sun must be well up. He had awakened on high alert, with muscles tensed and ready to go. But after taking inventory of the sights, sounds, and smells of his immediate surroundings, he calmed himself. Celine and the kits were still dozing in a jumble, and he could see Thor's sides moving in the steady rhythm of sleep. All seemed safe.

Domino tried to remain at ease, but he found it almost impossible when he was trapped in such close proximity to a dog, especially a dog he had spent a lifetime tormenting. As he lay there, his mind replayed the amazing parade of catastrophe he had endured over the past day and night, and he was momentarily crushed by the urge to give in to despair. Then Celine stirred and snapped awake. Since the first thing she saw was her mate's face, she was able to remain calm as she recollected where she was and how she had come to be there. "Oh, Domino," she meowed softly.

"Good morning," he answered. He touched her nose and rubbed his cheek along hers. Then he got to his feet and had a long, deep stretch. He was surprised at the stiffness and pain in his muscles.

As if reading his mind, Celine said, "Ugh, I ache all over."

"Prolonged times of tension will do that, I suppose," he reasoned. "We were probably even clenched up in our sleep. It will be a long time before we feel like relaxing again."

Soon the kits were awake as well. The big cats checked them over for injury. Their necks were sore and Catlyn had a rat bite on her leg, which Celine tended, but they were otherwise unhurt.

Still facing out the door, Thor stood. He turned his head to glare briefly at the cats then left the small building.

Celine and Domino looked at one another. It had been such a strange night that Thor's hospitality was just another point to ponder. Then Domino realized he was hungry. "How about we introduce these kits to the back porch?" he meowed.

"Yes, good thinking. I could use some breakfast." Celine nuzzled the kits to their feet. "Come on, Catlyn and Marble. We'll show you where the big cats are fed in this territory." She went to the door of the doghouse, looked around carefully, then glanced back and meowed for the kits to follow. They fell into place behind her. Domino brought up the rear.

Thor sat a little distance away with his back to them, staring out in the direction of the ruined barn. Domino couldn't bear to look at it. He began to slink away after his family, but he felt he ought to acknowledge the kindness the dog had shown them. He changed direction and went to stand alongside him. "Um, hey, Thor," he began. "I know I haven't always been very, ah, *polite* to you—"

"Listen, cat," Thor cut him off, "this doesn't mean that you and I are friends now."

"No, right, of course not. I didn't mean to imply—"

"I have no love for your kind," Thor continued in a low growl, "but I have only loathing for other kinds. At least you do your job and we can leave one another alone. But *that* ..." he nodded at the ruins, "...that is something I cannot tolerate."

"You'll get no argument from me about that."

The dog seemed to have nothing more to say. He gave no

further indication that he was aware of Domino's presence, so the cat turned and went after his family.

On the porch, the cats found a big bowl of cat food, a plate of chicken, and another bowl filled with fresh water. They set to. Almost immediately, Mr. Brown creaked open the kitchen door and came out to join them.

"Oh, there you are! I *knew* you got them kittens out of that barn safe. I just knew it. I told Mrs. Brown, 'I'm sure Domino and Licorice know what they're doing.' I *knew* you got out okay." He squatted alongside the ravenous cats and scratched vigorously behind their ears with both hands. "I just knew it," he went on.

Domino and Celine flattened their ears and switched their tails in annoyance—food was their only interest at the moment —but the kits stopped eating to twine themselves around Mr. Brown's calves and mew fetchingly at him.

"Oh, you good little baby cats. Oh, I am so glad to see you," Mr. Brown babbled. "I knew you got out, I just *knew* it."

"Oh boy," muttered Domino so only Celine could hear.

With full bellies, the cats herded their kits down the stairs and into the yard. Muscle memory and habit bent their steps toward the demolished barn, but halfway there they halted beneath the sheltering branches of the old hickory tree.

The view before them was surreal. Where once the safety and security and permanence of the enormous wooden structure had loomed, there was now just open space above steaming ash and cinder. Collapse and ruin was layered upon the charred frames of the burned-out vehicles, still recognizable in shape even if no longer functional. Through the haze above the debris, the cats' view went over the distant meadow, all the way to where it lifted itself into gentle hills, met the sullen sky at last, and vanished.

Gone were the cooler-den and Domino's beloved pile of blankets in front of the hayloft door. Gone was the nest where Celine had raised and cared for the kits. The kittens' impressive stash of toys, their small, brightly colored food dishes, the clutter and old cartons among which they once hid and played —all were destroyed. The stink of raging flame and ruinous danger hung over the yard. Domino realized there was no place on his entire territory he could go to get away from the stink or the danger. As he stared dismally at the devastation, he felt Celine shudder beside him. They had been fortunate to escape the conflagration with their lives.

Celine, too, gazed dejectedly at the smoldering remains of their home. She meowed without inflection or emotion, "Maybe I should take the kits and go."

"Maybe you should." Domino could practically feel his heart rip in two.

He and Celine herded the kits across the grass, down the dusty lane, past the chicken coop, and around behind the children's clubhouse. They paused beneath the oak tree to sniff at the stone and cross left over from the previous day's funeral. Domino watched Celine warily. Her head hung low over the grave for several moments before her expression changed. He was relieved to see a sharpening of the senses come over her as she lifted her snout to scent the air and swivel her ears. "Ugh, all I can smell here is that awful burning stench."

"I know," meowed Domino.

Celine led the way to the stone wall. She leaped up on top of it and turned to her kits. One after the other, they hopped up to join her. It was more of a scramble in Catlyn's case; Domino hoped yet again that she would get some more size someday. But faced with the deprivation of feral life, this seemed even less likely now.

Domino looked up at Celine and she bent her head to him. "Take care of these kits," he told her. "You're sure you'll be okay in the woods?"

She touched his nose with uncommon tenderness. "Yes, of course. I wasn't much bigger than them when I started spending most of my time in the woods. And they have me to care for them. We'll be fine," she continued. "I know some nice, safe hidey holes, and I have one or two dens we can shelter in, as well. I know the clean streams to drink from and the seed-rich places to hunt birds and rodents."

"Okay, then."

"You get things sorted out here and as soon as it's safe for the kits, I'll bring them back."

"Okay."

She touched his nose one more time, turned, and vanished. Marble nodded at his pawpaw, turned, and followed his myu. Only Catlyn lingered.

"What is it, kit?" Domino asked.

"It's just that—I'm worried about you," she mewed. "Will you be safe here?"

Domino's heart throbbed, once, leaving a painful lump in his throat.

"Yes, kit, I'll be fine," he answered in as soothing a voice as he could produce.

"I could stay and help, you know. I'm an excellent fighter." Her small voice shook slightly, and he knew she was thinking of the horror of the rats hiding in the smoke, materializing to nip and bite before vanishing again. But she stood courageously atop the stone wall, ready to fight by her pawpaw's side. "Remember how I took down that big, old moth?"

Domino actually smiled. "I remember," he said. "You are a

very promising little fighter. Someday you will be quite formidable indeed."

"So I should stay to help you?"

He put his forepaws onto a stone and stood on his hind legs to touch noses with her. "No, kitten, not this time. Please go with your myu so she can keep you safe. Go get big enough to fight."

"Okay, Pawpaw." She looked at him one more time with large golden eyes full of anxiety. Then Catlyn, the kitten of Domino's heart, disappeared over the wall.

FIFTEEN

Domino passed the day in a daze. In the past twenty-four hours, he had lost his strongest kit, his home, and his family. His mind knew that the danger had not been addressed, that it was indeed plotting and gathering somewhere at this very moment, but he could not bring himself to care.

He spent the sunlight hours lolling on the gray boulder between the old oak and the stone wall that bordered the woods. From here, Domino could watch over Tam's burial site, and he could simply swivel his head to scan the woods for signs of Celine and the kits. He was glad they were safely away from this place, but he still missed them. He had no stomach for anything except simply allowing the sun's rays to pass through him on their way to warm the stone and the earth. He closed his eyes, let his body go limp, and dozed on and off. He turned his mind off along with his heart, his instincts, and his muscle tension. He simply couldn't sustain it all another minute.

And miraculously, the day spent resting did its work. Over time, the fog of grief was burned off by a blazing hot sun of anger. In the late afternoon, Domino sat up straight, briskly bathed his paws and face, and took a moment to survey his territory.

Over by the coop, the chickens were pecking peacefully at the ground. When they had come down their gangplank that morning, the shock of the demolished barn had kept them clucking all day, but now they seemed to be talked out. Beyond them, Domino could see people working over the ashes and cinders. The entire Brown family was there, as well as several men. Mr. Brown, the oldest boy, and the other men were wearing turnout pants and boots, and they were raking and examining the blackened footprint. Thor lay in front of his doghouse, near the end of his leash, with head high and ears forward, watching the work.

Domino stood and stretched. Then he turned to face the woods and sat down again. He spent a long time gazing in among the trunks as far as he could. His head swiveled to follow any movement: the flit of a fluttering cardinal, the rustle of a foraging squirrel. There was no sign of Celine or the kits. Good. Now the warm sun on his flank was giving way to cooling shadow. Domino sent thoughts of safety and plenty to his unseen family, as they prepared to spend their first night in the woods.

He leaped off the boulder and stretched again, a good, long, cleansing stretch. Then he ambled in the direction of the back porch, ruminating.

Socrates had to go. But to get to him, Domino would need to get past countless rats. He could kill some, but not enough. Maybe he could get Cricket to help. She was the fiercest rat killer he had ever seen. But she wasn't entirely sane, so she might not be reliable if a plan depended on her doing something specific.

Probably the best way to neutralize the rats was to kill their leader, so-called Sunflower Seed, a.k.a. Rip. Maybe he should also kill those other rats who had been meeting with Socrates in his front yard that time when Domino had been gathering intelligence—Cloud, Chipper (or whatever their real names were), and some others. But Domino doubted he would recognize them if he saw them. Better just to focus on killing Rip and whoever was closest to him, if he got the chance.

The chickens looked up as he passed by them without a glance. "Domino," they clucked, "what happened to the barn? Was there a fire?" Not in the mood to answer fowl questions, he flattened his ears and picked up his pace without turning his head.

And what if he got to the rat leaders? He'd still have to get past that drooling beast, Max. This was by no means a given. Domino knew that sometimes a fierce and determined cat could drive off a dog, even a big one. But if the dog was also fierce and determined and anxious for the fight, it might not be possible. Furthermore, Domino knew he might already be weakened from battling rats. So for all Max's lack of intelligence, his sheer size and hatefulness made him a problematic obstacle.

By now, Domino had sprinted up the Browns' back steps and begun fortifying himself with kibble. But his mind kept working.

If he could just get to Socrates, he could take him. Like Celine had said, Socrates was an apartment pussy with no skills. All he had going for him was his mouth, but Domino was one of the few cats on whom Socrates's weaponized words had no effect. If he could just get that cat into a fair fight.

Dusk came on and people began to wander toward the house. Mrs. Brown bent to scratch behind Domino's ears as she came up onto the porch. "Poor guy," she murmured. "You've had a tough time." She sighed thoughtfully. "You and Mr. Brown. He lost all his 'babies' in the fire—no more jeeps. I wonder what he'll do with himself?" She stood and went into the house.

Then came Mr. Brown. "Hey, boy," he said in a gruff voice. Domino kept eating while his neck was rubbed yet again. "Where's Licorice and the kittens? Off hiding, huh? I don't blame them. That was sure scary." Domino swiveled an ear toward the man, whose voice seemed stuck in his throat for a minute. Then he cleared his throat and said, "I hope they come back soon." He straightened up and pulled open the door, calling, "Here, Jen, let me help you with that."

Domino ate his fill and leaped up onto the porch rail, where he could monitor the people standing in the yard. In their big boots and thick pants, they stank of burned wood and charred metal. Domino nonchalantly cleaned his face so he could eavesdrop.

"...sure looks like it started in the workshop."

"Bill's no idiot, though. He's been to enough fires that were started by stupidity."

"...found a wire that sure looked like something had chewed it. Over where he kept them oily rags ..."

"...how's that? What could have chewed it? The Browns always keep barn cats. There's one of 'em right there on the porch ..."

Domino hung his head in shame. He had been asleep up in the loft, indulging himself in his own grief, instead of paying attention and doing his job.

Oh, how he wished Celine were here. She would purr and lick the back of his neck and tell him he shouldn't blame himself. She would say any cat is entitled to mourn the loss of a kit, especially one as promising as Tam had been. And she'd point out that no normal cat could ever have imagined another cat doing such a thing—explaining to rats how to start a blaze—so no one could have expected him to be on the lookout for it. Socrates was freakishly intelligent, but he was also disturbingly immoral. Combine him with the cunning and breeding capacity of rats, and you get the sort of thing that had happened last night; destructive, unnatural, unimaginable evil.

Mr. and Mrs. Brown came out of the house carrying bottles, which they passed around to the men in the yard. The grownups all stood around drinking and talking.

"...get the backhoe up here sometime this week..."

"...You gonna look at getting one of those steel garages? ..."

"...I dunno, I hear they get awful hot in the sun..."

The older girl came up the steps and began to pat Domino. "Hey, Domino," she said. "Good news. We got you a new cathouse. Come see." She lifted him and carried him to the quiet back corner of the porch where Domino seldom went. Now he saw that a store-bought cat condo had been placed against the wall in a spot that was protected by the overhanging roof. The den portion of the cathouse was elevated several feet off the ground on a sturdy post. The entire structure was covered in carpeting. "See, Domino? What do you think of this?" asked the girl.

She set him on his feet on the porch floor facing the cathouse. He sniffed at it for a moment. It smelled horribly new and clean and a bit like chemicals. He turned to go.

"Where are you going? You have to check out your new house," instructed the girl.

"Yeah, carpet is all well and good for an indoor cat like Meg to scratch," Domino explained. "But why would I bother when I have tree trunks all around?" He made to slip between the girl's feet.

"Oh, come on, Domino. Just try it." She picked him up and jammed him, head first, through the round opening and into the den.

Sighing, Domino indulged her and examined the small space. He had to admit it was cleverly made with a cat's comfort in mind. The floor was soft and nap-worthy, and the walls were covered in more of the plush carpeting, which gave the tiny room a quiet, secure feel. It might do in a pinch.

But Domino still didn't care for the new carpet smell. It just made him miss his pile of old blankets in front of the hayloft door with the commanding view of his territory. Anyway, he had already spent the day napping and he was energized and motivated. He had work to do.

He stuck his head out the hole and perched at its edge. The girl was still standing there, watching him. "Thanks it's great I'll be sure to check it out more sometime," he meowed. With a mighty leap, he sailed past her. He kept the momentum going upon landing and dashed down the steps and past the chatting group of people in the yard. Mr. Brown was lighting the grill and more bottles were being passed around. "Here, kitty, kitty," one of the men called. Domino flattened his ears and kept going.

He spent the evening and half the night patrolling and pondering. But no matter how he turned the problem around in his mind, there was no way a single cat like him could take on the cat-rat-dog coalition in the Neighborhood. He was utterly baffled about how to stop them. He began to despair that he would only be able to sit and watch as they eventually took over his territory, eating his food, stealing the hens' eggs, terrorizing his family, and doing as they pleased. He began to wonder if he would be allowed to stay. He couldn't see himself living like that, though. He could never stand by like Flufferdoodle while all around him wrong was considered right and the good, natural order of things was turned on its head. Gloomily he pictured the alternative; himself, his mate, and his kits living a life of feral exile and all it entailed—cold winters, hunger, fleas, predators—and he shook his head miserably.

"No!" he meowed aloud. "By the Great Cats, this is *my* territory. I will not sit by or run away while it is taken from me."

He would fight. But he could not do it alone. And so he paced to the far side of the driveway, where he did something he would never even have considered doing before these strange times: he talked to Thor.

DOMINO'S first steps past the invisible line that demarcated the no-go zone around the dog were nerve-racking. He didn't know if the magic spell from the previous night still held, and if Thor would allow him onto his territory without snapping his neck.

The German shepherd ignored him at first. Thor lay in the doorway of his doghouse, keeping watch on the hydrangea border between lawn and meadow. He only gave evidence he was aware of Domino's presence with the flick of one ear.

"Good evening, Thor," began the cat. He was embarrassed by the weakness and apprehension in his own voice, and he made an effort to speak more assertively. "How are you?" *Wow, powerful opening remarks,* he thought.

"What is it, cat?" Thor turned to regard him briefly, then looked away again.

"Oh, okay, well, you see ..." Domino fumbled for the right way to phrase it. After all, it is not in a cat's natural vocabulary to admit weakness. "I guess the truth is, I was hoping you might, um, help me with something."

"I'm listening."

"Oh, good. Well, it's sort of a problem that I—we—may have here, and I'm not sure what I ought to, that is, maybe you have an idea—"

"My paws, spit it out! Are you worried those rats and that weird cat will come back?"

"Yes. And their dog."

"Dog?" Thor's head snapped up and he gave Domino his full attention.

"Yes. Back in the Neighborhood, where they all live, that cat—the Siamese, the one who was here last night—he lives with a dog. But not like you and I live on the same territory and ignore each other. They actually live together inside the house, and they're, um, *friends*. They do things together."

"Disgusting," huffed Thor.

"I know, it's stomach-turning," agreed Domino. "But the fact remains that they do this. Now ordinarily, I'll set any cat straight if he thinks he can come on this territory. I might even take on a dog that tried it. But a cat and a dog together—"

"—with all those rats, too," continued Thor in a low growl, "that's a lot for any cat to take on. I've never seen anything like it, I tell you. They came through the hydrangea hedge just over there last night, a cat actually moving along with a pack of rats. Highly unusual."

"Yes, well, that's how they do things over in the Neighborhood. They don't seem to have the same understanding of the proper way of things as we do."

"That's because they're so far removed from it," said Thor. "I've seen similar things before. I haven't always lived here, with the Browns, you know. I had several other homes before this. I used to live in a tiny apartment in a city, where I had to stay inside all day. The person I lived with came home after dark and walked me on a leash. That was it; that was my life. It was horrible."

"Indeed!" exclaimed Domino, genuinely appalled.

"On weekends, sometimes my person would take me to a dog park and let me off the leash so I could run around in a fenced-in area. But it was small and full of irritating little dogs that wanted to play. I wanted to *run*. I wanted to sniff and hunt and jump. I wanted to clear every creature out of that dog park and secure it. None of the other dogs understood me. And worst of all, they were all *happy*. Life on a leash—that was good enough for them." Thor's lip curled briefly with contempt.

"My person cared for me, though," he continued, "and he saw I wasn't happy. Well, maybe the torn-up sofa and broken crockery helped him figure it out. But the point is that my nature was stronger than my surroundings.

"My person took me to the local shelter and turned me in. I was adopted twice more and went through pretty much the same thing. Sometimes I was forced to spend entire days locked in a crate. And one house I lived in had many animals living as you say—cats who thought they were my equals, a large, white rat who slept with the cats, a bird even. But I was still leashed and restrained. In fact, I was expected to befriend all those vermin."

By a supreme act of will, Domino let it go that Thor had lumped cats in as *vermin* along with a rat and bird.

"Finally, I saw my chance and I ran away," Thor continued. "Every time I spotted a tree, I went in that direction. If I saw noisy, smelly cars or people, I headed away from them. I got as far from the pavement and noise and stink as I could. When I finally reached a nice blend of houses and wild places,

I let a kind person feed me and take me to the local shelter. They tried to find my last owner but had no luck. So they put me up for adoption and before long, the Browns came and took me home.

"And now I have a purpose. I keep their territory safe by warning them of intruders. I have a nice outdoor run of my own that I share with *no one*." He gave Domino a significant look as he said this. The cat nodded agreeably for him to continue. "I have my own house, but I am also welcome in the Browns' home if the weather is harsh. There are children who need to be watched over when they go for walks or throw sticks into the meadow for me to fetch. There is activity to keep an eye on at all times." He sighed contentedly. "I have people, yes, but they're the right people for me. I have a job and a territory. I get to be a dog."

Domino thought of his own life, at least before the barn burned. "Me, too. I have a job and a home here. I am not only allowed to be a cat, I am expected to."

"Right," woofed Thor. "But that cat that came here from the Neighborhood, he's all messed up."

"Socrates," meowed Domino. "His name is Socrates."

"Oh, well, la-di-da," sniffed Thor. "Anyway, my point is, this *Socrates* simply has everything given to him that he could ever need, and he has lost touch with the natural order of things. In fact, he doesn't even think it's right. He thinks he knows better how things should be."

"He calls it *transcendence*," explained Domino. "He says creatures can transcend their nature." Thor huffed at this. Domino continued, "When he was new in the Neighborhood, he amazed all the cats by being friends with a dog. They all thought it was the greatest thing ever, like Socrates could do magic or something. Then he talked them into giving up all the things cats normally do, especially hunting. He made them feel like any cat who hunts is a backward, cruel, base creature. And I can almost understand it, because all the cats in the Neighborhood are pets. That's their only job—to be pleasant companions to their people—so they don't need to hunt in order to be fed. But anyway, they all bought into his nonsense."

"Hence the rats," deduced Thor.

"Hence the rats," agreed Domino. "At this point, I think some of the cats understand why they used to do things the way they did, but now it's too late. They're afraid to kill any rats. Socrates will sic the dog on them, or the other rats will swarm them and kill them." He went on to tell Thor details of life in the transformed Neighborhood, including what had happened to Cricket and her kits when she stood up to Socrates.

Thor listened to Domino with his mouth agape. "So that's why that skinny cat is so crazy," he muttered. "I hear her out in the meadow or in the north woods some nights, with that awful howl of hers. Makes my fur stand up."

"Yes, it's a terrible story," said Domino. "So now you see the problem. I had hoped we might be able to ignore the situation over in the Neighborhood—each to his own and all that. But after what happened here last night, I don't believe we can any more."

"No, it doesn't look that way. It looks like we will need to do something about them." Thor stood and shook off. "Tell me more about the dog."

"Max," said Domino. He described the yellow cur to Thor, concluding with, "You could definitely beat him in a fight."

Thor held his head high as he listened, the better to display his impressive size. "There's no doubt I could." Then he looked sadly at the cable that ran from his collar to a coiled pile on the ground. Both animals traced it with their eyes to the other end, which was fastened to a steel eyelet that was screwed into a solid wood beam that framed the doorway of the doghouse. "If he comes onto my territory, I mean," added Thor.

"But that's just it—we can't wait until they are ready to come here again and do more damage," wailed Domino. "I can't stand being a sitting duck, just waiting for them to attack on their terms, hurting us a little more each time. I want Celine and the kits to come back and live in peace and safety, like before." He could see Thor thinking it over, but the dog didn't look completely convinced. "Do you really want to be trapped on your tether here, watching helplessly as Max runs freely around the Brown territory? Do you want to be shamed by another dog marking the area all around you for himself?" Domino looked Thor in the eye. "Next time, it could be your doghouse they burn." He was gratified to see comprehension dawn on Thor's face at last.

"You make a good point, cat," he woofed. "The time has come to bring the fight to them. Let's catch them off their guard. Let's mark up *their* territory. Let's have a fair fight." Then he sat down abruptly as the momentum left his voice. "But how can I help you? I'm either on this tether or in the Browns' house."

"Well, sometimes the kids take you into the meadow to chase sticks. Maybe you could run off then?"

Thor seemed conflicted. "I could," he said, "but then I would break their trust. You see, the Browns let me off my leash sometimes because I am a good dog. I never leave the Browns' territory and if they call me, I come. If I just ran off one day, and worse, if I left the territory with you and went to the Neighborhood, I don't think they'd trust me anymore."

"So what? I go where I want whenever I want. No person tells me what to do."

Thor gave him a patronizing look. "Spoken like a cat," he said. But Domino could see him thinking about it. "Hey, what if we went over there at night, while the Browns were asleep?" suggested Thor. "They'd never know I had been gone."

"And they say dogs are stupid," meowed Domino.

"Who says that?" barked Thor.

"Oh, I don't know, I've just heard it around," Domino said nonchalantly. Thor growled low in his throat, and Domino adjusted his attitude. "Okay, so let's try it at night. Now, how do we get you off that tether?"

"Well, now, I thought cats were so smart. After all, didn't you say that Socrates opens the door for Max? So I'm sure it would be no problem for you to figure out a way to get me free." Thor grinned at him.

Domino's pride kicked in and he became determined to figure it out. He looked at Thor, his collar, the tether, and the steel eyelet. "Can you slip your collar over your head?" he asked. "What if you go to the end of your tether and try walking backward? Then the tether could pull the collar over your head."

"Hmm, now you're thinking. I've never tried that." Thor trotted to the end of his lead, stopping expertly at the place just before it would pull him up short. He swung his hindquarters away from the doghouse and began pulling backward against his collar.

Domino watched intently. The collar slipped forward to the base of Thor's skull, scrunching skin, fur, and ears up onto his forehead. But although Thor's loose hide bunched up in front of the collar, the leather ring would not slip over his head.

After trying for several more minutes, Thor gave up. He looked dejectedly at Domino and woofed, "I can't do it,"

"Okay, okay, so that won't work. Let's see here." Domino walked back along the length of the cable to where it was fastened to the eyelet, about three inches off the ground on one side of the doorway. "If the rats nibbled the wire in the barn to start the fire, maybe we could nibble this cable?"

Thor bounded to Domino's side, picked up the cable in his front teeth, and began chomping at it. Domino watched with a critical eye, hiding his disgust as slobber flew. But the slender cable simply bent around Thor's large, pointy teeth, and the dog could get no purchase on it. When one glob of drool too many landed on Domino's head, he hissed, "Okay, stop. It's not working. We have to try something else."

Thor dropped the glistening cable on the ground and barked at it twice.

"Look, forget it," said Domino. "We don't have the right teeth for this kind of work. And we don't have any gnawing rats at our command to do it for us. Hmm, let's see..." He followed the cable to the eyelet, which he sniffed and tested in his teeth. "Ouch! Nope, no way. This eyelet is as hard as a rock."

Thor watched him smugly. "Puny cat," he snorted. He nudged Domino out of the way with his snout and gave the eyelet a test bite of his own.

"Thor, no," meowed Domino in alarm. "You'll break your teeth." But Thor's large mouth missed the eyelet altogether, and there was a splintering sound as his teeth connected with the wood into which the eyelet was fastened. "Thor, that's it!" shouted Domino. "You've figured it out."

"Figured what out?" asked Thor glumly. "I couldn't even get the eyelet into my mouth. I'd have to chew away all that wood to get to it."

"Exactly! Chew away all the wood, and the eyelet will come out," explained Domino.

Thor just seemed perplexed. Domino waited while the dog looked back and forth from the eyelet to him to the eyelet. "So if I get the eyelet loose from the wood, then I can chew it?" he finally asked.

Domino rolled his eyes and shook his head impatiently. "No, Thor, you won't need to do anything else to the eyelet. Once the eyelet is loose, you're free." Thor still didn't understand, so Domino tried again. "Think of it this way; the eyelet is just a part of the tether. What you need to do is get the doghouse off the eyelet. Then you can run around freely, just pulling the tether and the eyelet with you."

"Oh!" Thor got it at last. "I could do that. I'm an excellent chewer."

"I know. I've seen what you do to those rawhide bones."

"Okay, here I go." And Thor set to, gnawing and chewing at the wood. Domino watched him work, admiring the size and strength of Thor's flashing white fangs, if not the drool that darkened the wood around the eyelet. Domino imagined what it must be like to have strong jaws full of teeth like that. *If I had that mouth, I could take care of Max myself,* he mused.

Before long, Thor took a break to pant and rest his jaws. "Mr. Brown must've made this doghouse out of very hard wood," he complained. He walked over to his water bowl and lapped up a good, long drink.

Domino switched his tail with impatience and went to inspect Thor's work. The edges of the beam were splintered and slightly rounded, but that was it. This was clearly going to take some time. Domino's plan to launch a preemptive assault would not happen this night, after all. Maybe they could do it tomorrow during the day, when all the people were away. But then Domino remembered Rudy saying that Max was locked in the house during the day when the people were away, and even Socrates couldn't get the door open when it was locked up tight. And leaving Max alive to threaten the territory was not a satisfactory outcome.

No, it would have to be tonight or tomorrow night. Domino didn't think they had much more time before the hordes would be upon them. Thor simply had to free himself in time to help.

The dog went back to his work in earnest, lying on his belly with his big paws on either side of the door frame, gnawing and chewing as though the wood were one of his rawhide bones. Antsy, Domino watched as long as he could bear it. Finally he meowed, "I'm going to go patrol for a while and make sure nothing is happening. I'll be back."

"Okay," mumbled Thor around a mouthful of two-by-four. Then he sneezed and spattered the wood with mucous and slobber.

"Ugh," muttered Domino. He turned and cantered away toward the hydrangea hedge.

DOMINO FOUND the territory eerily empty that night. No mouse, vole, or rabbit crossed his path. Neither owl nor bat plied the air. Not even a raccoon or a possum waddled into view. A consummate professional, Domino set his distraction aside and systematically worked the perimeter, ensuring himself thrice over that no unauthorized (or tasty) creature violated his domain.

At sunup, Domino decided all was in good shape for the time being. Weary and short-tempered, he headed back toward the doghouse to check on Thor's progress with the eyelet. But when he got there, the dog was asleep.

"Thor, you idiot," he meowed before he could think better of it. Luckily, Thor had been deep in slumber. When he leaped to his feet with a yap, he was confused and unaware of the exact words Domino had spoken.

"What is it? Are they here?" Thor woofed. He spun about, looking around for signs of the enemy.

Domino just shook his head, waiting for the dog to get oriented and wake up fully. Then he explained in an irate tone, "You fell asleep. You haven't gotten the eyelet free from the doghouse yet."

Thor glared at the barn cat then shook himself off vigorously. He turned and went to his water bowl for a long drink. Then he turned back to Domino. "I worked on it for hours. My mouth is sore and full of splinters. Why don't you take a turn?" he added sarcastically.

Domino returned his glare before walking over to the work site. Upon inspection, he saw that Thor had made some progress; the wood on both sides of the metal eyelet had been chewed away to about the depth of one of Domino's paws. But more than that would need to be done before the tether could be loosened. Domino sighed and composed himself before turning back to Thor. The dog was ignoring him, scanning the territory with a searching gaze and a scenting nose. "Okay, Thor, I see that you did get a lot done," he meowed in as contrite a tone as he could muster.

The dog's posture softened. "Yes, I did," he huffed.

"Yes, I see that now. Well, maybe you can work on it some more today, and we can get over to the Neighborhood tonight and take care of business."

Thor lifted his chin and met Domino's gaze. "I was planning to work on it after breakfast."

"Okay, that sounds great. I'd really appreciate it." At the

end of his patience, Domino headed to the porch for a mouthful of kibble. Then, tuckered out from the all-night patrol, he slouched into the yard. As he passed the chicken coop, he heard the porch door open. He paused and turned to watch the older boy come outside and walk toward Thor. Domino held his breath, hoping the boy wouldn't notice the damage to the doghouse. He exhaled in relief as Thor thought to meet the boy before he got too close to the worksite.

The big kid patted Thor on the head and scratched his ears. "Hey, boy," he said. "You ready to come in for breakfast?" Thor whined his approval and the boy unhooked him from the tether. Like he did every morning, the dog loped across the backyard and onto the porch. Before the boy caught up, Thor made sure to catch Domino's eye before dipping his snout into the bowl of cat food for a quick appetizer. Domino's ears went back, but there wasn't anything he could do anything about it.

"You get out of there. That's not yours," the boy admonished as he mounted the porch steps. "Come inside now." He opened the door and Thor vanished into the house, where he would be fed and brushed before rolling around with the kids for a while.

Domino turned back to his search for somewhere private to sleep. He ached to be able to slip inside the barn and pad upstairs to his cozy blankets and den. "Oh well, I guess I'll just have to find another spot," he grumbled to himself.

He came to the children's clubhouse and went inside. A powerful leap set him on top of the scarred, old worktable. He went to the far edge where the table was pushed against the window and lay down. He had intended to spend some time looking out at his territory, but he fell asleep immediately.

. . .

NOISES from the direction of the house, muffled by passage through the ancient panes, woke him. Domino lifted his head, yawned, and peered out the window. The light was brighter but it was still definitely morning. Through the grime and across the sizeable yard, he could barely make out the forms of the entire Brown family as they walked from the house to Mrs. Brown's car. The males all wore long trousers and jackets, and the females wore skirts. The younger boy had Thor by the collar. He walked the dog to the tether and reattached it before joining his family in the vehicle. Then they drove off.

Domino jumped to his feet. It must be the weekend! He should have realized it yesterday, when the Brown family had been in and out of the house all day, but the burning barn had thrown his brain all out of whack. But today was the second day of the weekend. And if it was the weekend, then there was every possibility that Socrates and Max would be out and about. But with people everywhere, the rats would need to stay out of sight. This might be the perfect time to catch the cat and dog alone, without their rodent thugs to protect them.

Urgency vibrated through Domino. He stood, stretched quickly, and jumped down from the table. Outside, he trotted past the bothersome hens without sparing them a glance. Up ahead, he could see Thor working at the wood around the eyelet again. Good. Domino's stomach was growling and if Thor was already at work, perhaps he could detour onto the porch for a quick meal.

Anticipating a fresh pour of cat food and maybe even some leftover scrambled eggs, Domino sprinted up the porch steps. Then he froze in disbelief.

His food dish, water bowl, and a small plate of leftovers were all in their customary spot near the door. And with its back to him, oblivious, an enormous rat was feeding.

Outrage burst into Domino's skull like a thunderclap so that he never even thought of stealth. "Hey," he roared, "what do you think you're doing?"

An ordinary rat would have jumped a foot into the air and hit the ground running, but the arrogant creature didn't even deign to turn around until it had finished its mouthful. Flummoxed, Domino wondered if it had even heard him. At last, slowly and deliberately, the rat rotated its oversized body to face him, and Domino recognized the elongated, crooked snout and devious, beady eyes of Rip.

"Mm, great vittles you got here, Dom," sneered the varmint.

"*How dare you?*" Domino hissed. He had to remind himself to shake off the bizarre inertia these rats induced in him with their unnatural, familiar behavior. *This is a rat,* he reminded himself. *It's prey.* At last, his instincts began to take over and the tunnel vision kicked in as his eyes locked on to the target. His ears went back, his carriage lowered, and he took three fast steps toward the rat. His heart pounded and his muscles tightened as his subconscious calculated the amount of battle a rat this big could bring.

Rip didn't seem in the least bit alarmed. As he watched Domino approach, he broke into a coarse laugh. Baffled yet again by the unexpected reaction, Domino lost his concentration once more. He forced himself to stay in his crouch and kept his vision locked onto Rip, but he faltered in his advance. Rip noticed. "What are you gonna do, attack me?" he taunted.

"Oh, I'm not just going to attack you," Domino said in a low growl. "I'm going to break your neck and tear your throat out and shred the greasy meat from your filthy bones." His tail switched wildly from side to side as excitement for the kill mounted in his body. "Then I'm going to pull out your innards like a slimy ball of yarn and—"

Rip's raucous laughter cut him off. But this time, the drive to kill was in full gear and Domino's concentration was not disrupted. "Really?" the rat jeered at him. "You really think you're gonna do all that to me?"

Domino's teeth were chattering, so powerful was the lust to slaughter. His words came out in a low moan. "If I were you, I'd be a lot more afraid right now."

The rat shook his head in mirth. "And if I were you," he squeaked, "I'd look behind me right now."

At that instant, Thor's full-throated barks of warning split the air. Domino felt the fur rise on his back as he turned and beheld a horrifying sight.

Rats were boiling up onto the porch from the steps, the edges of the decking, the posts and the railings. More rats than he could count, certainly more than he could hope to fight. They swarmed every side of the porch so that Domino had no possible route of escape. Beyond them, Max could be seen in the yard, lifting a leg to piddle on Mrs. Brown's little herb garden before approaching the porch stairs.

And cresting the top step in a posture of victorious leadership, with the most disagreeable and arrogant smirk on his face, was Socrates.

SIXTEEN

Domino skittered backward, away from the advancing army, tumbling over Rip's heavy body in the process.

"Hey, watch where you're going, you stinking bunghole," grunted the rat. "I ought to tear your face off."

Domino kept going until his backside smacked up against the house. He scuttled along the angle between wall and decking, away from the steps, until he was brought up short by the base of the new cathouse the Browns had gotten him. He halted in the insufficient cover of wall and post, facing as many of his enemy as he could at once. His back rose toward the porch ceiling, his ears flattened until they appeared to be part of his neck, and every strand of fur stood at full attention. His mouth hung open, lips drawn back from fangs, hisses and spittle issuing forth. His eyes however were not slitted in rage but round with fear, the pupils dilated so they almost covered the entire iris.

The rats carpeted the decking of the porch but left a circle of empty space around Domino, into which stepped Socrates. The smug grin remained on his face as he gloated over the barn cat's predicament. Rip pushed his way through the rodents and came to stand beside Socrates. Then Max came up behind them, stepping on more than one rat as he took up his position.

"Well, well, well," smirked Socrates. "Looks like the Lord of the Territory is, perhaps, dispossessed?"

Domino fought down panic and struggled to turn his rational brain back on. He forced himself to disregard the peril of his situation and focus only on Socrates. He collected himself for one second more before replying, concentrating so that his voice would come out strong and assured sounding. "Is that what you think?" he meowed. "That trespassing on another cat's territory somehow makes you its new owner?"

"Not at all. We don't hold to such archaic ideas as owner-ship of territory. As usual, you are behind the times, Domino. What is now understood is that everyone must be free to go where he or she wishes."

As always, Socrates had an answer so smooth and slippery that Domino could gain no purchase on it. So, he answered with simple defiance. "Not around here, it's not." Domino's mind scrambled for a plan, but none was forthcoming. Thor's earsplitting barks were so loud that it was hard for him to think. He glanced over the ring of rats and saw the German shepherd dancing furiously at the end of his tether, froth flying from his mouth, desperate to reach the porch and engage the dog intruding on his master's territory. *Would have been nice if you had barked to warn me before the invasion had me surrounded,* Domino thought.

Socrates spoke, reclaiming Domino's attention. "Come, now, Domino, are you still intent on playing this game of yours? The time has come for you to get with the program. You've had your fun, but no one lives your way anymore. Even your friend, Flufferdoodle, has accepted the new way of doing things, and he is happy and peaceful in his home. Safe and sound," Socrates added with pointed emphasis.

"He most certainly is not," hissed Domino. "And neither are the other cats in the Neighborhood. They're just afraid to say anything because there are so many rats everywhere."

"Nonsense." Socrates dismissed his words with a flick of his tail.

"Are you kidding, cat? Really?" Rip shook his head in disbelief. "You want us to believe that cats are somehow afraid of rats? As if it has ever been that way in all the history of animals! We're small rodents who just want to survive. You cats are bigger and stronger. You're the ones with the claws and teeth. You're the ones who have always killed us. And now you want us to believe that the cats in the Neighborhood are afraid of *us*?" He gave an exaggerated guffaw.

Socrates snickered at Rip's remarks. "Really, you sound ridiculous, Domino," he chided.

"Oh, yeah? Then why aren't any of the cats here with you?" Domino asked. "If they all think this new way of doing things is so great, why aren't they here, too?"

"They chose not to come, that's all. In our way of doing things, everyone is free to do what they like. Everyone is free to join us while we pay you this courtesy visit, but at the moment, clearly the cats are occupied with their own affairs." Socrates's answer sounded less certain than his previous assertions, but he gained conviction as he argued, finishing with, "As I said, all creatures are free to do as we please. *All* creatures, not just cats."

The rats screeched their approval, drowning out any answer Domino might have made. After some time, they quieted down to angry murmurs among themselves and inched closer. Hundreds of beady black eyes fixed on Domino. He changed his posture to a defensive fighting stance, but he could do nothing to make his fur lay flat. Terror squirmed in his bowels and twisted his stomach, but his heart pounded resolute and true. He might be overwhelmed and outnumbered but if it came to a fight, by the Great Cats, he would take Socrates with him, and any of the rats he could reach as well, before Max got around to snapping his neck.

Socrates perked his ears forward and curled his tail in a genial, inquisitive manner. "So, what do you say, old friend? Will you join us at last?"

He had striven to add warmth to his meow, but it sounded artificial to Domino. And no amount of oratorical skill could add warmth to those cold, colorless, slightly crossed eyes. Domino noticed once again that they never looked straight at him; they always seemed to be looking just past him or on either side of him, never quite seeing him as a fellow creature. He shivered.

The rats closed in still more as they waited for his answer. Socrates's cross-eyed gaze was locked on him and unwavering, disturbingly the closest thing Domino had ever seen to a predatory stare from the Siamese. Behind Socrates, Max was at full attention, lips back, mouth watering, and muscles tensing in anticipation of a command to attack. His low canine growl was just audible above Thor's thunderous rage from across the driveway.

Domino swallowed with difficulty. He stood big and hulking as possible and focused a glare as sharp as a hawk's beak into Socrates's demented eyes. His words came out in a gravelly growl: *"Get these disgusting vermin off my porch, take your turd-eating, idiot dog, and get your crazy, ball-less backside off my territory."*

The intensity of Domino's barely suppressed wrath was

almost palpable. The rats backed into one another as they fell back in uncertainty. Max didn't move but his growling ceased and his lips smoothed down over his fangs.

Socrates went rigid and his eyes became even colder with rage. His ears flushed red through their velvet fur.

Only Rip seemed not to be intimidated. The big rat actually snickered at Domino's words, which made Socrates even more furious. Then Rip turned to the Siamese and said, "I don't know, Socrates. I just don't think he gets it."

Socrates struggled to regain his composure. "No, Sunflower Seed, I don't think he gets it at all. I suppose we have no choice but to remove him." He glanced at the rat. "What do you recommend?"

Rip gave another grating chortle. "Well, we gotta kill him, basically. Now, let's see... we could give him the swarm treatment. Rats are great at dispatching bigger animals, when we work together."

Excited squeaks sounded all around. Domino's ears ached from the noise.

"What about me? I'd love to do it," yipped Max.

Rip considered it. "Huh, yeah, that's a good idea. Okay, here's what you're gonna do—"

"I notice Socrates hasn't volunteered," Domino meowed loudly.

All eyes turned in Socrates's direction. For a brief moment, he actually looked frightened. For once, the Siamese seemed to have nothing to say.

"How about it, Soc?" Domino pressed. "You and me. Wanna do this?"

Socrates found his voice at last. "Oh, Great Cats, no. Not me. There are so many good creatures here who deserve to do the honors far more than I. I would never presume to take that away from them."

"Yeah, that's what I thought." Domino sneered at the haughty Siamese.

Rip snickered again. "Okay, then," said the rat. "I vote we let Max have him. A good, clean kill, outcome pretty much guaranteed, less chance of injury to any of my rats. Sound good to you, Socrates?"

"Oh boy, oh boy," drooled Max. His lips pulled back from his fangs as he tensed to lunge.

Domino appraised the size of the dog's teeth, and his throat went dry. He could hear Rip giving instructions to the rats to hem him in if he tried to bolt, telling them to swarm him, grab onto him, and hold him down so he couldn't get away. In the distance, Thor's impotent raging went on unabated. Domino thought the dog must surely go hoarse soon. If only he had gotten the eyelet free in time.

In a desperate last search for options, Domino scanned the yard around the porch and beheld the worst possible thing he could think of: Catlyn, no bigger than one of the rats, stalking unnoticed toward the bottom step. Her little kitten eyes were locked onto the nearest rat at the top of the stairs, which was facing away from her like all the others, watching the drama unfold on the porch. Catlyn's tiny features were set and determined as she moved forward, intent on assisting her father once the fighting started.

Domino heard nothing and saw nothing but the kitten. He felt like vomiting. He was frozen, riveted, not even keeping an eye on Max, concentrating all his will on somehow warning his kitten away.

Socrates noticed his odd expression and turned to see what

had distracted him. "Oh, I say! Hold on a minute, Sunflower Seed. I think we have a real treat here."

"What is it?" grunted the rat, clearly annoyed at the interruption.

Socrates stepped through the crowd of rats, descended the porch steps, and halted in front of Catlyn. "Why, hello there, kit," he said in his phony jovial voice. Confused at seeing a cat among all these rats, Catlyn gave a tiny, confused hiss. The much bigger cat stepped briskly around her, picked her up by the scruff of the neck, and carried her up the porch steps. He placed her on the decking in front of Rip.

Catlyn looked around. No longer unobserved and plotting to pick off a rat from the back of the pack, she was now the center of attention from the hundreds of rats surrounding her. There, too, was the oddly cold cat who had dropped her in the center of the sordid gathering. And behind him was a cruel-looking dog. Domino could see her begin to tremble as she glanced frantically from creature to creature. At last, she saw him. "Pawpaw!" she mewed. She took two running steps toward him before Socrates jumped in front of her and swatted her back. She landed on her back, paws in the air, with a tiny thump. The rats burst into uproarious laughter.

Domino headed for his kit but before he had taken a step, Max was in front of him. "Stay where you are, cat," he growled. "Wait until Socrates tells us what to do."

Domino stared into the dog's eyes then snapped his head down as though seeing something move behind him. When Max turned to see what he was looking at, Domino ran through his legs and had almost reached his kitten before the swarm started. One rat grabbed onto his tail and held on. A second clamped onto the flesh of a hind leg. More of the heavy rats attached themselves to his legs so that he could barely lift them.

Then a horde was on his back, weighing him down so that at last he collapsed onto the planking of the deck, unable to move. He was barely a length away from his kitten. The rats made sure not to block his line of vision, and he could plainly see the look of terror on her face. "Pawpaw!" she mewed.

"Pawpaw," mocked Rip. All the rats screeched with malicious laughter.

Catlyn spun and swiped the nearest rat in the face, then turned to run to Domino. Socrates neatly swatted her off her feet and pinned her to the ground with a paw on her back. "Settle down, kitten," he intoned. "That is not how cats treat rats anymore." He gave Domino a malevolent grin. "You know what, Sunflower Seed? I just got the best idea."

"Oh, yeah? What's that?" squeaked the bloated rat.

"How about we show Lord Domino here what we do to cats who think they're better than rats."

Rip chortled, and it was the ugliest sound Domino had ever heard. "Are you thinking what I'm thinking?" he asked.

"I am indeed."

Rip shook his head in admiration. "Socrates, I gotta hand it to you. You know how to handle these uppity cats." He scurried up to Domino's face and addressed him. "You see, cat, it's nothing personal. It's just that your kind has always killed my kind, and no one ever thought twice about it. You guys never stopped to think of us as fellow creatures. But thank goodness a brilliant cat like Socrates here came along and helped all the cats think different. Now we got this wonderful new system where the killing has finally stopped. We're at peace with one another."

He paused as if to allow Domino time to digest the import of his words. Domino had been struggling against the weight of the rats that held him, but now he forced himself to relax. He could not move them, so he decided to save his strength and watch for a chance to do something, anything. While his mind was working, he kept his eyes focused on Rip.

Satisfied that Domino was listening, the rat continued. "But every now and then, we get one of these cats who thinks he is better than his fellow creatures. And we need to teach him the error of his ways. We find that the best way to do this is to give him a demonstration. We like to demonstrate how very painful it is when he feels so superior to other creatures that he kills them."

Domino forced himself to suppress the hysteria that wanted to rise in him. He didn't like where this was going.

"So now, Domino, we are going to demonstrate for you how very painful it is when one of your kind is killed by other creatures."

As if I didn't already know, thought Domino. The image of Tam in the hawk's talons was still fresh in his mind. He didn't think he could bear to see another of his kittens violently killed before him.

Rip turned to Socrates, who still held Catlyn pinned beneath his paw. "What do you think, Soc? Shall I call in my demo team?"

Socrates stared at Domino, his eyes still burning with cold rage. "No. In fact, you know what? Our friend here," and he nodded at Domino," has suggested that I am unwilling to do any of the physical work associated with our positive movement. So I think it best that I handle this little detail."

"Ah, right you are, Socrates. You always were the brains of the outfit," agreed Rip in the reverent tone he used when addressing the Siamese. His obsequiousness now sounded so blatantly phony, Domino marveled that Socrates still didn't pick up on it.

Domino watched as Socrates lowered his snout to the back of Catlyn's neck and sniffed. The kitten remained sprawled on her belly, her skinny legs spraddled in all directions. Only her perfectly round eyes moved freely, and she stared into her pawpaw's face in terror. Immobilized himself, Domino could only return her look, pouring every ounce of strength and courage he had into it.

Socrates straightened up again and removed his paw from Catlyn's back. The kitten immediately sprang to her feet, only to be swatted up into the air. This time, she landed badly on her back. Socrates's heavy paw was on her belly in an instant. The rats guffawed at the kitten's predicament. Max bellowed, "Oh, yeah! Yeah!" And ever present in the background was Thor's howling frustration at his confinement.

Socrates met Domino's gaze. "Hey, Domino, watch this," he purred. He raised his free forepaw and, with one vicious swipe, rendered Catlyn's delicate ear a collection of bloody tatters. Her mew of pain and fear was a bolt of searing pain in Domino's heart. He clenched his eyes shut.

"Screee!" screeched all the rats in a drawn-out wail of approval. When Domino looked again, Socrates was bowing his head in acknowledgement of their enthusiasm for his performance.

The Siamese turned to Rip and meowed, "What do you think, Sunflower Seed? Any requests?"

"Yeah, I got some ideas. Let's see, what was that again? Oh yeah... how about you 'break her neck and tear her throat out and shred the greasy meat from her filthy bones.' Then you 'pull out her innards like a slimy ball of yarn.'" He looked at Domino. "Did I get that right, cat?" He leered with evil delight. "See how bad it sounds when it's one of yours?"

"I only see that now it sounds too good for you," growled

Domino. The rats blanketing his body bit and scratched, but he did not give them the satisfaction of crying out in pain. He forced himself not to think about the blood he could feel soaking his fur in several places.

"You hear that?" Rip squeaked to Socrates. "He says that's still too good."

Socrates looked down at the wriggling kitten pinned beneath his forepaws. "Very well, I shall skip the step where I break her neck first. That would end it much too quickly, and she would miss out on all the other pleasant sensations. I've got it! How about we start at the end and work our way backward, yes?"

Rip shook his head yet again in admiration, and this time it looked genuine to Domino. "There you go again, Soc," he said.

Pleased, the Siamese lifted a paw and extended his claws, each long enough to do mortal damage to a small kitten. He held the paw in front of Catlyn's eyes so she could see it. Speaking to her now, he drawled, "So I shall start by pulling out your innards, foolish kitten. Are you ready?"

Catlyn succumbed to a seizure of terror. Her body flailed and a scream of terror escaped her. Domino couldn't stop himself from trying to get up and attack Socrates, but the rats who were holding him down chided and bit and would not let him go. A particularly heavy rodent on his neck sank its teeth into Domino's ear and tore. He could feel hot blood soaking the fur on his cheek and neck.

Then the entire gathering became still, waiting. Socrates made sure to look into Domino's face as he raised the pawful of claws to deliver the first swipe to Catlyn's fuzzy belly. Only at the last second did he lower his sight to the target as his paw descended.

Suddenly something happened so fast (and Domino's mind

was so addled with horror) that at first he couldn't understand what it was. There came a blood-curdling yowl of such rage and volume that all the creatures froze in terror. Socrates was knocked several feet sideways by something that moved so fast, it appeared to be a blur. Rats scattered in confusion as the Siamese was engulfed in a whirling, spitting ball of claws and teeth. Fur and spittle and specks of blood flew in all directions. Max and Rip both held their ground, trying to make sense of what was happening. Socrates's shrieks of pain were deafening.

There was a flash where the combatants held still long enough for all the creatures on the porch to see what was going on. Socrates was on his back with a murderous, matted, foaming monster atop him that could only be what was left of Cricket. Her fangs were clamped on his throat, her forepaws wrapped securely around his torso. She was just bringing her hind legs up to rake his belly. In that one moment of clarity, Socrates's wild eyes locked onto Rip's beady ones and he gagged out the words, "Get this crazy she-cat off me." Then Cricket began tearing at his stomach, he writhed in agony, and the mad struggle started again.

Rip called to the dumbstruck rats that were scattered on the porch, gaping at the vicious combat. "You heard him—get her off him." He gestured furiously. "Go! Swarm!"

As if a spell had broken, ten, twenty, a hundred rats flung themselves into the brawl. Cricket seemed to have the strength of a mountain lion in her madness and Socrates was too hyster-ical to hold still, so the rats became part of the raging battle. Domino watched, nauseated, as the spinning mass reddened and slowed at last. Before his eyes, the creature that had once been a sweet-tempered feral cat called Cricket was disassem-bled into a skinless, gory, flailing thing. Then the flesh was stripped away until her very bones were exposed, and she found peace at last.

But something odd happened; the rats didn't stop. The orgy of slaughter continued unabated, now consuming Socrates as well. "Sunflower Seed!" he screamed. "Max! Help!" The rats went on with their ecstatic slaughter, and soon Domino heard only wet, rasping cries that could no longer be identified as feline.

Domino tore his eyes from the spectacle and glanced at Rip. The huge rat watched the carnage with delight, his features alive with evil amusement. "Yes, my rats! That's it!" he squeaked excitedly. Max was also captivated by the cats' demise, a mixture of confusion and fear on his face.

The rats on Domino's back and legs were plainly fascinated as well, and he could feel their grip on him slacken. He seized the moment, shook violently, and leaped in the air, twisting and raking rodents from himself before he landed. In one bound, he reached his dazed kit. Her scruff safely in his jaws, he spun and shot to the base of the new cathouse then sprang cleanly up and through the opening. The entire maneuver had taken only an instant, leaving the collection of malevolent animals on the porch no time to react. Inside the cathouse, Domino dropped Catlyn and spun to face the entrance to the space. Any creature that tried to get in would have to deal with his claws and teeth.

From a height of several feet, Domino could look down at the scene on the porch. A mass of blood-darkened, gore-slimed rodents writhed among the remains of what had recently been two cats. They bit and snarled at one another and fought over scraps. Max sat staring at them, baffled, as though he couldn't comprehend where Socrates had gone. Rip was cuffing and nipping the rats who were supposed to have kept Domino pinned. In the distance, across the yard, Thor strained at his tether, his barking now a series of apoplectic croaks.

Rip finished disciplining the guard rats and turned to Max. "Well?" he squeaked.

Max's ears perked forward inquisitively. "Well, what?" he woofed.

"Well, what are you going to do about *that*?" Rip gestured up at Domino in the cathouse.

Max shrugged. "I dunno."

Rip reached him in two rat skips and sank his teeth into Max's foreleg.

"Owowow!" howled the dog. He lifted his leg and shook it vigorously. Rip sailed into the air, bounced off the decking in a single leap, and landed on Max's shoulder. He scrambled up to the top of the dog's head, lifted an ear with his clawed forefoot, and yelled, "Get that cat down here so we can finish this!"

The high-pitched screeches of a rat's voice are unpleasant at a distance; projected directly into a dog's ear at close range, they are intolerable. Max whined, lowered his head, and swiped at his ear with a paw. Rip had already jumped down and stood before him, glaring. Max scowled at him and snarled, "All right, all right! For scat's sake, you don't have to be such a bunghole. I could kill you with one bite, you know."

"And I could have my rats make you look like Socrates."

"Yeah, but then we'd both be dead."

"Yes, we would."

A brief staring contest ensued, which Max gave up on quickly. "So what should I do? I can't get him out of there without losing my face, you know."

"Just knock that thing over that he's hiding in," explained Rip impatiently. "Once it's on the ground, I'll send my rats in and we can get this over with."

"Fine." Max stepped over to the cathouse, halting just out of range of Domino's claws. The barn cat opened his mouth wide, displaying his impressive teeth and hissing a warning. Max just smirked. "I can't wait to watch you turn into red slime," he growled.

Domino ignored him and pulled his head inside to check on his kit. The interior of the cramped space was hot with fear and sweat, and the chemical new-carpet smell was mixed with the reek of blood. "Catlyn, listen," Domino meowed urgently.

She looked up from a scratch on her flank that she had been licking. Domino flinched at the sight of her shredded ear. "Yes, Pawpaw?" she mewed.

"They're going to knock this cat tower over. I want you to dig into the carpeting and hold on with all four paws, okay?"

"Okay. Then what?"

"Then they are planning to send in a swarm of rats to drag us out, so they can—" but even now, he wouldn't scare his kitten with the truth. She hadn't seen the horror of Cricket and Socrates's end, and Domino decided she didn't need to be even more frightened than she already was for her last few moments alive. He spent an instant hoping that she would be finished quickly before continuing. "—so they can fight us. But I'm going to surprise them."

"What are you going to do, Pawpaw?"

Outside, the rats were chanting loudly, "Knock it down! Knock it down!"

Domino meowed urgently, "The instant this thing hits the ground, I'm going to run out and kill the rats' leader, Rip. Without him giving the other rats commands and disciplining them, they may not know what to do next."

"Okay. What should I do?"

"You will take up my position in the entrance here and tear up any rat that tries to get in."

"So I get to help you fight now?"

"Yes, kitten, you get to fight now. And you had better fight like everything good in the world depends on it."

Catlyn stood in a brave posture, but her voice was shaky. "What about the dog? Won't he get you?"

Domino forced a smile. "He won't be fast enough. I'll kill Rip and come right back in here. When you see me coming back, get out of the way. Then we can block the entrance together."

"How long do you think we can hold it?"

"Long enough—until the Browns get home and see what's going on."

Catlyn splayed her legs and fastened her sharp little claws into the carpeting. "Okay, Pawpaw, I'm rea—" The tiny sanctuary pitched wildly to the side and slammed down onto the decking.

"Scat," yelled Domino. He hadn't been positioned properly and was caught unprepared. His head had smacked against the wall when they hit the ground and he saw nothing but floating white motes. He shook his head desperately to clear it. "Are you okay, Catlyn?" he meowed before he could even see again.

"Yes, Pawpaw, I was holding on like you said."

"Okay, then, get ready to guard the door."

Outside, the rats roared at the toppled cathouse. Rip's abrasive voice blared over the din, commanding his team, "Go! Swarm! Drag them out!"

Still dizzy but out of time, Domino got to his feet, spun to face the door, and launched out of the hole as the first rats were coming in. The force of his hurtling body blasted them out of the way. Domino's vision was coming back but he used the screech of Rip's commands to home in on the bloated beast. A startled scream of terror told him he was over his mark. Maybe it was instinct or maybe it was guidance from the Great Cats themselves, but Domino's jaws were on Rip's neck, and he shook his head violently from side to side, like a dog. With a wet, satisfying snap, the evil rat's spine gave at the base of his skull. Domino, finally able to see again, dropped the monster onto the ground and looked to make sure he was dead. Rip's beady eyes, wide with dread, looked at Domino just long enough for the rat to comprehend what had happened before they began clouding over.

Domino spun to return to the safety of the cathouse, but Max was on him before he could take a step. The dog slammed him down with heavy paws, snarling ferociously with fangs bared and drool flying. Domino was flipped onto his back and his head smacked onto the decking. He gazed up into the approaching jaws of death. He spent his last moment alive begging the Great Cats that his kit would die quickly.

There was a report like a pistol firing, and an eerie silence fell over the scene. Domino had barely realized it was the absence of Thor's barking when the German shepherd was all over Max. Dazed but still conscious, Domino flipped over and belly-crawled into the cathouse. Catlyn made way for him, and he was just able to turn and face out the doorway again before he collapsed. The myriad injuries he had sustained, blood loss from countless bites and scratches, concussions from banging his head twice, and exhaustion combined to overcome him. Semiconscious, he watched the dogs fight, comforted by the fact that if the rats killed him, his body would be a barrier between them and his kit.

The war between the dogs raged loud and bloody. It ranged all over the porch and cascaded down the steps to tumble about the yard. Domino faded in and out of consciousness, but he was relieved to see that the rats had fallen out of order without their leader. Some fled in fear and some stood fascinated by the canine brawl, but all forgot what they were supposed to be doing. Apparently, in their lust for power, Socrates and Rip had never appointed seconds-in-command. Just as Domino was drifting back into a spell of blackness, he heard tires on the gravel driveway. The Browns were home.

Domino forced himself to stay awake. In the yard, the fight seemed to be over; Max had been vicious but, in the end, Thor was just a larger, more powerful dog. His jaws were clamped onto Max's throat and he growled and shook the yellow dog, but Domino could see that the intruder was nothing more than a body at this point.

There were running footsteps and shouts. Mr. Brown's commanding voice called, "Thor! Stop it! Settle down, boy! Sit! Kids, stay away from the dogs! Go inside."

The children skirted Thor and ran up the porch steps. They skidded to a stop and began shrieking.

"Ew! Rats!"

"Oh my God, what is that mess?"

"Gross!"

"Mom!"

Mrs. Brown came up the steps. Her face seemed to elongate with horror at the sight of her back porch, splattered with gore and fleeing rodents. "Good Lord, what has happened here?" she exclaimed.

Rats scattered in all directions as the children squealed. The older girl noticed the knocked-over cathouse and went to investigate. "Mom," she called over her shoulder, "Domino's hurt."

"Oh, no." Mrs. Brown was beside her daughter immediately, peering at the semiconscious barn cat. "Domino, sweetie, what happened? Are you okay?" Domino responded to her words with broken purrs and blinking eyes. "Did you fight all those rats? Oh, you good boy!"

In the yard, Mr. Brown had gotten Thor under control. He led him back to his doghouse, looped the loose tether around the entire structure and tied it, and left Thor in his territory to cool down. The big dog paced back and forth, pausing occasionally to give a short hoarse howl in the direction of Max's yellow corpse.

Meanwhile, Mrs. Brown stood up. "Billy, take your brother and sisters into the house. Make sure everything's okay and that the rats didn't get in there." The older boy did as he was told, and she turned to her husband as he came up the steps. "My God, Bill, what in the world happened here?"

The man just shook his head. "No idea. Never seen anything like it."

"How's Thor?"

"He's got some bites that might need a stitch or two. I'd like him to get some shots, too. Who knows what kind of filth that other dog was into." He paused to glare at the corpse on the ground. Then he asked, "How's my Domino?"

"Well, I'm not sure. He's in that cathouse thingy the kids got him. I think he's hurt, but he won't come out."

"Here, I'll get 'im." Mr. Brown knelt in front of Domino. "Oh, yeah, his ear's tore up bad. Come here, boy. Come on out and let me take a look at you."

The man had always been a source of comfort and security to Domino, ever since he had come here as a kitten. He trusted the man. Gathering the last of his strength, he stood on shaky legs and crawled out to meet the outstretched hand. "I'm so glad to see you," he murmured. Mr. Brown moved to pick him up, but Domino turned abruptly and tried to reenter the cathouse. "Wait!" he meowed.

"Come here, you," said Mr. Brown. Strong hands held him still.

"But my kitten is still in there, and she's hurt, too," Domino explained.

"He wants to go back into the cathouse," chuckled Mr. Brown.

"Well, why? Is there something in there?"

"I don't know. Lemme see." Mr. Brown bent low to peer into the round doorway. "Oh, my goodness, yes. He's got one of his babies in there!"

"Oh, no! Is it okay?" Mrs. Brown was beside her husband in a flash, fishing Catlyn out with gentle hands. "Oh, look at its poor little ear! Oh, the poor little kitten."

Mr. Brown continued to hold Domino with his strong hands, checking the cat over. Domino knew his body hurt in many places, but it seemed to be less and less of an issue. He was floating on a cushion of softest fleece, softer than his old blanket pile back in the barn. He purred louder as he drifted further and further away. The last thing he heard was Mr. Brown saying, "Why don't you call Dr. Mundy and see if he'll meet us in his office on a Sunday? Tell him it's an emergency."

THEREAFTER

The next thing Domino remembered was the car ride to the vet's office. He was wrapped in a warm towel and stowed securely in his cat carrier. He could see out through the wire door. Thor sat on the seat next to him. The big dog glanced down.

"Too bad they stuck you in that cage, cat," he gloated. "The view from here is amazing."

"I've seen it before." Or that is what Domino would have said, but he was asleep again.

Then Catlyn was beside him on the stainless steel surface of the examination table. Mr. Brown stroked the kitten gently, carefully avoiding her damaged ear, while Mrs. Brown watched anxiously. Dr. Mundy prodded at Domino's multiple injuries.

"Ow! Watch it, klutz," Domino growled. He tried to stand up, but Dr. Mundy had anticipated the move and kept him pinned on his belly.

"Yeah, stitches, antibiotics, the works. I'm going to need to put him out for a while so I can get him fixed up. He'll need to stay overnight." He nodded at Catlyn. "Her, too. But Thor should be able to go home with you today."

The next morning, a sore but alert Domino rode home on the back seat in his carrier. Beside him, Catlyn mewed a stream of questions and observations from the lap of the young girl who held her.

Once the car stopped, Mrs. Brown got out and carried Domino's kennel up onto the back porch. The girl followed, carrying Catlyn.

"There's someone here to see you, Domino," sang Mrs. Brown as she set the carrier down. Domino could see the rest of his family through the wire mesh.

"Celine! Marble! You're here," he meowed. As soon as Mrs. Brown opened the door, he sprang out and head butted his family affectionately, knocking them over several times in his delight. The young girl set Catlyn among the purring gathering and stepped back by her mother to watch.

The joyous reunion went on for quite some time. "Domino, I'm so glad you're alive," meowed Celine, running her cheek along his neck. "When Catlyn went missing, I was beside myself. Her trail was easy to follow but Marble couldn't run fast enough, so I carried him all the way back here. The Browns were putting you in the car and leaving when I got here. Marble and I spent the night in the house, in a box. It was warm and safe and quiet, but I am glad to be outside again." She touched noses with her mate. "And I am so glad to see you."

"Me too, me too!" he purred. He knocked Marble to the ground once more with a zealous head butt then stood. "Okay, what's to eat?"

Mrs. Brown had just come back out with a dinner plate covered with chicken shreds, tuna fish, and scrambled eggs.

"Welcome home, tiger," she said. "You did such a good job! Mr. Brown had to go to work, but he left instructions for a special meal for you."

A curious feeling came over Domino, like a sudden weakness that caught at his throat but somehow felt really good. "Great," he meowed in a choked voice.

The plate hit the decking and it was big enough that all four cats found a place to eat.

That afternoon, with a full belly, Domino lounged in the sun atop the porch railing. Facing him, Celine tended to his wounds. "Dr. Mundy did such a great job cleaning you up, there's not much for me to do."

"You could wash the back of my head," he suggested.

Celine gave him a coy smile. "You always were a sucker for that," she purred.

"Hey, I can't reach it myself."

Below, the kittens frolicked in the dusty yard, under their parents' watchful eye. Domino was amazed; Dr. Mundy had stitched Catlyn's ear back together so skillfully, it almost looked normal again.

Mr. Brown pulled into the driveway earlier than usual. Just behind his car was a white truck. Domino shuddered at the picture of a giant, scary rat on the side of the truck. The rat was in a red circle, and there was a red line through it.

Mr. Brown spent some time talking to the men from the truck. Then he went into the house. The men began working around the foundation. Domino was too warm and content (and still sore) to investigate, so he and Celine monitored the situation from the railing.

The two younger children came outside and picked up Catlyn and Marble. They brought the kits back into the house. Celine jumped off the rail and followed them inside.

Then Mr. Brown came out with the older boy and girl. The boy was carrying a rifle. Curious now, Domino jumped down gingerly and went to sit in the sunny yard where he could keep an eye on them. The Browns followed the men as they worked around the base of the house. Every now and then, a rat would break from cover and dart away. The children took turns picking them off as they fled. Domino purred appreciatively as he enjoyed the show.

That night, Domino crept over to visit Thor. With things settling back to normal, he chose to respect the invisible border that delineated the dog's range of mobility. But Thor surprised him by coming to sit right next to him. "The boundary has changed, cat," he woofed. "Mr. Brown attached my tether to a metal spike in the ground, so now I can reach a little farther. In other words, where you are sitting is no longer a safe place for a cat."

"Good to know," meowed Domino. He rose and moved back three paces before sitting and speaking again. "Been meaning to ask you, dog... how come you didn't warn me that those foul creatures were invading? It might have been nice to know. You kind of have one job, after all."

Thor ignored his insulting tone. "They didn't come this way."

"What? But they always come this way. They've been setting up routes in those north woods for months."

"They've been setting up decoys for months, you mean."

The truth dawned on Domino. "My tail. All this energy and time I wasted monitoring their activities in those woods." He thought some more. "And all the rats' lives *they* wasted, sending them into the woods to be torn to ribbons by me, Celine, and Cricket, just to set up a distraction."

"Yup."

"Ugh." He shook his head. "But that's how rats work, I guess." He almost felt sorry for the countless rats who had been duped by their leader into throwing their lives away on a false mission—but not quite.

Finished with the dog, Domino got up and headed back to the house. He spent an hour inspecting the perimeter. He found numerous rat feeding stations that the men from the truck had left seemingly in every crevice and overhang. Rat food did not interest him, however, and he moved on.

The house had a wide front porch, but he had never been able to get through the lattice protecting the space beneath it. Now that he was taking the time to look, he found five different places where rats had clearly been entering the space. He followed trails of pellets, fur, and stench from the front porch, along the edge of a flower bed, to the pavement of the road that ran past the house. While he had been distracted monitoring the north woods, he had never thought to keep an eye on the front yard. Now that he was looking, the rat trails were as obvious as if they were lit up with spotlights. Domino shook his head. He hadn't been paying attention to the right things, and the invasion had been staged and executed right under his nose. He had been played.

MRS. BROWN often sat on the sunny back porch steps and talked on the phone. Her conversations over the next few days generally involved the enormous, unprecedented rat infestation in the area. Referrals for exterminators and tips for rodent prevention were exchanged liberally.

Because all the cats in the Neighborhood had been neutered, kittens were in high demand. Within a few weeks, Marble went to live with a family not far from Flufferdoodle's house. Catlyn was adopted by the people who lived on the far side of the north woods.

The Browns had a modernized replica of the barn built on the footprint of the old one. It was completed in time to house the boat, once the cold weather returned. There was a smart, new cat door alongside the main doors. Once again, Domino and Celine could doze in the afternoon sun, but now they slept on a fleece bed in front of the grand glass window (no longer simply an opening that let in cold weather, bats, and rain) that protected the loft door. One morning, Celine padded down the barn steps and went to the back porch for breakfast. She didn't return until the following day, and after that there were no more kittens.

The two barn cats were gifted with many peaceful years in full feline flower on the Brown territory. Celine went back to working her woods, and Domino easily handled his patrol duties. He often had enough free time to range, and he enjoyed meeting up with Catlyn in the north woods between their homes to hunt sparrows and chipmunks. Her people had given her the name Sugar, and she had a fine territory of her own.

Flufferdoodle was not sorry to see the rats go. Domino made the trek many times to spend pleasant afternoons strutting the streets of the Neighborhood alongside his enormous friend, and he was grateful for every minute of it. After a while, Prowls even made a comeback, and Domino attended a few. It took a while to dispel the bad feelings that lingered from the Great Infestation, and for years afterward, the older cats told the younger cats the story of what had happened. Lily never came to a Prowl again, which was fine with Domino, but he was happy to see Tiger and Mister return after a while. Their playfulness and frisky attitude helped rebuild the spirit of the gatherings. Marble (whose people called him Onyx) even turned up at one or two of them, but he generally preferred to stay in his home to be patted and eat treats.

The Brown children grew as big as their parents, and one by one they left the territory. They often came back to visit, though, eventually bringing children of their own.

Thor grew shaggy and gray. As his health declined, he spent more time in the house. At last came his final ride to Dr. Mundy's office. That afternoon, all the Brown children returned to the house. There was a long, solemn funeral near the boulder under the ancient oak, and all the people's eyes watered. Celine and Domino sat nearby respectfully until it was over.

Celine, too, was struggling. Her once-fluid movements that had long ago thrilled a young Domino had become stiff and hesitant. Domino wrapped himself around her at night in their fleece nest. She said his warmth helped her aches. But it became too difficult for her to climb the stairs to the loft every evening. The hard years of her youth, before she came to live with Domino, took their toll on her body in her old age. Her trips into the woods became longer each day, and eventually she stopped coming back.

Domino missed her terribly, but now all the work of patrol was his responsibility. He was not as energetic and strong as he had been, and it became an all-consuming task to keep the area free of vermin.

Mr. Brown sat on the back porch one autumn afternoon. Uncharacteristically, Domino let the man hold him in his lap and scratch behind his ears. "How you holding up, old boy?" asked Mr. Brown.

"Old? You should talk," growled Domino.

A few days later, Mr. Brown brought a new kitten out onto

the porch. "Domino," he said, "this is Cheez Doodle. I want you to take good care of him."

Domino was taken aback. "You do know you're on my territory, kitten, do you not?" he growled.

"Now, Domino, you be nice," warned Mr. Brown.

The kitten looked at Domino warily then glanced away to survey his surroundings.

Domino was offended by the young cat's lack of respect. "I'm talking to you," he meowed.

"That's better," said Mr. Brown.

The kitten looked at Domino again, and the older cat took a moment to assess him. He was a decent size for a youngster. He had a bright orange coat that reminded Domino of his old friend, Flufferdoodle, except the newcomer's fur was short. He didn't seem frightened of Domino, which was upsetting. Rather, he appeared pleased to meet a new cat. He spoke at last, his voice still the high-pitched mew of a kitten. "Hi. Do you play?"

"Do I play? Of course not. Do I look like a kitten to you?" Domino sputtered.

"No. But you can still play." Cheez Doodle reared up on his back legs, raising his forepaws and showing his teeth though leaving his ears pricked forward.

Disgusted, Domino turned to walk away. He had barely taken a step before the rude newcomer assaulted his tail.

Mr. Brown laughed. "Aw, now ain't that cute. Cheez Doodle wants to play. You be nice to him, Domino."

For the first few months, Cheez Doodle was insufferable. Domino hissed and swatted, but the youngster came back time and again, looking to frolic. Then he would pass out cold and nap deeply, no matter where he was. Exasperated, Domino showed him how to find a safe spot before falling asleep. When the snow flew, he even let the orange kit curl up with him on the coldest nights. By springtime, Cheez Doodle was nearly as big as Domino and showing signs of becoming an apt hunter.

Cheez Doodle didn't keep the territory quite as orderly as Domino would have, but the old cat welcomed the help. He began to spend more time than ever napping in the fleece bed by the loft window (where Cheez Doodle was now expressly forbidden to go). The summer seemed endless, warm, and deeply restful.

Domino hadn't seen Celine in over two years but with so much time to himself, he had begun to miss her a little more every day. He dragged himself up the back porch steps for a snack of kibble, allowed Mr. Brown to give his neck a good rubbing, then made his way across the yard and past the chicken coop. The late summer sun slanted across the lawn as he passed the great oak. Distantly, he recalled the creatures slumbering beneath the earth here; Thor the German shepherd, and a promising but impetuous kit named Tam. Domino touched nose to earth and continued on his belabored way.

He came to the sun-warmed boulder, planning to leap atop it and bask while scanning the woods for signs of Celine. But over the years, the stone had grown high. He could neither jump onto it nor climb it. Giving up, he lay in the warm grass in front of it. The lowering sun showered him with gold. All across the meadow, the late-summer insect orchestra played the age-old song of evening, and the music filled Domino's head to the exclusion of all else. The breeze dipped and sighed and disappeared.

"Domino."

He snapped his head up from where it had been resting on his paws. "Yes?" he meowed. He blinked in the rays of the setting sun, which now angled directly into his eyes. Among and within the light was the shape of a large and powerful crea-ture, only a few feet away. Alarmed, Domino leaped to his feet.

A long-lost feeling of well-being came over him; it had taken no effort to jump up. The customary pains in his hips and back had failed to materialize, and his muscles had performed as well as in his youth.

The creature in front of him was enormous, certainly large enough to devour a barn cat with ease. The sun dropped away and the animal itself was revealed. Domino gasped in amaze-ment. A gleaming black panther stood before him, blinking at him with friendly golden eyes. All fear left him, replaced by joy. "Celine!" he meowed (and his voice sounded strangely loud and deep), "Look how big and healthy you've grown."

"Speak for yourself," said the panther. Her voice was powerful yet somehow it still held the same old lilting quality he remembered.

Domino glanced down at his forelegs. Before his eyes, the white spots shrank and disappeared as his coat filled in solid black and glossy as Celine-panther's. His paws enlarged and got farther away as his legs lengthened and thickened. "What's happening?" he roared.

Celine-panther stepped forward and gently touched noses with him. He had to tilt his head down slightly to meet her. He closed his eyes in ecstasy at her touch rediscovered. Then he looked back at his body, and it was long and rippling with muscle. "Ha!" he roared again.

He turned to Celine in delight. She began pacing away across the meadow. Domino was beside her in a single bound. *That leap must have been as long as a car,* he thought, *and it was nothing to me.* He threw his head back and roared again, a joyful noise at the rightness of it all. Celine butted him in the shoulder, hard, but his magnificent new form balanced against it with ease. Celine leaped ahead, and he caught up effortlessly.

Laughing, they loped across the waving grasses, leaping tussocks and shrubs and boulders. Domino felt more alive than he ever had, and he pushed his gleaming new body to greater speed. Celine matched it, and they raced over the ground, going faster and faster, leaping higher and higher. The world rushed past in a blur. Domino glanced at Celine and she nodded: *Yes, we can do that now.*

With a smooth and powerful leap, they left the ground altogether. Unencumbered by the need to touch earth, they sped faster still. Ahead, a new sun rose over the distant horizon. The cats streamed toward it, ever at whiskertouch, hurtling at a pace unheard of for cats. They reached the new light, passed into it and through it, and arrived, at last, in Africa.

AUTHOR'S NOTE

Many people who have read *Domino* have misunderstood what it is about.

Some equate the animal species with human races and claim *Domino* is a book that supports racism. This is untrue. The various animal species do not represent human races; note that different animal characters within the same species think and do quite different things.

Other readers angrily insist this book is anti-immigrant. Again, untrue; my own father and my in-laws are immigrants. Immigrants bring fresh energy and a true understanding of the value of liberty to America. Suggestions that I would write a racist or anti-immigrant book of any sort are deeply offensive.

Here's the key that unlocks the tale: the animals in *Domino* embody schools of thought. They represent ideas. Which ideas do they represent? I leave that to the reader to figure out.

Thank you for reading!

GRATITUDE

I'd like to thank Yuri Bezmenov, who had the courage to tell this story in the first place.

I am in debt to my feedback readers for their thoughts and advice on how to make *Domino* the best story possible. Thanks to fellow author and friend Jack July for demonstrating in his *Amy Lynn* series that stories can be wildly entertaining and told in entirely new ways I'd never have thought of. Thanks to author/friend Daniella Bova for her thoughtful comments and enthusiastic encouragement. Still more thanks to author/friend Sheryn MacMunn for countless lunches spent dreaming and scheming. Additional feedback thanks to John Earle, and, as always, to Karen Tsakos for developmental assistance and invaluable encouragement.

I am grateful for the readers and writers' community of the CLFA. I have made some great friends there! I appreciate everyone's encouragement and support, and I am thrilled to see better and better books from CLFA writers all the time. (Shout out to Marina—good luck with your book relaunch!)

Finally, and most importantly, thanks and love to Jim for unwavering support and faith throughout my writerly adventure.